Mia From the Eastside 2

T.May

ISBN: 978-1-7369606-1-5 (Paperback)

Printed in the United States of America

This book is dedicated to everyone who purchased this novel after waiting over 4 years. That's real and I definitely appreciate it. After reading this book though continue reading to catch the sneak peek of Nearee, i'm excited to write an anthology where every character essentially has their own standalone series but they won't have to be read in any certain order but at the same time their stories, intertwine and overlap because the town is so small. These kind of books and series have always been my favorite. So let me know what ya'll think.

Much Love, T.May<3

Contents

Mia from the Eastside 2

An I'm from Da' Bury novel

By: T. May

Proverbs 4:23 NLT

"Guard your heart above all else, for it determines the course of your life."

Chapter 1

Mia sat in front of the computer monitor sweating like a run-away slave, as she took the three-hour placement test to begin her college journey. She was halfway through and just as she had expected the writing portion of the exam was a breeze. She hadn't started sweating until she hit the math section, and prior to that moment she thought she had always been good at the subject.

"Binomials? The fuck?" She whispered to herself in the practically empty, silent testing center. She recognized the math problem as being an algebraic equation, but she had never seen a problem so advanced that she didn't know where to start. She sat back in her seat and laughed to herself already knowing it over for the math portion. She knew that missing the last few years of high school would be a setback, but she was determined not to let it hold her back. She clicked the finish tab at the bottom of the screen and waited for the professor to come explain her scores to her.

Five minutes later the short, petite professor walked over to her and sat down.

"You did exceptionally well on the reading and writing portion of the exam so with that you will go straight into English 101. As far as the math though dear," she said looking up from the sheet of paper, "you'll have to start from the beginning. Don't worry it's not unusual, math is the hardest subject for people to retain. So congratulations you are all set, now you can go downstairs take your photo for your school identification and get your classes scheduled. You'll be assigned an advisor, what is your major dear?" She asked Mia.

"Chemical dependency." Mia answered, after witnessing the stronghold that drugs on Corrie, she sympathized with drug addicts and wanted nothing more than to help them.

"Okay that'll either be Dan Ryan or Amy Linn, they're both great. Good luck Mrs. Truitt." She said flashing her coffee-stained teeth.

"Thank you." Mia said, gathering her items before grabbing her book bag, slinging it onto her back and heading out into the hallway.

"I heard they eat the bats and that's how someone contracted the disease in the first place." She heard one professor say to another in a hushed tone, as they stood out in the hallway.

"What the hell are they talking about?" Mia thought to herself as she walked past them looking down at the shiny waxed cream colored floor as she headed towards the staircase. The thought left as quickly as it came as she began to think about her own life, everything seemed to be lining up perfectly at the moment. Malakai was happy, her relationship with Reese was drama-free, her face was clean and clear like a neutrogena commercial, her weight was up in all the right places, her hair was getting longer, all of her

bills were paid ahead and now in two weeks she would finally be getting back to the thing she had always loved the most… school! She was thrilled and couldn't wait to get to work and tell everybody.

Dax

A couple hours after the judge ruled his case a mistrial, Dax looked down at the monitor on his ankle as he jogged down the concrete steps at the courthouse. With spring just a few weeks away, the sun was beaming on Dax but the wind made the cool 44 degrees feel like a cold 30, still he wasn't fazed by it, he was to pumped up. He couldn't even describe the immense amount of relief and joy he felt walking out of the courtroom a free man. He knew the officers in his city hated him and were just waiting to bury him under the jail, fortunately for him they weren't so lucky today. So now all he had to do was figure out a new way to get money without indicting himself in the process but first things first… Mia.

When he made it down to the crowded parking lot he realized he didn't have his phone and since no one came to support him in court, he didn't even have a ride. He decided to just take the short walk across the highway, to the Eastside when T Grizzley's, *"First Day out,"* began to blare from one of the parked cars.

Dax squinted his eyes as he scanned the parking lot trying to see who was playing his shit. He fell out laughing after Spook popped out of a white dodge charger, dancing as the beat dropped.

"They let my nigga out!" Spook shouted,

throwing his hands in the air.

"Huh!!? They can't hold a real nigga down!" Dax yelled back, pounding his chest and cracking up.

All eyes were on the duo as they embraced and gave each other dap before jumping in the whip and skidding off.

"Yooo!!!" Dax yelled at a white lady in a suit, headed towards the courthouse, as he hung out of the window.

"You better chill bro, that bitch look like the district attorney." Spook said with a smirk.

"Shit I'm out here now!" Dax said, sliding back down onto his seat. "How the fuck you know they was letting me go?" Dax asked, turning to Spook. "I ain't see nobody in that mahfucker."

"I didn't know for real, you know I don't be doing this courthouse shit unless I'm coming to see my P.O. but Shariece was in there you know that's Mercedes

peoples and shit. She called her." Spook said, looking straight ahead as he drove.

"Well nigga I wish you could've saw that shit, the judge had them mothafuckers mad as shit." Dax said smiling, "Especially that bitch ass nigga Davis!" Dax said, referring to the cop that always seemed to personally arrest him. "But yo I need to find some molly or at least some perks. Let's ride through the hood while I wait for Mia to get off work. "

"The single life ain't THAT bad bro." Spook said, snapping his head around to look over at Dax. "The hoes still asking about you nigga," Spook continued, the whole hood had been talking about how Mia was on some new shit boo'd up with Reese. She seemed content and Spook doubted she would even take Dax back at this point. He looked at Dax and then back at the road. Wondering what kind of voodoo Mia had between her legs because she definitely had his nigga gone.

"Fuck them hoes, them bitches never even picked up the phone half of the time," Dax said as he glared out the window. He had been blowing Ashley's phone up during his bid but she rarely answered the phone but after he got the paternity test results for the baby in the mail, he knew why. She was a skeezer plain and simple, but he wasn't sweating it. He knew the papers inside of the manila envelope was just the golden ticket he needed to get Mia back. She would've been right by his side thuggin' it out with him if things hadn't went down the way they did. He knew that Spook and the whole city would probably think he was crazy for wanting Mia back but he didn't give a fuck. In his eyes they would never understand just by judging from the outside looking in. Yeah, she was out here doing her thing but in his eyes she was just doing him how he had done her for years, but now that he was home it was time to dead all that. Fuck what everybody thought, Mia belonged to him and there wasn't a doubt in his mind that she would drop Reese like a bad habit as soon as he popped out.

Spook glanced over at Dax before refocusing his attention to the road again not knowing exactly what to say to him.

"So what are you gone do when you see this nigga?" Spook finally asked him quizzically.

Dax pulled on his beard and laughed at the thought.

The half-shift Mia worked after leaving the college, went by like it was nothing as everybody laughed and joked on the line like always. Once she clocked out, she headed down the hallway to the warehouse to find Reese. He always got off an hour after she did and it was convenient for the couple.

"Ay Mia, you got everybody around this mothafucker talking about you going back to college but I ain't seen shit yet." Eddie said as soon as he saw Mia.

"Dang my bad, here it go." Mia said, whipping out her college i.d. and handing it to Eddie.

"Check you out." Eddie said pointing at the I.d. as he held it up, "Ya smile big as hell." Eddie said, revealing his crater-sized dimples as he laughed.

"Look who's talking." Mia said, pointing to Eddie's wide grin.

"I'm just fucking with you," he said still laughing as he handed the I.D. back her. "Seriously though, I'm proud of you." Eddie said before turning to walk away.

"Thanks E," Mia said, sliding the i.d. back into the front pocket of her lab coat before she continued to look for Reese.

"What do you want to eat tonight? And can we finally watch, "*Their Eyes were Watching God*?" They added it on hulu." Mia asked Reese after she spotted him heading towards her. Romance dramas were her favorite after horror movies, and she loved the fact that he would attentively sit and watch them with her all the time.

"Yeah we can watch it, and I'm good with the leftover lasagna. I told you everything tastes better the next day." Reese said, leaning up against the wall in the hallway.

"Ayo, we done ate that for two days. What else do you have a taste for?"

"Come on LB, he'll be home in less than an hour." Chanel said, looping her arm around Mia's, slowly dragging her away.

"Chill Chanel, we trying to figure out the food situation for tonight." Mia said, pulling away.

"Fat ass is always eating. Come on college girl," Alyssa said walking up to the trio.

"Don't worry about it, whatever you cook tonight I'm eating it." Reese said laughing.

"Alright cool. See you in a few babe." Mia said, before finally giving in to Chanel.

"Ya'll still trying to do the Laser tag shit this weekend?" Ballow asked as they headed out to the parking lot.

"Yeah, Saturday right?" Lola asked.

"Yep," Ballow told her.

"I can't wait, imma light yalls asses up too! So be ready!" Alyssa said.

"Man ya'll forgot, Cali's house warming is this

weekend across the bridge. So me and Reese will be up there." Mia told them. "I thought ya'll were coming. We turning up."

"Damn! I forgot all about it! Why you ain't remind us?" Chanel asked.

"Dang Mia, me and Lola just signed the overtime sheet for Saturday." Alyssa said.

"My fault. It's alright she don't need anything for real anyway, she was asking everybody to bring her wine or weed!" Mia said, making everybody laugh.

"We'll give you some to take to her." Lola said looking at Alyssa, who just nodded in agreeance.

Twenty minutes later Mia pulled onto her street wondering why Spook was parked in her front yard. She pulled in behind him and hopped out, but everything seemed to move in slow motion after Dax emerged from the passenger side door. She hadn't talked to him in almost a year and thought that not seeing him or talking to him would make all of her feelings for him somehow diminish, at least a little bit. But it became clear after seeing him that no amount of time or space could lessen the profound-love they shared with one another.

Although Dax wanted Mia back more than anything, he still had every intention on snapping on her for hurting and making a fool out of him while he was locked up. He didn't give a damn that he had embarrassed her first. He would've never in a million years thought that she would actually move on and get into a whole 'nother relationship. The thought of her with another man was the only thing Dax had thought about for the past year. He fixated on the topic so much that he smoked K2 and drank jailhouse hooch during the majority of his bid to cope. He wanted to whoop her ass for all the internal distress, and heartache he suffered in silence but at the same time he was afflicted. The desolation made him realize just how much he took her for granted when he previously came home and he promised himself that he would never make the same mistake again.

Spook sat in the car breaking a blunt down, as Mia and Dax embraced in silence without a care in the world. *"These mothafuckers here boy..."* he thought to himself as he looked over his shoulder at them and shook his head.

"Look," Dax said, pulling the rolled up, manila envelope from his back pocket and handing it to her. Mia took a step back, before pulling the white sheet of paper out of the sleeve and unraveling it.

"Daxton Truitt vs. Ashley Steward paternity test for Daxton Truitt Jr. The alleged father is excluded as the biological father...." Mia paused and looked up at Dax before she continued to read the paper aloud. "Probability of paternity 0.00%." Mia stood there at a loss for words.

"I- this- man..." Mia said, stuttering as she slowly shook her head.

"I- I- I- my ass! What did I tell you babe!?" Dax said leaning down to eye level with Mia. "You forgive me now?"

"This shit gotta be fake." Mia said, flipping the

paper over front to back and back to the front before rereading the results.

"You know it ain't fake, come here!" He said, pulling Mia into his arms. "Just admit it babe. You left me for nothing. It's all good though, I'm back." He said laughing, "You forgive me?"

This shit can't be happening yo. She thought to herself, as she put her face into her hands. Dax having a baby outside of the marriage was the only thing she wasn't willing to accept but with that being out of the picture she instantly knew that it was over for her relationship with Reese but she had no clue how she was going to break it to him. He deserved better.

"Nah don't get quiet now," Dax said laughing. "You want me to tell his bitch ass?" He asked. He knew she probably wouldn't want to hurt the niggas feelings.

"Nah," Mia sighed, "I'll do it. He's nice man, he deserves-"

"Fuck that nigga." Dax said, spitting on the ground, "talking about he's nice. I don't give a fuck about that nigga Mia. You lucky I don't bust your fucking ass for all the shit you done put me through." Dax said, snatching the paper from her.

Spook sat in the car listening and cracking up to himself.

"Bust who's ass?" Mia asked, looking up at Dax with her eyebrows raised. "You see this is exactly how the fuck we got here in the first place." she said pointing her finger in Dax's face, "The disrespect leads to violence, the violence leads to us separating, the separating leads to cheating. Do you see where

I'm going with this?" Mia said using her hands as she explained.

"I ain't trying to hear that shit." Dax said, before walking around to his side of the door to reach into the car to get a newport. "I ain't the violent one, you are. I'm a changed man," He said, placing the cigarette between his lips. "And all that cheating shit is dead, you leaving me this time opened my eyes. I need my wife. So I'm going to go ride around and let you tell that nigga what it is. Your husband is home and if he cherishes his life he better be far from this mothafucker when I get back." He said pointing at Mia with the cigarette between his two fingers, before getting back in the car with Spook.

Normally Mia would cuss Spook out for driving across her grass but today she breathed a sigh of relief as she watched them drive off.

Reese walked into the house shortly after Malakai's bus dropped him off. Mia had just stopped pacing the living room floor long enough to take a seat on the edge of the couch, as she contemplated how to deliver the news to him. Her conscience was eating her up as she reminisced on how much fun she and Reese had during their short relationship. Anywhere she wanted to go, he'd make sure he took her. She never had to question his loyalty, he always made it very clear that he had her back and would always be there for her and somehow, here she was about to walk away from him. She wanted to smoke or drink to calm her nerves but she knew if she was high, she'd come off as chill and nonchalant. Whereas if she drank, she knew she'd become overly emotional, crying and carrying on, which she felt she didn't have the right to be, so she remained sober in her thoughts. Deep down, she knew she loved Reese... just not more than Dax.

"Why you sitting like that?" Reese asked as soon as he laid eyes on Mia. Normally she'd already be showered, changed and starting dinner.

"I need to talk to you," Mia said after he closed the front door.

"What's up?" Reese said, taking off his jacket and sitting next to her.

Mia looked over at Reese and began to fidget in her seat before she clasped her hands together.

"Come on, talk to me. What's up?" Reese said in a gentle tone as he placed his hand on her thigh.

"They let Dax come home today." Mia softly blurted out.

"And?" Reese said with his face frowned up as he observed Mia.

"Well since he's on the box, he'll have to be here." Mia said, continuously wringing her hands.

"So basically, you're taking the nigga back?" Reese asked her with one side of his top lip raised.

"I didn't say that." Mia said looking down at the black faux sheepskin rug on the floor.

"What exactly are you saying than Mia?" Reese said standing up.

"I don't know, I just feel like-"

"Let me stop you right there," he said, holding up his hand, "since you don't know. I'll make it easier for you." He said, before walking to the back of the house towards the bedroom.

Mia put her head back and exhaled before getting up to follow him. "So what are you about to do?" she asked him.

"What do you think? I'm leaving. I tried to show you how you're supposed to be treated this past year but if that wasn't enough than clearly you're still in love with the nigga." Reese said, snatching the closet open. "I ain't gonna front, I figured this day would come but I ain't think it was going to be anytime soon. Shit he just came home today! That right there tells me everything I need to know." He said with his nose flaring as he pulled his clothes off the hangers and threw them onto the bed.

"It's just easier this way Reese, I don't want you to keep having problems with him because of me." Mia said.

"I'm a grown ass man." He said, throwing the hangers onto the bed before stopping to look at Mia. "You ain't gotta look out for me, you think I ain't never have to deal with niggas like him before? I saw the Access Corrections app on your phone, I knew you were still sending him money but I chose to ignore it." He said, shaking his head. "I'm not even mad at you, this is on me." He said heading to the kitchen to get trash bags.

"I didn't send him the money with the intention of getting back with him." Mia said, following closely behind him. "I just know nobody looks out for him when he's locked up and i'm pretty sure if I were to get locked up, he'd make sure I was straight."

"Yeah, keep telling yourself that." Reese said while stuffing his clothes into the black force flex bags.

Mia just shook her head in response, the two remained silent for the next fifteen minutes as he took multiple trips from the house to his car carrying his shoes and clothes. When he was done, he stopped at Malakai's room to say goodbye.

"I'll see you later Kai." He said, holding out his fist in front of Malakai.

"See you later poopy head." Malakai said, oblivious to what was going on, he quickly fist bumped Reese before returning his concentration to his game.

"I'm sorry about all this Reese, I really care about you. I just-"

"Word of advice Mia, any nigga that would get you to risk your freedom, smuggling drugs into prisons for years," he said in a soft tone, clinching his jaw, "for their benefit, never gave a fuck about you or the child you could potentially be taken away from." He told her, before walking out and slamming the front door behind him.

"Uuggghhhhh!" Mia groaned, before falling face down onto her bed and screaming into her pillow.

Chapter 2

The sharp and sudden sound of the shower curtain skating across the metal rod, startled Dax out of his sleep. He looked over at the alarm clock on the nightstand and realized that Mia must've been getting ready for work. He had returned right before nine last night to a sleeping Malakai with Mia sitting on the couch with a pint of fireball and a lit blunt. She was happy to see him but he could tell that the situation with Reese was bothering her. Deep down he knew that she probably had feelings for Reese since he had been there for her through his most recent fuck ups. And Dax had been in similar situations himself with females that he would see on the side over the years. It'd start with just the sex and eventually evolve into feelings, he just would never allow his to grow to the point of no return. He had learned that lesson years ago, so the minute he'd feel himself starting to like a bitch or vise-versa he'd cut them off, at least until they got their minds right. So he empathized with Mia on the inside but that didn't mean he would go easy on her, he couldn't have her doing it again.

"Why you sitting in the dark?" Dax asked as soon as he walked through the front door.

"I was just thinking.." Mia told him before taking a

deep pull from the blunt.

"About?" Dax said standing in front of her. "Come here, give me a hug." He told her, before removing his gun from his waist and sitting it on the couch next to her.

Mia squinted her eyes as she looked up at him, "you know what I'm thinking about." She said softly, before standing up to hug him.

"Fuck that nigga babe. Don't worry about it. Ain't that nigga like 30 or something? He knew you were mine. Shit everybody knows that." Dax told her in a low tone. "He better pray I don't run into him anywhere."

"But that's what I'm saying. Okay we broke up, cool. He'll get over that but I don't want ya'll fighting or you trying to shoot him over me." Mia told him after she let him go and looked at him.

"Don't nobody gotta shoot his soft ass. I've never even heard of this nigga." Dax told her.

Mia didn't reply, she knew Reese wasn't from the hood but he wasn't soft by a longshot. Dax's way of thinking could get him hurt one day, just how several females judging Mia by her appearance had resulted in them getting their asses beat in the past.

"Man, what?" Dax asked, cocking his head to the side as they stood face to face. He could tell she wasn't saying what she was thinking.

"All I'm saying is don't sleep on anybody." Mia told him. Getting cocky could get you killed in her eyes, that was why she fought every battle as if her life depended on it, that's how she always managed to win.

"Shit I'm not underestimating the nigga, I just said I

don't know who the fuck he is," Dax said shrugging, before taking the blunt from Mia. "You looking good though babe, your hair got longer," he said, touching her pressed curls as he put the short blunt to his lips. Since they were teenagers, they had never went this long without laying eyes on each other. "I'm glad you're my wife Mia." He said before turning his head away to blow out the smoke, "I know that nigga is sick. I don't ever want to feel how I've felt this past year without you."

Mia looked Dax in the eyes, as she took a swig of her fireball, she hoped that he wouldn't make her regret her decision.

"You still love me, Mrs. Truitt?" Dax asked her, as he used his left hand to take the bottle from her and drank from it. While he used his to right hand to intertwine his fingers with hers.

"I do but this is it for me. No more back and forth, making up to break up. I'm done with that." She said bluntly. Her experience with Reese showed her that a relationship didn't have to be an emotional roller coaster. They had spent an entire year together and the biggest thing they'd argue about was what they were going to watch on t.v. There was no stressing, sitting up waiting for him to come home or riding through the hoods trying to find him. They'd go to bed together every single night and she didn't have to fight him to get the pin to his phone, he willingly gave it to her. Their relationship wasn't perfect by any means but it was a far cry from her and Dax's violent romance.

"I promise you, no more babe." Dax said, wrapping his arms around Mia and kissing the top of her head. Mia closed her eyes and inhaled the scent of the man she loved

more than anything. "Lay down right quick." He whispered as she felt for her panties under her silk gown.

Mia laughed as she sat down and laid back onto the sofa, already knowing she wasn't wearing panties. She knew that Dax keeping his promises would be a long shot, but it was a chance she was willing to take.

"You should wake Kai up for school." Dax heard Mia say as she entered the bedroom in her towel and shower cap.

"Yeah let me wake him up, but come here right quick." He told her, leaning up to grab a handful of her towel from behind.

"Stop crazy," Mia said laughing, while holding onto the front of her towel.

"Why are you going to work anyway? Take a few days off with me." Dax told her, getting up from the bed.

Mia stopped to think about it, she did have 30 hours-worth of sick time so she could take at least 3 days off, and she didn't really want to face Reese immediately anyway.

"You're right, I'm about to call them right now. You still have to get Kai up though." She said, grabbing her phone and heading into the kitchen to call out.

Dax went across the hall to Malakai's room to wake him up.

"Big man." Dax said, gently shaking the bed. "It's time for school, Kai."

Malakai jumped up as soon as he recognized that it was his dad waking him. He was six and a half now, and in the 1st grade.

"Dad!" Malakai said hugging Dax, "can I stay home today, so we can play fortnite?"

"I'll be here when you get off the bus, we can play all night if you want to." Dax told him.

"Okay bet it dad," Malakai said, nodding his head as he held out his fist to give his dad a pound, causing Dax to laugh.

"Alright, so put your clothes on and brush your teeth. What do you want to eat?" he asked.

"I eat at school now dad, today is pizza for breakfast." Malakai said.

"Oh okay. I like them one's son, I'm going to have to go get me some so we can take a picture for the 'gram." Dax said looking at the outfit Mia had laid across his gaming chair and the shoes on the floor.

Malakai laughed as he pulled his nightshirt over his head.

Twenty minutes later Mia stepped off the front step with Malakai as they saw his bus making its way down the street.

Malakai looked up at Mia as she grabbed his hand and headed towards the street. He remained silent as he remembered that Reese had left the night before. Although he was happy his dad was back, he had quickly grown accustomed to having Reese around to take him places and spend time with them like a family.

"When will Reese come back mom?" Malakai quickly blurted out as the bus's yellow amber lights came to life pulling in front of them.

Mia looked into her son's big brown eyes and recognized the sadness behind them as she registered what he asked. Caught up in her own feelings, wants and needs she had never even thought about how switching between Dax and Reese would affect her son. She was just following her emotions, which clearly was mistake number 1 as she stood at a loss for words as Malakai waited for a response and the bus driver waited on him. She squatted down to be at eye level with him before she pulled him close to hug him. Her selfishness was hurting her baby boy.

"Um, I'm not sure yet Kai but don't worry about it. Just have a good day at school. I love you okay?"

"Okay," he said, before he turned to run towards his bus.

Mia waved and mouthed "*sorry,*" to the bus driver who in return rolled her eyes and pulled away.

"Mm." Mia laughed loud to herself as she headed back into the house.

"You want me to roll up?" Mia asked as she walked back into the house. She needed to put her mind at ease asap, thinking about what Kai asked.

"I'm already two steps ahead of you lil mama." Dax said as he patted to the empty spot next to him on the couch and sparked the blunt.

Mia walked over and sat down beside him, contemplating on if she should bring up Malakai wondering about Reese or not.

"Here babe." Dax said, reaching the blunt to Mia.

Reese decided to sit away from the group to avoid the interrogation he knew Mia's friends would impose on him. Mia had his head fucked up a lot more than he cared to admit. He started to just call out of work because he figured that she wouldn't come in anyway but since he wasn't sure, he came in with his game face on. He refused to give her the benefit of seeing him hurt. He blasted Rooga and Lil Moe's "*Scrappers*," to drown out his thoughts of Mia as he sat at the end of the table.

Lola, Alyssa, Chanel and Ballow sat in the break room wondering why Mia didn't come to work and why Reese was sitting in on the opposite end of the table alone, listening to music. They knew that normally if one of them called out they would both call out. After Lola noticed that Mia left her text on read, they knew something had to have happened.

"Where you at today Mimi?" Mia read the text from Lola and decided not to reply. She didn't feel like explaining everything she had enough going on as it was. She knew they would all be taken aback by her decision, including Corrie and Egypt. She could only imagine what would come out of her mom's mouth when she found out. She sat down next to Dax on the sofa and just shook her head at the thought. After inhaling the thick smoke, she melted into the couch and her thoughts drifted off to Reese. She wondered if he was good but she knew she was the cause of all everything and definitely the last person he wanted to hear from.

Mia fell out laughing, after hearing Chief Keef's, "*Understand Me,*" began to play through the soundbar, interrupting her thoughts. Chief Keef had been both of their favorite artist at one point and time. They would ride around the city blasting his old mixtapes as Dax would bust his licks. Nobody could tell Mia she wasn't Dax's trap queen as a young teen. She looked up after feeling Dax tap her on the knee as he stood in front of her, cupping his meat and playfully rocking back and forth as he rapped the song to her. She pointed at Dax with the blunt between her fingers, as she began to recite the song word for word back to him. She squinted her eyes as she watched his swole, tatted chest through the smoke as the blunt dangled from her lips.

"Here hubby." Mia said, reaching the blunt up to him. Licking her lips after they made eye contact. "Let me play something." she said.

"What do you want to hear babe?" Dax asked after taking the blunt and putting his arm around her to pull her closer.

"For the night, by Pop Smoke." Mia said, watching Dax.

"Alright I got you." Dax said, before searching the song.

"Give me a kiss." Mia whispered, after she heard the melodies of the flute and guitar come to life.

After waking up and picking up her phone, Mia snuggled up closer to Dax as she scrolled through her facebook timeline.

"What the hell," she said, stopping at a post with Dax posing holding his middle finger up with Spook and two other females. She recognized Spook's babymom Mercedes but she didn't know the chick that Dax had his arm draped across her shoulders from a can of paint.

"Ayo." Mia said, using her elbow to nudge him awake.

"What babe damn. You all rough." Dax grumbled.

"Who the fuck is this bitch with the stale red bob that you got your arm around in a picture?" Mia said as she rolled over and stuck her phone into his face.

"Yo she was Mercedes' homegirl, all we did was take a picture." Dax said, in a nonchalant tone.

"Oh, ok so now you're a celebrity, and random bitches just want to take pictures with you?" Mia said sarcastically. "The hell?" she continued, while reaching over Dax to their night stand to grab her pink blunt cutter, her weed and her pack of watermelon Game blunts.

"Babe stop it, you know I been that nigga man. I can't help that I'm hood famous." Dax told her, sitting up in the bed.

"The fuck outta here. After all the embarrassing shit we've been through on social media, going back and forth, arguing and putting all of our business out there. You would think that the last thing you would want to do is post up with some random ass bitch. You ready to have the whole city thinking this bitch is your girl.

Especially since we haven't even announced that we're back together. My family don't know," Mia said, pausing to lick the blunt paper. "Your family don't know, my friends don't know."

"Man everybody knows Dax and Mia are always going to be together! The hell? Who cares!" Dax yelled, "We're not married to them, we're married to each other. See that's your problem right there, you're always worrying about what mothafuckers think." He said, before getting off the bed.

"I'm going to take my shower. Then we can take pictures and post them but niggas know what the fuck it is." Dax said before heading out of the bedroom.

Chapter 3

"I know ya'll saw Mia's facebook yesterday?" Alyssa asked, looking at Chanel as they worked on the line.

"Yeah I saw that shit. I ain't even say anything, I just liked it and kept it moving. They look happy as hell and what can we say for real? That's literally her husband." Chanel said, shrugging.

"Husband or no husband, that nigga dogged her and she takes him back just that easy?" Alyssa said with her face twisted in disgust. "We gotta get her to come to her senses about this shit."

"Man, she ain't going to be trying to hear what you have to say Lyssa. She been with that nigga since she was 13." Ballow said, carrying a stack of boxes.

"Mia is old enough to make her own decisions. Us debating about it ain't going to change nothing. That's her business." Lola said glaring at Alyssa.

"Hey O.G.!" Alyssa said, looking down the line over at Mrs. Pat, an older black lady that worked beside Mia for the past few years. She was in her mid-50's and had a gold tooth, the rumor on the job was that she had been wild when she was coming up so Alyssa liked to call her O.G. but Mrs. Pat was normally quiet. She minded her business and stayed quiet as she soaked up everything Alyssa, Lola, Chanel, Mia and Ballow would say.

"You think you could talk some sense into Mia for me whenever she gets back?" Alyssa asked.

"There's not much I can tell her Alyssa," Mrs. Pat said. "trust me, I used to be just like Mia if not worst. That's how I got some of these old scars across my face," Mrs. Pat said as she ran her finger over a scar across her left eyebrow. "but honestly there's not going to be much neither one of us can say to her right now. She's in love and she's going to have to come out of it on her own because I've been there and done that so our words won't really affect her."

"Bingo!" Lola said, pointing to Mrs. Pat.

"Yeah that's true." Chanel said, agreeing. "At least now we know why Reese was looking like that yesterday. We should've never tried to hook them up." Chanel said, shaking her head.

"Nah, she gave Dax a taste of his own medicine. I'm glad we did it." Alyssa said.

"Me too." Lola said, nodding her head.

Mia stood under the steaming hot shower water with her eyes closed as Dax ran a lathered rag across her back.

Dax admired Mia's silhouette from behind as he worked his way down, to his name tattooed on her ass surrounded by her light tiger stripes.

"Let me wash your back babe." She finally said, turning around to face him.

"Aight." Dax said, handing her back her rag, before they switched sides.

"Damn this is why I don't take showers with you, you'll give a nigga 3rd degree burns." He said laughing as he reached for the knob to change the water temperature.

"Uh uh babe, you're used to those lukewarm prison showers," Mia said, reaching over his shoulder to swap her rag with his and grab his body wash from the shower rack. "That shit was feeling good to me," she continued.

Dax put his head under the shower and let the warm water run down his face as he felt Mia scrubbing his back.

"You got bigger babe." He heard Mia mumble before he felt her thrust her pelvis into him.

"What the fuck are you doing man!?" Dax asked, cracking up.

"Hitting it from the back," Mia said as she continued to try to hump Dax from behind.

"Come on Mia chill!" Dax said, turning around to his side to hold Mia back. "You always on some gay shit." Dax said laughing as he struggled to maintain his balance, wrestling with Mia in the sudsy shower.

"Ahhh!" Mia cried laughing after she slipped and

grabbed Dax causing them both to come crashing down onto the floor, snapping all the shower curtain hooks on the way down.

"Ayyooo!" Mia yelled, cracking up as she and Dax laid on the floor laughing. "My back!"

"I think my shit broke," Dax hollered, between laughs putting his hand on his hip bone.

Mia laughed even harder when she looked over at Dax and saw him twisted up inside of the shower curtain with both of his feet still hanging over the tub.

"I fucked the shit out of you." She said as they both continued to lay there, laughing through the pain.

Mia slipped into an oversized t-shirt as Dax stepped into a pair of nike pro boxers after finally getting up from the floor.

"I'm about to order something, what do you want to eat Dax?" Mia asked, as she strolled through denny's menu.

"I ain't hungry yet babe." he said, before he pressed play on moneybags.

"Well i'm ordering french toast, eggs and hash browns. When my food comes don't be breathing all on my neck and shit trying to ask me for mine." Mia told him.

"I wont, but you trying to drink babe?" Dax asked, looking over at Mia.

"It's too early, it's not even 12 yet." Mia said, before she continued to rap along with the music, deciding to make a video on snapchat.

"Well i'm about to pop me a yerky!" Dax said hopping up off the bed to run and get his pills.

"Oh lord here we go." Mia said, shaking her head.

"I ain't trying to hear that shit babe, i've been chilling for real. And I wouldn't need one if you hadn't made us fall out the fucking shower." Dax yelled over the music, as he stood at the fridge opening a bottle of water.

"Yeah aight!" Mia hollered, before pulling her phone out.

After ordering two breakfast plates, Mia walked around and lit her candles all throughout the house. After finding Dax on the couch smoking another blunt with his bottle of water, she took the blunt from him and sat down beside him, "You want to watch something with me?" she asked him.

"Yeah, go ahead and pick something." Dax told her, before reaching for the remote.

"Man you ain't gone do nothing but complain about what I pick." Mia said, pouting before retrieving the remote from him.

"Babe you do be watching some weird ass shows," Dax said laughing. "But I'll watch it with you today, put it on." He told her.

Mia went through her list on Netflix and found, *"The originals."*

"See, what the fuck is this? Some damn vampires and werewolves?" Dax asked.

"Yes yo, but give it a chance." Mia said, elbowing Dax. "They be wrecking shit I promise you."

"Nah lil mama, put some gangsta shit on." Dax said, taking the remote and pointing it at the television.

Mia yawned after Dax chose a regular hood classic. She didn't understand how he didn't get tired of watching what they already lived or at least witnessed day to day.

Twenty minutes into the movie Mia looked over at Dax, who was nodding out from the effects of the prescription pills. She huffed and rolled her eyes, while she waited for their food to arrive.

That night, Mia stood at Malakai's door and watched Dax as he tucked him in. Their father and son bond was what separated Dax from any other man in her eyes. She remembered times when she was growing up, where she'd wonder where her own father was and whether he loved her or not. So she cherished that she married the father of her child and was able to give Malakai the experience of living with both parents. She knew first hand how gangsta Dax could be at times so watching him dote on their son, gave her an overwhelming sense of love and appreciation. Unconsciously putting Dax on an unparalleled pedestal above the rest.

"What babe?" Dax asked, with a smirk after he caught a glimpse of Mia's enchanted stare.

Mia smiled before looking down at her pink toe nails sitting inside of her peek toe fuzzy slippers.

Dax walked over to her and stopped in front of her before he leaned his head into hers.

“What babe?” He asked again, smiling.

“Nothing, I just love you that’s all.” Mia said before leaning in for a kiss.

“I love you too little mama.” Dax said, before he softly patted her ass.

“How far can you go outside? Can we sit on the step and smoke?” Mia asked.

“Yeah, we should be good. I think I can’t go outside the yard of some shit.” Dax said, grabbing his lighter and cigarettes as Mia grabbed her blunt.

After stepping outside, Dax sat on the top step and Mia sat down on the second step in between his legs. Dax lit his cigarette and passed the lighter to Mia as she sat looking up at the moon.

“Hey babe? Can I ask you something?” Mia said, staring off in a daze.

“Yeah babe, what’s up?” Dax asked, blowing out the smoke and looking down at her.

“How come you’ve never showed me how to shoot a gun? Can you?” Mia asked, struggling to light her blunt.

Dax leaned forward and shielded her blunt from the night air with his hand as she lit it. “Nah babe man. You will fuck around and shoot me.” Dax said laughing but deep down he was serious. He’d seen Mia’s anger get the best of her countless times before and putting a gun in her hand was the last thing he wanted to do.

Mia inhaled the thick smoke before she turned to face him. “Why would you say that?” she asked, with a frown. “I would not.”

“I don’t think you ever would do it intentionally babe. But we both know how you get when you’re mad. How about this, right, how about we both work on our anger issues and then i’ll teach you.” Dax said, nodding his head after Mia grinned in response. She put her arms over his knees and relaxed as the weed finally began to mellow her out. She leaned her head back into his lap and gazed as the bright stars in the dark sky.

“I got you babe.” Dax said, as she passed the blunt to him. He retrieved the blunt before looking up to join her as she watched the stars.

Chapter 4

Mia walked into work Friday morning already knowing what the topic of discussion would be on the manufacturing line. *"They not finna get me outta character today,"* she thought to herself as soon as she walked into the room. She and Dax had had a ball the entire three days that she took off and she was convinced that she made the right decision. Now all she had to do was try to apologize to Reese again and pray he forgave her.

"Mia back!" Lulu their room's line leader said in her heavy Filippino accent, as she got up from her desk to meet Mia.

"Lil sis!" Alyssa said from across the room, throwing her hands in the air.

"You take husband back?" Lulu asked as the whole room got quiet.

Mia's eyebrows furrowed as she smiled and looked down at Lulu nodding.

"Ohhh, no good. Reese sad." Lulu continued as she looked up at Mia.

"Lulu how do you know my business?" Mia asked, walking past her towards Alyssa, Chanel and Ballow who were cracking up.

"Everyone know, you get close to Reese and stop wearing, ring." Lulu said pointing to her own ring finger.

"Well damn," Mia said, shrugging. "Alright ya'll let's just do this work." She said pointing towards the line. The last thing she wanted to think about was how she had made Reese feel, but she knew it was inevitable.

Deep in thought, the first break bell rung before Mia knew it. Just last week she would be flying out into the hallway to wait for Reese but now everything had changed and she felt like it was time for her to face the music.

She decided to stay behind and wait for Reese in the hallway as everybody headed upstairs to the break room. She fidgeted with the buttons on her lab jacket as she thought about how to say everything.

Reese hit the corner with his face planted inside of his phone.

"Reese." Mia softly called out.

"What's up?" he said dryly as he looked up at her.

"I just wanted us to talk so that we can just clear the air and avoid the tension everybody is probably expecting between us." She said, scratching a spot in her head that wasn't itching. "I know things won't be the way they were, and we don't have to be the best of friends but I don't want us to be enemies or for you to stay pissed and upset with me." Mia told him.

"It is what it is Mia." Reese said, sliding his phone into his pocket. "You can't help who you love right." He told her, blowing out his breath before allowing his eyes to meet hers.

"So we're cool?" Mia asked him as she searched his brooding eyes.

"As a fan." Reese said with a half-hearted smile as he reached his hand out to shake hers.

"Reese, I hope you really forgive me and you're not just saying it. I know how you are." Mia said, searching his eyes.

"This ain't about nothing Mia, so don't even stress it aight?" He said smiling to reassure her.

"Okay," Mia said before they headed towards the break room in silence together.

"It's only been 5 days and I'm ready to get the fuck out of here already." Dax said to Spook as they sat in the living room smoking and drinking.

"I know this shit is killing you bro, how long they got on you this shit." Spook asked.

"It's supposed to be two or three months, but this shit is crazy though. I didn't even want Mia to leave for work, you know normally i'd be leaving right behind her ass," Dax said laughing. "And then tomorrow night she's going to Baltimore to go to her sister's house for a little party, so i'm just going to be stuck in this bitch looking crazy."

"Damn so what's up with that work shit anyway bro? You ain't worried about yo? You know them 9 to 5 niggas don't be playing fair." Spook said, looking over at Dax.

"I ain't worried about that shit bro, that nigga ain't retarded." Dax said, folding his arms and leaning back into the couch.

"Yeah aight nigga," Spook said standing up and stretching his arms to the ceiling, "but look, I got some running around to do bro. You need some bread?" Spook asked.

"Don't come in here trying to son me nigga, I ain't broke. Fuck you talkin bout." Dax said, laughing before pulling out his last roll of hundreds that he had stashed in the pantry while he was away.

"Bluffing ass nigga man." Spook said, before heading towards the front door. "And look I almost forgot, I found you a couple." Spook said, pulling out a sandwich bag with 5 yellow tiny pills.

"My mothafuckin nigga." Dax said, doing his little two-step before giving Spook dap.

"Alright bro, but listen take your time with these. I heard them shits are some pressure, so they'll have you tweakin' if you don't." Spook said, pointing to the baggie before walking out.

Dax stood in the empty, silent house and decided to test the pills out right then and there. He popped two and grabbed his sprite to wash them down. He decided to lay down and wait for them to kick in. Eventually his imagination took hold as he pondered on how Mia and Reese were in fact interacting at work. He folded one of his arms underneath his head, as he stared over at the muted television envisioning all the various scenarios and possibilities.

"You good Mimi?" Lola said after Mia walked into the crowded break room behind Reese and sat in her normal seat.

"I'm straight." Mia said, pulling out her phone.

"You and Reese cool?" Chanel asked, looking at Reese who sat a chair away from Mia with his headphones still in.

"Yeah, I apologized again." Mia said, looking over at him.

"That's what's up." Alyssa said across from Mia. "I'm going to invite him to the laser tag shit Saturday, since he ain't going with you across the bridge now."

"You think he'll come?" Lola asked.

Alyssa shrugged and looked at him, "he might be glad to shoot some shit up."

"I think he'll go." Mia said, looking at her phone wondering why Dax texted her, *"Fuck you doing!?"* With a dozen suspicious face emojis.

Reese drove the forklift in the warehouse, with Kc & Jojo's *"Crazy,"* rattling his ear drums. He resented the fact that he couldn't express his true feelings to Mia. He told her he was alright but what he really wanted to tell her that he missed her, missed talking to her, laughing with her, chilling with her. Deep down he missed waking up to her, he missed their smoke sessions and of course their mind-blowing sex.

He shook his head at the thought. He prayed that Dax would somehow mess up enough for her to be done with him for good. He knew it was wishful thinking and he was aware that he sounded foolish but he couldn't help how he felt. Mia had permanently stolen his heart under temporary circumstances.

Mia was excited to be home knowing Dax was inside waiting, before he got on the box he would never be home when she got off work.

After walking through the front door, she walked through the empty living room straight down the hall to the bedroom but he wasn't there either. She walked backwards and turned the knob on the bathroom door. She found Dax sitting face down hugging the towel bowl as he threw up.

"What the heck?" Mia said, with her nose wrinkled as she slowly approached him.

Dax wiped the sweat forming on the bridge of his nose after lifting his head up.

"Fuck no." Mia said, backing up before she covered her mouth.

"What the hell did you eat?" She said, pinching her nose.

"I will throw the fuck up." She continued, swallowing slowly.

"I was drinking and popped to many pills I think." He said, before laying his head back down onto his forearm.

"But what did that nigga Reese say to you today? I know he said something. He ain't gone let you go that easy." *Immu kill that nigga.* Dax thought to himself.

"He didn't say anything, leave them pills alone." Mia said, before turning on her heels and walking out the bathroom. *He didn't say nothing, I did. Leave him alone.* She thought to herself. She couldn't imagine Dax doing something to him because of her dumbness. She closed the door behind herself, praying they would never run into each other.

Chapter 5

Cali's Housewarming Party

The following afternoon, Mia pulled up to Corrie's house and braced herself for the conversation that she knew was inevitable. She beeped the horn and just shook her head as she waited for her to emerge.

"What's up mom? Hey lil sis!" Mia said, after Corrie and Keegan came out and opened the passenger side front and back door to climb in.

"You tell me Mia. I mean shit, you left Reese for Daxton?" Corrie asked, slamming the door. She leaned her back into the door as she turned and looked at Mia.

Mia threw her hands up.

Corrie sucked her teeth while repositioning to grab her seatbelt.

"He ain't going to do shit but drag you down! Why you don't see that is fucking beyond me." Corrie yelled.

"Alright so mom, did you or did you not have three kids by our dad even after you saw that he wasn't the best man in the world? How do you explain that? Love right? That's all this is man." Mia said, hoping that Corrie would understand.

"So you really think that because he's Malakai's dad you have to stay with him?" Corrie huffed.

"Not have to but I want to mom, I love him. He's my soulmate," Mia said in a high-pitched tone, "and I don't want my kids to have different father's mom, i'm trying to be like you!" Mia said, with her hands on her chest.

"Be like me huh, so you want to raise three kids alone? Struggling and trying to make a dolla' outta fifteen cents your whole life?" Corrie scoffed.

"It wasn't that bad mom, we turned out alright but let's just change the subject big Corr." Mia said, putting her truck into drive and slowly pulling off.

"Hmmp." Corrie said, before pulling out her phone and ignoring Mia.

"So what's going on Keegan? You good back there?" Mia said, adjusting her rearview mirror to see Keegan's face.

"I'm good, did mom tell you that we're moving to Atlanta in a couple months? We all are transferring our jobs, we thought you would come too but now that you're back with Dax, that's dead." Keegan said, before looking out of the window.

Mia squinted her eyes as she processed the news, first Egypt moved to Baltimore, then Cali and now Corrie and Keegan were moving 12 hours away.

"Ain't this about a bitch. I guess it really is me, Dax and Malakai against the world." She thought to herself.

"Nah I ain't know that Keegan." Mia said, catching Keegans gaze in the mirror before refocusing her eyes on the road.

They all remained quiet for the remainder of the ride, fixated on their own thoughts and social media timelines.

Cali stood at her kitchen counter twerking to her favorite rapper as she made her infamous jungle juice. She mixed 2 bottles of Ciroc, one bottle of bombay sapphire and a bottle of Absolut before mixing it with 3 small cans of pineapple juice and a carton of peach minute maid. She cut up fresh pineapples, tossing them into her punch bowl as well before she placed them in the refrigerator.

Her boyfriend Zay walked into the kitchen with his homeboy Black in tow as they headed out the back door. Zay walked over to the counter and picked up the empty bottle of bombay sapphire.

“You know this is Gin right Cali?” He asked, looking over at her as she pulled ground beef, onions and green peppers from the fridge.

“Mhmm.” Cali said, while nodding as she looked over at him.

“You mixing vodka with dry gin, ya’ll gone be fucked all the way up.” Zay said, looking over at Black who was standing by the back door.

“Slim said she turnin up.” Black said, with a chuckle.

“Ya'll crazy but we bout to ride over to the liquor store on green ave.” Zay said, walking over to Cali and kissing her on her cheek as she stood at the sink rinsing the vegetables.

Cali waved them off as she continued to rock to Kevin Gates.

"Put my City girlz on!" Corrie yelled over the loud music that was already playing. It was a little past 7p.m. by the time they arrived and by now everybody was already halfway lit, just waiting for Cali to finish cooking so they could really turn up.

"Look at Corrie!" Egypt said laughing, "Ayyeee get it Corrie!" Egypt said as Corrie attempted to twerk.

"Mom is lit." Keegan said calmly as she laid back on the couch.

"Ayo," Mia said, laughing before she took a shot of her apple ciroc, "Cali you still frying the chicken?" Mia yelled so Cali could hear her from the living room.

"I just got finished, alright come on ya'll. I made meatballs, greens, hot wings, fried chicken and corn on the cob." Cali said walking into the living room.

"Now we talking." Mia said, hopping up and running towards the kitchen with everybody else not too far behind.

"Alright ya'll, now let's just do the movie charades." Cali suggested, after everybody was done eating.

"All we do is come up here, say a line in a movie and if nobody can guess the movie then we all have to take a shot." Cali explained after she saw Keegan's face screwed up.

"Well Imma be drunk as hell because I don't watch t.v." Keegan said, raising her cup, "shit let's do it."

"Ya'll wanna do partners to make it easier?" Egypt asked everybody.

"Yeah, let's do partners." Corrie said.

"Alright cool well I'll just do one to show ya'll what I mean." Cali said getting up and going to the front of the room.

"Ya'll wanna see a bitch go down the slide?" Cali said obnoxiously with one hand on her hip, "I'll show you how a bitch-"

"Norbit!" Everyone yelled at once.

"Even I knew that one!" Keegan said.

"Yep," Cali said "see it's fun! Your turn Mia, I know you got one!" Cali said, walking over to her. "Pick one that they won't guess." Cali whispered into Mia's ear.

Mia smiled and nodded her head, "Alright ya'll hold on. Let me get on my acting shit." She said, putting on her resting bitch face as she traded places with Cali.

"I hate you!" Mia yelled, in her best southern accent after a few seconds, "you're only here because mom says it's our Christian duty!" she said before acting like she was crying.

"No she didn't say, *Christian dooty.*" Corrie hollered, mimicking Mia's accent, causing everybody to fall out.

"Damn sis," Cali said, giving Mia the side eye as she scratched her head.

"I knew ya'll wouldn't know that one, it was from the old version of the movie *It!* See ya'll ain't fucking with me." Mia said laughing, "now everybody take a shot!"

"You're phone's ringing Mia." Egypt said, handing it to Mia.

"What's up babe?" Mia said after answering.

"Answer your facetime, let me see who all in that mothafucker." Dax said.

"Babe you trippin'. This is a girls' night little house warming it's all females." Mia told him as she walked into the kitchen.

"Facetime me." Dax repeated.

"You trippin," Mia said while requesting to facetime him, "now look!" Mia said after he answered and could see her. She headed back into the noisy living room with an attitude.

"You satisfied or what man?" Mia said, showing him everybody all around the room talking and laughing.

"Yo go ahead with that insecure mess Dax," Egypt said, snatching the phone from Mia. "We chilling, having a good time. She'll be home tomorrow." She said, rolling her eyes and handing the phone back to Mia.

"Didn't nobody call to see you Egypt, ya'll both in there with them short ass dresses on but aight, I love you babe call me before you go to sleep, I'll be up." Dax said.

"Alright hubby." Mia said before disconnecting

the call.

Work crew

"But did ya'll see Chanel run into that wall trying to get away from Ballow though!?" Alyssa asked, as they all sat around the oversized hibachi table in the Japanese restaurant, after leaving laser tag.

"I told ya'll we shouldn't of drank that much before we started, shit I got dizzy and some more shit. It felt like I was going to throw up for real!" Chanel said, before leaning down to sip out of her volcano bowl.

"But your ass is still drinking though!" Alyssa said, laughing.

"That shit reminded me of the time, we all got drunk before going to that haunted cornfield that year. Ya'll remember that shit?" Ballow asked, looking around the table.

"Oh my gosh, yes! I forgot about that, that was the year Mia lost her shoe right?" Lola asked, leaning up in her seat.

"Hell yeah, that nigga with the chainsaw was chasing her. Mia is funny as shit man, swear she tough and scary as hell." Ballow said, laughing.

"Chill on my lil sis. But yo so Reese, how do you feel man? I ain't trying to be all in ya'll shit but are ya'll good now? We see that she took that lame ass nigga back but we can all tell you that she does really care about you." Alyssa asked, looking around at the group.

"Hell yeah man, don't give up on her yet because it's only a matter of time before Dax fucks up again." Chanel said, pointing at Reese.

"Real shit, it's only a matter of time." Alyssa said, nodding in agreement.

Reese sat up in his seat a little bit as the question swiveled in his brain. He knew it would come up eventually but he was glad they had all been drinking, which made it easier to let down his guard.

"I can't lie, I was mad as shit at first but now i'm realizing that I put myself in this situation from the jump. She's young and that nigga is all she's ever known, so it's going to take a minute for her to finally ever be done with his ass. But like ya'll said, it's only matter of time." Reese said, before shrugging before leaned back in his seat with his legs wide open. "But yeah so when that time comes, I got her for sure."

"That's what it is." Ballow said, realizing that Reese was a stand up guy. He couldn't say the same if it had been him, he wished one of his hoes would try to carry him.

"Real nigga shit!" Alyssa said, cheesing, "we gots to toast to that."

"All we're saying is, you can't change a man! If they don't want to do right then you can't force them," Egypt said holding her hands up as if to surrender, "let his ass go."

"Exactly," Corrie said, turning to Egypt, "why

would she leave a nice working man like Reese for lying, cheating, disrespectful ass Dax?!" Corrie yelled, throwing her hands in the air and shaking her head.

"Mom why are ya'll talking about me like i'm not present? We already had this conversation on the way here. I can't explain something that I don't understand myself. You don't think I know that Reese is a good man? I was the one with him for a year." Mia said pointing to her chest, "yeah we had hella fun and he never disrespected me but it just still wasn't enough to replace the love I feel for Dax. I can't even explain it, that's just how deep that shit is big Corr." Mia said, looking down at her phone and laughing.

"I don't see a damn thing funny," Corrie said looking around the room, "seriously Mia have you looked in the mirror? I mean really sat and looked in the mirror? You can have anybody your heart desires, okay? Don't forget that the next time ya'll are fighting like Ike and Tina." Corrie said.

"Nah Ike used to whoop Tina's ass, I always get my licks in believe that." Mia said, causing Keegan to bust out laughing but she was dead serious. She didn't look at her and Dax's fights as abusive or a domestic violence type situation, she knew that nine times out of ten she always threw the first blow and to her it was normal.

"My sister is crazy." Keegan continued, covering her mouth as she laughed.

"Don't laugh at her, I be trying to tell her Corrie, she don't be trying to hear it though." Egypt said, shaking her head.

"Are ya'll still talking about relationships?" Cali

asked with a frown as she came downstairs with Zay and Black.

"Not relationships, just *my* relationship." Mia said, rolling her eyes to the ceiling. She couldn't stand that she constantly had to defend her and Dax's relationship to the people she loved. They would never change the fact that Dax had her heart no matter what they said.

"I just want to know how mom is so judgmental about the fighting aspect of it all when she used to do the same stuff when we were growing up. I learned from you mom." Mia said standing up, "if you can't beat a man what do you do Cali!?" she said, walking over to Cali and shrugging her shoulders.

"Pick up something and bust they head to the white meat." Keegan said, chiming in as Cali stood there sipping her wine.

"Exactly! Even little sis knows!! Come on now!" Mia yelled.

"Nah! But hold up though my situations were always different I was defending myself! Don't make it seem like I'm out here teaching ya'll that having a violent relationship is normal! That shit ain't cute!" Corrie said standing up as well.

"I never said that! But look, Dax likes to cheat and sometimes he's disrespectful out of his mouth so of course I'm throwing the first punches!" Mia said defending her actions.

Black stood back with Zay listening to the unfamiliar women debate, while observing Mia, wondering who she was and who was crazy enough to be straight up disrespecting her to the degree that she was speaking on but since he didn't know her it wasn't his place to step in or get involved.

"Nah that ain't it bestfriend. I'm with big Corr on this one." Egypt said, shaking her head. "Listen to how you sound though, he's cheating and calling you out of your name, if that ain't enough to leave than what is?" Egypt asked.

"Exactly!!" Corrie said, throwing her hands up in the air. "I told you before not to be stupid! I didn't raise no damn dummies!"

"Who the fuck is dumb though mom?" Mia questioned, looking across the room at Corrie.

"You!" Corrie hollered.

"Alright now mom chill." Cali said, walking over to Corrie.

"No fuck that, that's what it is! I'm tired of everybody beating around the fucking bush!" Corrie said, slamming her cup on the table, causing beer to splash everywhere. "You're being fucking dumb! And I didn't raise no stupid ass bitches!"

Mia's nostrils flared as she squinted her eyes, glaring at her mother. Tears of humiliation slid down her check before Mia charged at Corrie ready to fight.

"No ya'll!"

"Nah!"

"Chill!" Everybody said getting between Corrie and Mia.

"Nah let me go," Mia said, struggling to break free

from Egypt and Black's grip as they held her back.

"Na slim, that's ya mova." Black said, stepping in to grab Mia.

"I wish the fuck you would Mia! He split your shit wide open, cheats on you, disrespects you for the whole world to see, and you're ready to fight ME to defend that mothafucker!" Corrie screamed as she tried to get past Cali, Keegan, and Zay. "A stupid bitch like the fuck I said! And I ain't one of those little bitches you be fighting on the street. I will fuck you up Mia!" Corrie yelled pointing at Mia.

Sober Mia had common sense and knew she wasn't seeing Corrie but drunk Mia saw red and felt like she had a chance. Black bear hugged her from behind and dragged her out of the front door with Egypt behind him.

"Get off me! I'm good!" Mia yelled through her tears, after they got her outside to her truck.

"Can you stand here with her while I get her coat and stuff?" Egypt asked Black.

"Yeah slim." Black said, looking over at Mia who was leaning up against her passenger side door with tears still in her eyes. He felt sorry for her but decided to just stand there with her in silence, not wanting to make the situation worse.

The silence made Mia self-conscious after she had peeped how attractive Black was standing across from her underneath the street light, in his black and grey nike jogging set with silver chrome foamposites. He was as dark as his name suggested and she appreciated his height and the neatness of his two strand-twist styled dreads. She quickly tried to wipe her eyes and pick at imaginary lent on her dress, before folding her arms.

After calming Corrie down, Cali came outside to check on Mia and bring her belongings to her, "you good lil sis?" she asked, coming down the pathway.

"I'm good, but mom won't ever have to worry about me again." Mia said, before snatching her keys, backpack purse and distressed jean jacket from Cali.

"Come on Mia, you know how mom is." Cali reasoned.

"It's cool Cali," Mia sniffled and shrugged.

"Thanks for helping us, what did you say your name was again?" Egypt asked Black after she returned.

"No problem, but my name is Black." He said.

"Alright, good looking." Egypt said.

"Keep your head up slim." He said, turning to Mia before heading back inside.

"Why the hell did you do that?" Mia whispered, after Egypt was in talking distance.

"Do what?" Egypt said smiling.

"You gone leave me outside with this nigga," Mia said pointing towards Black as he walked inside, "I'm out here looking ugly as shit crying, you left and I had to take a double take of this nigga," Mia said laughing, "like, wait a minute! Let me pull myself together and why ya'll ain't have my back in there yo?" Mia asked, looking from Egypt to Cali.

"Ahh! You were crying your ugly cry too!" Egypt

said as she bent over cracking up at Mia. "And don't get mad at us you know me and Cali don't condone that violent bullshit you and Dax be on."

Normally Mia would just go stay the night with Egypt but she was in a hurry to get back to Dax.

"Yeah whatever. Well, i'm out, let me get home to Ike." Mia said, before hugging Cali and Egypt.

"Mom why did you have to say it like that?" Cali asked, looking at Corrie. "You know she takes everything to heart."

"I said what needed to be said! She needs to get it through her head!" Corrie said, pointing to her temple. "He ain't the one!"

"That was a little messed up though mom," Keegan said.

"I don't give a damn, ya'll won't understand until you have a daughter of your own who grows up and lets a man treat her like trash, it hurts me for real! This is the only way I know to get through to her." Corrie said.

"I've been asking myself, where did I go wrong in raising her." Corrie continued before walking out shaking her head.

Dax threw his clothes into the dirty clothes hamper after hopping out of the shower. He opened his top drawer and slipped on his boxer briefs before facetiming Mia.

"You ain't call me." He said as soon as she picked up.

"I'm already on my way home." Mia said.

"What ya'll got into it again?" Dax asked her through the phone, he could tell she had been crying and he knew how she and her fam had a tendency to get physical from time to time.

"Man something like that but, I'll talk to you when I get home." Mia said.

"Are you sure yo?" Dax asked her.

"Yeah, I'm cool." Mia said, but deep down she kept replaying what Corrie said to her over and over in her head. For as long as she could remember, she had always felt like Corrie was more strict with her and treated her differently than Cali and Keegan and she had a good idea as to why that was.

"Cali, Mia, Keegan! Come down here for a second." Corrie yelled from the bottom of the steps.

Ten-year-old Cali, 7-year-old Mia and 5-year-old Keegan came running down.

"Aight listen up, I'll be right back. Ya'll don't answer the door for anybody, stay off that house phone and there is cereal and noodles that ya'll can eat." Corrie said, looking at the three girls.

"I mean what I said, you hear me Mia?" Corrie asked, pointing at her.

"Yeah." Mia said, looking over at Cali.

The trio watched as Corrie grabbed her purse and head out of the front door.

Sunday morning, the next day Corrie still hadn't returned. Mia was the first one awake and as usual she headed downstairs to the kitchen. She opened the refrigerator door and saw that the milk was gone. She folder her arms, she knew Cali wouldn't be up for another couple hours. She grabbed a clean bowl from the dish rack and a pack of noodles. Ripping the plastic with her teeth before putting the noodles into the microwave and turning the dial for the timer. She looked over at the house phone hanging on the kitchen wall and grinned. She was going to do something fun to pass the time. She removed the phone from the jack and dialed 911, like she had so many times.

"911, what is your emergency?" She heard a lady say through the phone.

Mia hung up the phone and giggled.

She repeated the same process over and over until smoke started coming from the microwave.

**Boom, boom, boom* Someone was banging on the front door.*

"Salisbury P.D. is anyone home?" A male voice said through the door.

Mia marched up to the door in her flannel nightgown and unlocked the door before snatching it open.

"My mom always leave us and I'm hungry." She said, rolling her neck and her eyes at the officer.

"Is that right?" The officer said before stepping inside.

Mia put her hands on her hips as she looked up at the middle aged male officer with ivory skin and dry dark hair and brows.

"We have a possible 10-17 here at 303 East Church street." He said, into his radio as he sniffed the burnt aroma in the air.

An hour later, Corrie pulled up to her house surrounded by police cars, an ambulance and a fire truck.

She jumped out of the car, and saw Cali, Keegan and Mia sitting on the chairs on the porch talking to the officers along with a black lady from child protective services.

"Ms. Smith we came here to do a welfare check after someone called and hung up several times. We found your three daughters. Two sleeping, while this one was about to burn the house down. Turn around and put your hands behind your back you're under arrest for child endangerment. Do you have any family that would be willing to come pick them up? If you don't the social worker will have to take them…." Corrie drowned his voice out as she glared at Mia.

"This is on you, you're always doing something!" She said, stomping her foot.

Mia turned her music up to distract her from her thoughts of the past.

Dax was slumped in the dark living room, on the couch, when Mia got home at 2:45a.m.

"Come on babe," Mia said, nudging him so they could go to bed together.

"I was trying to stay up and wait for you little mama," Dax said, stretching his arms to the ceiling before standing to his feet.

"Let me guess, a perk put you down huh?" Mia asked, looking up at him.

"You already know babe," he said, before yawning as he followed Mia down the hallway to their bedroom.

"I can't with you man," Mia said sitting on the edge of the bed.

"So, what happened though? Why did you come back early?" As he joined her on their bed.

"Man, Corrie and Egypt was straight trippin' babe. Like now I'm being a dumb bitch for wanting to be with you, we're Ike and Tina and some more shit." Mia said, looking at the various framed pictures on the dresser of her and Dax posing at different prisons during their visits. Why they couldn't see that their love was real, blew Mia's mind. In her eyes they were obviously on their Bonnie and Clyde shit. "They just do not understand," she concluded.

"And they ain't got to," Dax said, putting his arm around her before pulling her into him, "the whole hood thinks I'm crazy for coming home to you in spite of everything but you think for one second, I give a fuck? Hell naw, and you know why? Because they don't know what we've been through together and they ain't doing shit for neither one of us. When i'm down who's riding at the end of the day? You are. So fuck what they think lil mama. They ain't doing nothing but making us even closer because at the end of the day all we got is each other. Think of it like this, who was at our wedding?" Dax asked, looking at Mia.

"Just us." Mia said, instantly reminiscing on the day they got married.

"Exactly and that's all we need. I know that's your family and everything but they will probably never understand us and that's cool as long as I got my wife that shit don't matter to me. Yeah we fight and shit gets crazy but I'll always choose you over everything." Dax said, lightly squeezing Mia after she put her arms around his waist.

"When have we ever needed anybody else? he whispered in her ear. "We don't lil mama, remember that."

Mia smiled and exhaled as Dax held her in his arms. In that moment she came to the conclusion that as long as she had her lover and bestfriend, they couldn't go wrong but little did she know, that assumption couldn't be further from the truth.

Chapter 6

March 2020

3 weeks later....

Mia pranced along the hallway, hiding her airpod's underneath her long, soft, black faux locs, humming along to Beyonce and Jay-Z's, *"On the Run 2."* Mentally she had been on cloud 9, Dax's current predicament was drawing them closer together. She couldn't remember the last time that they had gotten along for so long without coming to blows and she was loving it.

"Ya'll heard that this corona virus shit they been talking about on the news is getting more serious. That's probably what this shit is about." Alyssa said to everybody as they walked down the hallway towards the meeting their job had suddenly called.

"Yeah, I heard Trump tweeted that we're officially in a national emergency." Ballow said.

"We should've known shit was about to get real when they canceled my classes." Mia said, pausing her music and rolling her eyes. She was still mad that she was being forced to drop her courses or take them online after the college had 'temporarily shutdown'. She opted to drop her classes already knowing she wouldn't be focused or motivated to do a damn thing with Dax at home.

"Niggas dropping like flies, and they don't know how to stop the shit." Chanel whispered as they all walked into the packed meeting room.

"Yo is that Brian?" Mia asked, discretely pointing to the front of the room as she covered her mouth to whisper to Alyssa, "if he's here you know shit is finna get real."

"Hell yeah." Alyssa whispered.

Dressed as if he were about to play in the national golf tournaments, Brian was your typical fortune 500 company owner. A handsome white man, with white sandy blonde hair and blue eyes. Brian owned dozens of pharmaceutical companies along the east coast before the age of 40. He was filthy rich, living the American dream.

"Alright guys, it looks like everyone is all here," Brian said, clasping his hands together before he smiled, flashing his perfect set of veneers as he greeted the crowded room, "for those of you who don't know, My name is Brian Garrett the founder and CEO of the company, to start this meeting off and give you all a better understanding of what i'm about to say I have a short news clip here, that I want you all to pay attention to on the projector." He said, turning towards an oversized white screen before lifting a tiny remote aiming it at the projector in the back of the room. He pressed play and folded his arms, as his eyes pierced the screen.

"As of today, Maryland schools will be joining

dozens of schools around the nation in a temporary shutdown to stop the spread of the deadly virus. Along with all schools, gyms, bars, restaurants, movie theaters and any other nonessential businesses will also have to temporarily close their doors this afternoon at 5p.m. We understand that this is an inconvenience to many but it is our job to protect the health and well-being of Maryland residents." The state Governor announced as he stood in front of a see-through acrylic podium.

After the video paused, Mia leaned up in her seat to look over at Lola, who matched Mia's gaze and mouthed, "*what the fuck.*"

"So as you all can see, this Covid-19 virus has taken a turn for the worse. The death rates are climbing and the president has officially declared that this pandemic is a national emergency. While they are doing what they can to keep us all safe, we as a company have to make a ton of changes to our policies, as well as to our operations to prevent ourselves from getting shut down as well. Now because we are a pharmaceutical manufacturing company, we are considered an essential business and will remain open but the CDC is especially on our coattails about changing our cleaning guidelines. So we will be shutting the facility down for one week as of now to bring in a professional team to perform an extensive deep clean."

"Will we still get paid?" Someone blurted, from the crowd.

"Everyone will be getting paid, the bad news is that because of the new protocols we will have to downsize our number of employees for the time being. We do have to let our temps go for now to ensure that we are able to do our work at least 6 feet apart. I apologize to you all, I wish there were another way but as of now, this is the only option for us." Brian said.

"Damnnn." Ballow said, as the whispers and chatter started to pick up around the room. Mia nor any of her friends were temps so the news didn't really affect them but it was still crazy that it was even happening.

She turned around and scanned the crowd with her eyes and spotted Reese standing in the back with his arms folded, discussing the news with the rest of the warehouse men. She hadn't really talked to him in a few weeks but times like this she'd normally be texting him, already knowing he'd have something funny to say. Although she was basking in all of Dax's loving, she still missed Reese's friendship.

"Alright you guys," Brian said, holding up his hands to get everyone's attention, "so the production and warehouse crews can clock out in about a half an hour," he said, looking down at his rose gold Ulysse Nardin watch, "everyone else is free to go. Remember that the virus is serious, stay inside as much as possible, alright? See you all next week."

"Time to hit the liquor store." Alyssa said, rubbing her hands together.

"Period." Chanel said, sticking her tongue out as she bounced her shoulders.

"Ya'll crazy." Lola said, looking over at Mia who was deep in thought. She wondered what all these official changes would mean for Dax and his house arrest.

Dax

"So have you come into direct contact with law enforcement since our last visit?" Dax's parole officer mumbled through her surgical face mask, while simultaneously typing into her keyboard.

"Direct contact, nah." Dax said.

"Well it looks like it's your lucky day Mr. Truitt," she said, peering at him over her rimless glasses, "your ankle monitor will be removed today." She paused and sighed before she continued, "with this new virus in our midst, we are being forced to significantly reduce the amount of people coming inside of the office. So anyone with nonviolent offenses are being cut loose but to be honest Dax, if it were up to me you'd stay on the monitor. In fact I put in a personal request for it but it was denied." She said not bothering to hide the disdain in her tone.

"A racist bitch." Dax thought.

"So, your free to do the honors." She told him as she took a pair of scissors from her drawer, slamming them onto her desk and sliding them towards him.

The conversations in the ladies locker room were unusually loud as everyone discussed their plans for their unexpected paid time off. Mia stood at her locker leaning down to her pink mirror applying her watermelon lip gloss, she planned to pick Malakai up from school and head straight home.

"So what we doing ya'll? Ya'll trying to turn up? Spades? Movie night?" Alyssa said, looking from Chanel to Mia.

"Who's turn is it to host?" Lola asked, excitement lacing her tone.

"Don't look at me, it was Chanel's turn for real but I might have to take a rain check." Mia said, after she slammed her locker door while rubbing her lips together.

"Damn it's like that? That nigga came home and now you can't even fuck with us?" Alyssa said, leaning her head to the side with her face frowned up.

"Dang, I said might, I don't know yet for real." Mia said, sliding her hands into her pockets in the back of her jeans.

Chanel and Lola stood back and watched Mia and Alyssa bicker back and forth and just shook their heads.

"Let's go ya'll." Chanel said.

"They done fucked up now," Dax laughed as he bopped out of the parole and probation office, headed back to Spook's car. He was officially off the box and ready to get back to the way things normally went. No longer confined to his house he could do what he did best.. get money. He knew Mia would be tight but he figured they had spent enough time together to hold her over while he ripped and ran freely, at least for the day. Now all he had to do was figure out whether he was going back to pulling capers, trappin' or both.

"What we doing for em bro?" Dax asked, after he hopped back in the car.

"I'm dropping your ass back off bro, you won't have the boys tracking my shit." Spook said, pulling off.

"Oh yeah?" Dax asked, with a smirk before lifting up his left pant leg.

"The fuck? You the luckiest mothafucker I know bro. What's up with you?" Spook said, laughing while looking at Dax with the side eye.

"The fuck you mean nigga. It's this virus shit, they freeing all the real niggas. You trying to go to Delmar, to the liquor store bro?" Dax said, before turning the volume up on his nigga Boosie.

Spook nodded before they whipped out into the traffic on route 13.

"Can I stay up one more hour mom? Please? I almost beat this new level!" Malakai asked, later that night after Mia cracked his door open to tell him it was time for bed. It was already an hour past his bedtime but she had let him slide because of the shutdown. She had already started sipping but she was waiting to smoke until he went to sleep. She looked at Malakai's beaming eyes and didn't detect a hint of sleepiness so she decided to let him stay up.

"Alright one more hour but that's it." She said, knowing he'd ask for an additional hour when she returned.

"Thanks mom, one more hour and i'll be done." he said, leaning his elbows onto his knees as he laser focused in on his 32 inch t.v. in front of him.

Mia chuckled on the inside, before she closed the door. With it going on 10:30pm, she thought about what Dax could be doing and with who. She had been blowing him up, but he had yet to respond. The more she drank and the later it got the madder she became, she figured that his sudden disappearance had something to do with the virus. Even still, if the P.O. had given him some sort of pass or let him off all together, he had already reverted back to ripping and running in the streets, ignoring her calls and putting her last.

After throwing on her thick fleece knee length robe, she grabbed her bottle, along with the blunt she had rolled earlier and decided to sit on her front step to smoke, while she drank to calm her nerves. Under normal circumstances she would never sit outside in the cold but with the alcohol in her system the chill didn't bother her half as much.

Before she knew it a half an hour had passed and she shielded her eyes after recognizing Spook's white charger pulled into the yard shining his headlights in her face.

"Well nigga, it was nice knowing you." Spook said, as he shut off the headlights and put the car in park while looking at Mia as she sat on the step in the cold.

"Pull off nigga, she ain't see us." Dax said, in a

drunken slur, as he slouched down in the passenger seat.

Spook hollered laughing as he looked at Dax trying to hide in plain view.

"Fuck you bro, I told your ass I had to come home, hours ago!" Dax yelled, trying to play it off, as he climbed out of the car.

"Yo, whoop his ass babe because I told this nigga." He continued, as he used his thumb to point behind him towards Spook while he walked towards Mia.

"This nigga." Spook continued to laugh as he backed out of the yard.

"Man listen, i'm not in a joking mood. I've been off work since 10:00 this morning. Me and Kai been here but yet, I haven't heard from you since 9:00 maybe? Are you crazy?" Mia said, with her face screwed up.

"I know babe, it's my fault they let me off the box unexpectedly. I was too hype, we weren't doing shit though babe we went straight to the liquor store and it's a blur from there." Dax said, after he sat down and joined her on the step.

Mia shot to her feet so fast that Dax slightly flinched.

"The fuck are you flinching for? And don't you think your reaction to your excitement seems misplaced? When good shit happens to me the first person I want to call is you. But when good things happen to you, i'm the last person on your mind." Mia said, before she yanked the glass storm door open, forcefully slamming it into Dax's back.

"Come on babe," Dax said, reaching for Mia's arm.

"No, it's all good." Mia said, snatching away before disappearing into the house. She went straight into the bedroom, grabbed a pair of pajamas and headed into the bathroom, locked the door, turned on her music and turned on the shower. She knew that now that he was off the box, all the time they had been spending together would be over with. She was used to him ripping and running in the streets all day. She could deal with that but what she needed him to do was pick up the phone when he was out and about. She also refused to put up with the disappearing acts he was famous for, so if he thought for a second he was going to be able to go ghost for days on end, he had another thing coming.

Chapter 7

The next morning, Dax slid out of bed and he looked over his shoulder at a sleeping Mia before grabbing fresh underclothes, a pair of sweatpants and a white tee. He and Spook were supposed to meet up at Dre and Kion's to come up with a new game plan and he knew she was already mad at him from the night before, so he decided to get up, take his shower and leave before she woke up to avoid an argument.

After getting dressed, brushing his teeth, putting on his deodorant Dax went out to the truck but decided to send Mia a text before he pulled off so that she could read when she woke up,

Babe, i'm sorry about last night I was wrong for that but i'm going to make it up to you so don't be mad at me. I had to leave early to go handle some business. I don't want us fighting and arguing. Just be cool little mama and i'll be back as soon as I can.

After waking up to an empty bed, Mia sat up and lifted one of the slacks in the blinds and noticed that the truck was gone. She didn't plan on going anywhere but it would've been nice if she woke her up and gave her warning about him taking the truck. "It's too early for this." She said to herself before reaching for her phone on the nightstand. The first thing she saw was the message from Dax. "*Just be cool lil mama.*" She said, out loud before tossing her phone aside, she threw her head back onto her pillow and stared up at the ceiling fan, thinking about her hubby. After a few minutes, she decided to just go back to sleep and wait for Malakai to wake her up to cook breakfast.

"Ya'll are talking about dirty ass Sosa from middle school?" Dax asked, not believing his ears.

"Yeah bro, i'm telling you they're saying that nigga is getting bread. Yo' tell this nigga Kion." Spook said, waving Dax off. As they all stood, on the sidewalk in front of Dre's house.

"Yo, you know the lame niggas always grow up and get money. How else do you think they ever get some pussy. That nigga used to stink in school." Kion said, leaning on Spook's car.

"I was locked up with him during my second bid, he was dirty in the joint too." Dax said, frowning his face.

"I don't give a damn about that niggas hygiene preferences, we just need to see what he's on." Spook said.

"Damn right and he should be willing to meet up because I used to look out for him here and there in the joint. How the fuck is this nigga up? What the fuck is he pushing?" Dax asked.

"Shit they say that nigga sells a little bit of

everything." Dre' said.

"Damn how the fuck are we going to get up with this nigga? He ain't never around the way." Spook said, thinking out loud.

"What hoes do he fuck with? It ain't to many out here that we haven't cracked at least once." Dre' said, shrugging.

"This nigga." Spook, said laughing.

"Matter fact," Dax said, snapping his fingers, "I heard Nearee was fucking with him not to long ago She's probably over Kea's right now, let's go around there right quick." Dax said, before they all climbed into Spooks car.

"Yoo cuz," Dax said, knocking on the door as they all stood on Kea's porch.

"Damn nigga, I heard you were on lockdown in the house." Kea said, hugging Dax as soon as she opened the door.

"I was, they just let me off that shit." Dax said, following her into the living room.

"That's crazy they let you off house arrest and they just announced that they're shutting everything down anyway. What's up Dre', what's up Kion, Spook." Kea said, giving him a head nod.

"Damn what are they shutting down?" Dax asked.

"Schools, the clubs shit everything for real." Kea said.

"They shutting the clubs down for real?" Spook

said, wide eyed before he sat on the edge of her sofa.

"Bars, clubs, restaurants." Kea said, nodding before she looked over at Spook, "get ya' big ass off my couch before you break it."

"Shit you like it." Spook said, grabbing his meat after he stood up. Dre', Kion, and Dax all fell out laughing. The few of them were the only people that were aware that Spook and Kea casually messed around from time to time.

Kea stuck her middle finger up at Spook, with a bashful grin plastered on her face.

"Ya'll crazy, but what's up with Nearee cuz? Is she here?" Dax asked.

"Depends on who's asking." Nearee said, walking into the living room, holding a platter of wingdings and fried rice from the Chinese place.

"The fuck you eating?" Spook asked, looking over at her plate.

Nearee looked at him without replying.

"What's up Nearee? I need a favor." Dax said.

After waking up and realizing that it was almost noon, Mia hopped out of the bed to check on Malakai.

"You good Kai!?" Mia said, as she swung his door open.

Malakai laid in the bed in his white tank top and ninja turtle boxers as looked over at his mom with a confused look on his face.

"I'm good mom." He said, laughing.

"It's not funny, you had me a little worried there for a second. You usually come ask me for food by now." Mia said, joining him in his laughter.

"I was waiting for you to wake up." He said, leaning onto his elbows.

Mia's smile widened, his dad might be an asshole at times but her baby was the sweetest.

"What do you want to eat?" Mia said, before she headed into the bathroom to wash her face and brush her teeth.

"Can I have bacon, cream of wheat and eggs?" she heard him yell from his bed.

"This boy wants cream of wheat with everything." Mia said, grabbing her electric toothbrush.

Later that day, Dax drove with Spook in the passenger as they headed 15 minutes outside of town to a smaller town called Delmar, to meet up with Sosa. He turned onto a quiet street and found the house he was looking for at the very end of a large cul-de-sac. He slowly crept up, surveying every detail about the area.

He repositioned the gun on his waist after climbing out and heading to the backdoor. He thought about what happened the last time he met up with someone to buy drugs and just shook his head. Torri had fucked his head up from that day forth and he would never forget it. The fact that nobody had seen or heard from her ass since that day made it even worse, but he wasn't going back to jail regardless of what went down.

"I already know what you're thinking bro. Just be cool nigga." Spook said.

"I'm good nigga." Dax told him, before he climbed out of the truck.

After they knocked on the door a few times, a young nigga with long thick freeform dreads answered it, with an overstuffed blunt dangling from his mouth.

"He's in the basement." The guy said, holding the door open and standing to the side to let Dax and Spook walk in.

"What's good D?" Sosa said walking up to Dax and giving him dap. Sosa had cut off his dreads and looked a lot different than Dax remembered from a couple years prior. He still had the same buck fifty scar and dirty fingernails that Dax remembered but from the fresh shape up, Christian Dior scarf hanging around his neck and oversized diamond chain that simply said, "*SOS*," Dax could tell a lot had changed and he immediately began to plot on how he could rob him later on.

"This is my man Spook, Spook this is Sosa." Dax said, pointing the two out to one another. He looked around the basement as they spoke to one another. Aside from the two oversized metal file cabinets in the corner, the basement resembled a small modern apartment with it's spotless white wall to wall carpet, expensive vases and modern furniture. The place gave Dax rich white folk vibes and he wasn't feeling it.

"Let's go to the back," Sosa said, turning around, using two fingers to signal Spook and Dax to follow him as he headed towards a door that looked more like a closet.

Behind the door was a small room with a large metal table covered with giant zip lock bags full of various strains of weed, coke, dope, pills and blue crystal looking rocks that Dax wasn't familiar with. He also had several colorful small plastic vials with snap caps holding different pills.

"Now we talking." Dax said, rubbing his hands together.

"How much is your hard going for Sosa? What are you asking for a brick?" Dax said, looking over at Sosa.

"I didn't get to where I am by nickle and diming. I'm almost completely out the game but what I'm willing to do for you is give you that whole bag of molly." Sosa said, nodding towards the table. In fact, if Dax hadn't looked out for him when he didn't have shit in prison, he wouldn't have been doing business with him at all.

Dax looked over at Spook who looked like he was eyeballing Sosa's chain.

"All you have to do is bring me back a stack and you can keep the rest. By then I'll be completely done with everything else." Sosa said.

"So you ain't trying to sell me a lil bit of hard?" Dax asked, looking at Sosa.

"Bruh, I'm telling you this is where the money is at. I used to make a killing off of molly alone. You won't even have to give me shit until you sell out. I'm trying to tell you nigga, if you want to come up, that's how you do it." Sosa said, pointing to the bag.

"So how much can I make off of that bag right there?" Dax asked, folding his arms. He didn't want to cop molly because he knew that he would likely use more than he sold.

"At least four or five racks, easy. My nigga." Sosa said, holding up his hands.

"So what I gotta do to it? Cook the shit?" Dax continued to question. He had never seen molly in the crystalized form it was in now.

"Nah this is how it is. It dissolves when it's wet and some people put it in their water and make molly water." Sosa said, watching Dax.

"Niggas be putting that shit in their blunts when it's like that too bro." Spook said.

"Yeah nigga" Sosa said laughing and nodding his head, "I'm telling you it's money." He continued as he picked up the bag and handed it to Dax.

"Alright then, good looking." Dax said, passing the bag to Spook.

"No doubt, but yo?" Sosa said, as Dax dapped him up.

"What's up?" Dax asked.

"How the hell did you get my number?" Sosa inquired.

"A mutual friend of ours nigga. I got some connects to mahfucker." Dax said laughing.

"Yeah aight." Sosa said with a chuckle.

After they left with the gallon size ziploc bag inside of a backpack, Dax and Spook rode in silence until they were a few blocks away from Sosa's spot. Dax looked over at Spook before they both bust out laughing.

"That dumb mothafucker gave the wrong nigga some molly." Spook said, laughing.

"Did he!? Mannn! I ain't giving that nigga shit. The fuck he talking bout." Dax said, constantly checking his rear view and side mirrors.

"We good bro just chill." Spook said, recognizing the paranoia in Dax's eyes.

"We can never be too careful nigga." Dax said, opting to keep his head on a swivel.

After calling Dax a half a dozen times and getting no answer, Mia decided that she wasn't able to just sit around and fret. She saw on facebook that her work crew were all hanging out in Doverdale, at Chanel's and decided to call Alyssa and get her to come get her and Malakai.

Twenty minutes later Chanel pulled up in her silver ford fusion.

"Where's Alyssa?" Mia asked, after she and Malakai walked out to the car.

"She's already half drunk girl, hey Kai! Did you bring your controller so that you can play with Chase?" Chanel asked, turning to Malakai as he climbed into the back seat. Chase was her seven-year-old son.

"Yep, I got it right here!" Malakai said, holding his

playstation controller in the air.

"Thanks hoe! Let's go, Lyssa said she already bought me a bottle. Did you bring it?" Mia asked, looking over at Chanel.

"Yeah, but tell Dax that the next time he wants to make a disappearing act to get his own whip. How you look bumming rides, while he flossing in yo' shit." Chanel said, throwing a pint of fireball onto Mia's lap before pulling off.

Mia knew that her face more than likely turned red as she felt her anger boiling in her veins before the blood rushed to her face. She glared at Chanel, before she paused, she turned in her seat, glancing back at Malakai before she closed her eyes and sighed.

"Listen to me, I'm going to let you slide this one time, one fucking time tonight. I have enough problems. I didn't need you to come get me. I didn't even ask if we're being technical. Alyssa sent you!" Mia said, with her lip turned up.

"Here you go, nobody can't tell you anything without you being on defense mode. Coming to get you is not an issue. I don't mind looking out for you. I'm just trying to put you on game. I've been there and done that trust me." Chanel said.

"I'm not trying to hear this shit though. Is this why ya'll wanted me to come over?" Mia asked, bucking her eyes after she leaned forward in her seat to look at Chanel.

"Nah, you know what. It's all good don't even worry about it Mia." Chanel said, turning up the music.

By the time they pulled up to the house Mia had already drunk half of her bottle of liquor. She was mad at Chanel for putting her out there, especially in front of Malakai but she was more mad at the fact that the bitch was dead ass right. Dax had a lot of nerve and yet there she was defending his bullshit.

Mia slowly dragged herself out of the car, after Chanel and Malakai slammed their doors. She watched Malakai run pass Chanel, into her front door to find Chase. She walked into the house and found Alyssa, Lola and Ballow sitting around the table smoking, drinking and playing spades. She was relieved that Reese wasn't in attendance.

"Look who it is, we didn't expect to see you this whole week." Alyssa said, smiling as soon as Mia walked through the door.

"That makes two of us." Mia said, in a sarcastic tone before plopping down onto the couch.

"What's up? Where that nigga at?" Alyssa asked, as she shuffled a deck of cards in her hands.

"I don't want to talk about it, I came over here to drink and that's what i'm going to do." Mia said, lifting her bottle in the air before unscrewing the cap and guzzling.

Lola saw Chanel roll her eyes at Mia and decided to turn around in her seat to see why.

"What's going on Mimi?" Lola asked, with a frown.

"Man, what's up with ya'll man? Can't I just come over here, sit down and mind my business?" Mia asked, closing her eyes after she started to feel light headed. She decided to take off her flowered adida jacket before laying back on the couch.

"The hell wrong with her?" Alyssa whispered, looking at Chanel.

Chanel shrugged her shoulders and walked out.

Mia knew she was about to be sick after the room started spinning and she felt her stomach lining burning. She remembered that she hadn't ate since breakfast but had almost finished the bottle of liquor. "Shittt," Mia groaned, in a low tone before she put her arm across her forehead. She had broken out in a sweat, and slowly sat up after her mouth started watering.

"Already?" Alyssa said, with a chuckle as Mia ran pass the table towards the bathroom.

After Spook went to meet his babymom, Dax decided to stop by Kea's to see if she or Nearee knew anybody else who fucked with the molly heavy. He had taken a good amount of the *"blue magic"* as he called it, and was feeling a strong sense of euphoria. He felt like he was that nigga again, his restrictions were removed, he was back to getting money, and he could do whatever the fuck he wanted.

He got excited after he walked in and saw Nearee and her friend Mazi sitting on the love seat. Mazi was their city's version of Lori Harvey. Her exotic smooth caramel frappe skin tone, thick lips and honey butter colored eyes took her over the top. She rarely gave niggas the time of day which put them on her heels even more. She was a hot commodity in the city and Dax stayed ready to try his luck.

"Damn cuz is knocked out." Dax said, slightly laughing at Kea who was slumped over on the couch. "What are ya'll up to?" He asked the duo.

"Smoking."

"Bored as hell." Mazi and Nearee said in Unison.

"Damn, well ya'll come in here real quick, so we don't wake her up. Ya'll can help me with something." He said as he headed towards the kitchen, signaling for them to follow him.

"What is it?" Nearee asked as she entered the kitchen, following closely behind Mazi.

"Look." Dax said removing the bag of molly from the book bag, after he was face to face with them. Nearee's eyes lit up when she saw what it was, causing Dax to laugh.

"What is it?" Mazi asked.

"It's molly." Nearee confirmed.

"Why does it look like that?" Mazi asked, with a frown.

"That's that pure shit." Nearee said, licking her lips.

"Let me find out you're fiend out for the molly." Dax said, laughing at Nearee.

"Fuck no," Nearee said mushing his arm.

"Ain't nothing wrong with it, i'm fucking with it too." Dax admitted.

Nearee looked at Dax and twisting her lips to the side.

Dax looked at her and continued to laugh as he put the book bag down and opened the zip lock bag.

"You want to try it or you ain't fucking wit it?" Dax asked, looking at Mazi. He knew she normally partied but he wasn't sure from reading the skepticism on her face.

"Hell naw, that shit looks like crystal meth." Mazi said, shaking her head.

"You ain't never been around no crystal in ya life." Dax said, laughing.

Mazi shrugged, he was right.

"I'm telling you this is that good shit." Dax continued.

"I might try a tiny ass crumb." Mazi said, emphasizing the amount by pinching her fingers together. Dax dropped a single baggie into her hand, before turning to Nearee.

"Good looking on Sosa's number." He said, after he pulled out three 2-inch individual baggies he had bagged up earlier with Spook and handed them to her.

Nearee open one of the baggies, before holding her head back, sprinkling damn near half of its contents into her mouth.

Mazi licked her finger and stuck it inside the bag, she examined the crystal flakes stuck to her finger. Still suspicious that it was something else she wiped the drug onto the side of her A&F jeans and put the remainder of the small baggie in her purse. She would stick to her drink and weed.

"Alright so ya'll trying to help me bag some more up?" Dax said walking over to the light switch and turning it on.

"Yeah but why you ain't go home and let Mia help you do this?" Nearee asked, leaning on the table and putting one hand on her hip.

"Nobody ever told you that you should never shit where you sleep?" Dax asked her.

"And nobody ever told you, not to get high off of your own shit." Nearee said, pulling out a chair before sitting down at the table.

"You got that." Dax said, laughing as he pulled out the chair next to her.

"So what's up with my lil cuz anyway? I haven't seen her since that night ya'll both popped out in the club." Nearee said.

Talking about Mia, made Dax realize he never called or texted her back from hours ago. He quickly pulled out his phone and looked through his messages. She had called him a half a dozen times and messaged him even more cussing him out. He saw that she had gone to chill with her coworkers and instantly felt a twinge of jealousy wondering if Reese could possibly be there.

He wondered if she was crazy enough to continue to chill with Reese behind his back.

"But yeah Nearee i'll tell her you asked for her. She's doing good though. Staying out the way. You know how she is." He said, putting his phone down on the table.

"Yeah tell her for me yo, i'm happy ya'll worked it out because ya'll were both wildin' for a minute there! I was just like yo' they crazy as shit for this!" Nearee said, cracking up.

"I know you ain't talking yo, I heard you've been out here doing niggas dirty!" Dax said, shaking his head. "You and ya' cousin boy, gone make somebody fuck ya'll up."

"I don't even know what the hell you talking about." Nearee said, putting her hand on her chest.

"You got a lighter though?" she said, placing her blunt between her lips while laughing.

"Don't try to change the subject now. Ya'll females boy I tell you." Dax said, looking from Mazi to Nearee as he patted his pockets to find his lighter.

After Mia threw up what felt like her intestines, she sat on Chanel's yellow fuzzy bathroom rug, in front of the toilet, wishing she would have stayed the hell home. She leaned on the tub and cried assuming that she'd probably be feeling sick for the rest of the night. She decided to see if Dax would answer, so that he could come get her.

"Lola, can you bring me my phone please?" Mia groaned. She didn't want Alyssa or Chanel to come in and see her looking crazy but she didn't mind Lola or Ballow sitting with her. She knew the two of them always had her back and never judged. She was still sweating, so she pulled her black addidas t-shirt over her head and left her grey racer back tank top on.

A few seconds later Lola slightly knocked on the door, "it's me and Ballow." she said, rattling the locked door handle.

Mia opened the door, before sliding back to the floor and put her face in her hands, shaking her head.

"So what's going on Mimi? Why you crying?" Lola asked, in a concerned tone before she sat on the edge of the tub beside Mia and Ballow sat on the floor.

"I ain't never seen lil sis throwing up off the fireball!? The hell going on?" Alyssa said, through the door as she jiggled the knob.

"Ignore her, what's wrong?" Lola said, putting her hand on Mia's shoulder.

Before she could respond, Mia suddenly felt the urge to throw up again but began to dry heave instead. She laid her arm across the toilet seat and continued to groan and cry as Lola rubbed her back.

"How did you get this sick so fast, do you think you could be pregnant?" Lola asked.

Mia shrugged her shoulders.

"Did you eat?" Ballow asked.

Mia shook her head in response.

A few hours later, after drinking ginger ale, and taking a shower and a nap, Mia, Lola, Chanel, and Alyssa stood in the bathroom looking down at the pregnancy test on the sink.

When the clear blue test revealed, *"Pregnant,"*

Mia instantly started crying.

"I knew it!" Alyssa said.

"It's okay." Lola said, hugging Mia.

Chanel was still mad from earlier so she didn't say anything and opted to just look at Mia.

Mia wasn't sad about the fact that she was pregnant. She wanted another baby and prayed for a girl, but she was crying because of how she found out and the circumstances surrounding the situation. She had been calling Dax all day, only for him to ignore all her inquires about his where about's, only to respond several hours later on some bullshit about not being around Reese. The disrespect was evident but now that she was pregnant she knew she wasn't going anywhere, at least until she had the baby. It was about to be a long 9 months.

After returning home, the pregnancy test on the nightstand was the first thing Dax noticed as he walked into him and Mia's bedroom. She was facing the wall but he knew she wasn't asleep.

"You okay babe?" Dax asked, after he climbed in the bed behind her in the bed before pulling her into his arms.

"Get off me yo, don't do that. How the fuck you think you just gone come in here and act like shit is sweet when you've been ignoring me all day?" Mia said, while removing his arms from around her and sitting up.

"I was handling business babe chill." Dax said,

trying to make light of the situation.

"Man fuck that, what does handling business have to do with answering the phone? Oh aight!" Mia said.

"Alright babe damn my bad. I was feeling myself. I'm sorry you're right but my phone was dead though." He continued.

"Ay my nigga, it's 2020 they got fast chargers, portable chargers, wireless charging pads and some more shit. I'm not trying to hear that my phone died shit." Mia snapped, bucking her eyes.

"You got that little mama, just chill." Dax said, pulling Mia into his arms and rocking her back and forth. "We having another baby." Dax smiled.

Mia resisted, until she realized he wasn't going to let her go until she gave in. She sucked her teeth before she relaxed her muscles and softly exhaled. She hoped that her pregnancy would straighten him up a little more but deep down she knew better.

Chapter 8

Reese sat in the dimly lit living room of his childhood home as he reflected on the news, that Alyssa had just delivered to him through an imessage. Mia was pregnant. Silence filled the 4 bedroom, colonial style home before he began to throw a pocket sized red ball occasionally against the brick wall above the fireplace, causing a small echo to travel through the room each time the ball landed. The sound evoked a feeling of emptiness from deep within his spirit. He planned to raise children of his own in the large home and began to reminisce on the time he brought it up to Mia.

"MMmmm.." Mia moaned, as she dug her nails into his back.

Reese grunted as he released inside of her, before he felt his meat slowly softening up. He collapsed on top of her, out of breath.

"Why didn't you pull out!?" She said, slapping his shoulder as she wiggled her way from underneath his heavy frame.

"I couldn't help it." Reese said, rolling onto the mattress.

"Are you crazy? I told you I just switched my birth

control so it's not effective until another week. I'm going to buy a plan B." Mia said, getting off the bed and frantically picking up her clothes that were sprawled throughout his bedroom.

"Damn Mia you're acting, like i'm some deadbeat ass nigga." Reese said, before climbing off the bed.

"I know you're not a deadbeat but we've only been dating for 7 months. What the hell? I'm still technically married, i'm not having a baby like this!" She shrieked, before rushing to get dressed and go to the closest pharmacy.

Now it all made perfect sense, she wouldn't dare have a baby by him because he was never who she truly planned to be with.

"Call Kai in here, let's tell him." Mia said, the next morning as she laid on her side propped up on her elbow next to Dax.

"Kai!" Dax yelled, curious to see how Malakai would react to the news.

"Yeah?" Malakai said, after he walked in looking from Mia to Dax.

"Your dad, has something to tell you." Mia said, nodding her head towards Dax as she grinned holding in her laugh.

"Come here son son," Dax said, patting on his side of the bed.

"Aight, so you're going to be a big brother, your mom is having another baby." Dax said, after Malakai sat on the edge of the bed.

"Where is it sleeping?" Malakai said, with his eyebrows in the air.

Dax looked back at Mia after she fell out laughing.

"In here right?" Malakai continued as he pointed to their bedroom floor.

"Yeah the baby will sleep in here with us, we have to get a crib Kai." Mia said, in between her laughs.

"Are you happy?" Dax asked, leaning over to see Malakai's face.

Malakai walked over to Mia, and touched her stomach before he shrugged his small shoulders and walked back to his room.

"That's your son." Dax said, before they both silently laughed.

Now that Mia was pregnant he decided that he should try harder to keep her stress free and happy. After leaving while she was still sleeping yesterday, he had purposefully spent the morning in bed with her to remain on her good side and keep her in good spirits. He doubted that he'd ever be able to just lay around in the house for days at a time, as if he were still on the box but he planned to do his best. He wondered if she still thought about Reese and if she wished he could be more like him. After all Mia had always been a homebody, but Dax knew he was the opposite. She enjoyed her time alone, watching t.v. sitting around reading books and shit but he was a people person, he liked to party and get high. He enjoyed spending most of his days chilling in the hood, around the people that did the same kind of things he did.

He looked over at her and decided to avoid the topic. “When are you going to make the doctor's appointment little mama?” Dax asked, as he placed his hand on her thigh.

“I’m going to call today but hand me the remote babe, and what do you have to do today?” Mia asked, after Dax climbed out of the bed and began looking for something to wear.

“I’m just going to be moving around today, but i’ll make sure I go buy a portable charger.” Dax said, handing her the remote before he headed to the bathroom.

Mia scrolled through the vast variety of tv shows and movies on hbo as she searched for a new series to watch. She wished that Dax could stay home with her but knew that him being home was only a temporary situation. For as long as she’d known him, he’d never been the type of person that could sit still. She wished he was but seeing him lay in the bed that late in the afternoon showed Mia that he meant what he said when he promised to be home more while she was pregnant. That fact alone made Mia content.

Later that day, Dax sat in the truck with Spook in the passenger side as they tried to figure out how Dax could push larger quantities of the molly versus the petty amounts he had been getting out.

“Yooo nigga we must be high.” Spook asked, before turning his phone to Dax to show him the picture.

"Kizzy," Dax said, before leaning his head back and hollering laughing. She hadn't even crossed his mind, but now that Spook mentioned it, she could be the missing piece to his puzzle.

Kizzy was one of the females that Dax had been going steady with in the past behind Mia's back. Back in the day, Kizzy was one of the few sidelines that Dax had actually caught feelings for. She was bad as fuck, never the clingy or needy type, thick to death and her mouth skills were unmatched. Her only downfall was that she couldn't be trusted for shit. Dax hadn't spoken to her in a grip but Kizzy was known for gossiping and spreading rumors in the city with her connections to every hood. If you had something for sell, drugs, clothes, shoes, lashes then you would want Kizzy to know about it. She ran her mouth about everything, and Dax had learned the hard way years ago after Mia found out about their fiasco.

"I'm about to hit her on i.g." Dax said, picking up his phone. While driving with one hand, he quickly typed, *"Killa'Kizzy"* into instagram's search bar, he laughed to himself after her pictures popped up on her profile.

"Her fine big mouth ass." Dax said, as he drove and scrolled through the pictures on her page. I could tell that not much had changed, her ass was still fat but seeing her face made him remember how he slipped up and got caught up with her and her mouth game.. a true throat goat.

"Aight now, make Mia fuck you up, cuz she gone tell it." Spook said, leaning back in his seat.

"I ain't fucking with her bro." Dax said, before scrolling back to the top of her profile to hit her inbox.

"Yooo what's your number Kizzy, I need a favor." he wrote before hitting send.

"Favor for a favor...." She replied a few moments later with the eggplant and tongue emoji. Dax shook his head at his phone.

"*Where you at?*" he wrote back.

"You already know I'm on the southside. Pull up." Kizzy replied.

After agreeing to meet back up with Spook in a few, Dax headed towards Kizzy's infamous house. He decided to text Mia before he got there to lessen the chances of her calling while he was with Kizzy.

"You good little mama?"

"I'm cool, you alright?" She texted back a few seconds later.

"Yeah i'll be home soon." He replied before he put the phone on silent.

He pulled in front of the small, red house on Roger street and waited for Kizzy to come out. He relit his blunt and placed his phone face down in the cup holder before reclining his driver's seat.

Kizzy came outside wearing a long white fur coat with a jean bucket hat, a skintight white bodycon dress and a pair of denim slides.

"What's up stranger?" she said, as soon as she climbed into the passenger side.

"I heard that you're out here living the married

life and shit. You ain't want to wife me though." She said, playfully nudging Dax's arm.

"What's up Kizzy. You want some?" Dax asked, intentionally ignoring her last statement while leaning the blunt towards her.

"Yeah." She said, taking the blunt from Dax while looking down at his print in his black Nike sweats. She watched Dax as she hit the blunt. She could tell by his demeanor that he was trying to behave and not do to much and this just made her want to fuck with him even more.

"So what's up daddy? Why you so quiet? You pulled up on me remember." She said with a smirk.

"Why you out here dressed like it's summer time?" Dax asked, looking down at her french manicured toes.

"I was chilling inside making tik tok videos but I put a coat on." She said, grabbing the collar of her fur coat.

"Aight well look I got something for you if you tell your friends for me." Dax continued before she could respond.

"Alright, so give it here." She said, turning to face him, placing her elbow on the arm rest and opening her hand.

Dax reached into his pocket and removed the small baggie, "hmmp" he said.

"Alright, now let me taste it." Kizzy said, taking the baggie from Dax, before reaching over and rubbing his meat. She slowly licked her lips when she felt it quickly come to life.

"Yo, you wild." Dax said, slightly debating if he wanted to risk it all, as he looked down at the white and purple polish on her long acrylic nails.

Kizzy looked at Dax as she went underneath the elastic band in his boxers before swiftly pulling out his erect meat.

"One time won't hurt." He thought to himself before he lifted up in his seat to pull his pants and boxers down some.

Kizzy laughed to herself before she took her arms out of her coat and repositioned herself comfortably on her knees.

"Suck that shit," he said after he felt the warmth of her throat, effortlessly making his dick disappear.

Mia sat her phone down on the dresser as she talked to Egypt while standing in front of her mirror.

"I can't believe you're really pregnant that fast." Egypt said, in disbelief as Mia lifted her shirt and turned to the side in the mirror.

"Me either, you can't even tell. This is weird as hell, it's so early. Remember when I found out I was pregnant with Kai I was already almost 5 months." Mia said, before she dropped her shirt and picked the phone back up.

"Hey Pooka Wookaaaa!" Egypt yelled after she saw Malakai walk into the room behind Mia.

Malakai brought Mia a green apple and a bottle of

water and placed them on the dresser.

"Aww! Look what my baby brought me!" Mia said, before squeezing Malakai and kissing him on the cheek repeatedly.

"I love my little baby son!" Mia continued, still hugging him as tight as she could.

"He's the sweetest whittle baby!" Egypt said, in her baby voice.

"Hey! Stop it! It's for the new baby." Malakai said, before he ripped himself away and ran back to his room leaving Mia and Egypt cracking up.

Chapter 9

Instead of returning to work that following Monday, Mia sat in the compact waiting room at the OB/GYN doctor's office. Her legs bounced in anticipation, as Dax sat beside her cupping her hand and rubbing it softly with his thumb. When she was 13 she remembered being ashamed about being pregnant so young and having to only be accompanied by Corrie at each appointment because Dax was incarcerated. But now she was of age and she had her husband by her side, the memories alone sent waves of gratification through her spine.

"Mia Truitt." A mid-age white nurse called out, after opening a wooden door with a glass window from the side of the room. She stood sideways to allow Mia and Dax to pass through as she held the door open.

She had a clipboard in one hand and a specimen cup in the other.

"So Ms. Truitt i'm Nurse Rebecca and you've been assigned to Doctor Linsdey. I'm just going to need a urine sample from you to confirm your pregnancy and then Dr. Lindsey will be in to give you an ultrasound and tell you about how far along you are. Does that sound okay?" She asked, with a heavy southern drawl.

"Yep, no problem." Mia said, reaching for the cup

and handing Dax her backpack purse before she left the room behind the nurse.

Dax took her purse and sat down in the seat next to the examination chair as Mia walked out. He was excited to see the baby on the monitor but his mind quickly drifted off to the molly he had in the truck. After five minutes he finally decided that he would run outside and come right back. He stood to his feet and turned around to place Mia's purse on the seat but was interrupted when Nurse Rebecca suddenly returned with her clipboard and pen.

"Now dad, while she's in the bathroom I can ask you a few questions that will pertain to the health of the baby. The questions are voluntary and you can opt out of answering anytime you choose. Alright?" Nurse Rebecca asked, looking up at Dax with a smile.

"Aight." Dax said, choosing to remain standing before folding his arms.

"So do you drink alcohol and if so how often would you say?" She asked, while looking down at her clipboard.

Mia walked in and handed the cup wrapped in paper towels to the Nurse before she sat on the exam table and listened.

"I drink on the weekends," Dax said, he could feel Mia staring a hole through his face but he deliberately kept his eyes on the Nurse.

"Okay, do you do any drugs regularly? If so what kind of drugs and how often?" She asked.

"What the fuck? Man this bitch is the police." Dax

thought, as he swiped his left hand across ripples in his hair. He looked over at Mia with his face frowned up but she simply shrugged her shoulders and smiled at him.

"I ain't got time for this shit." He thought.

"You can ask Mia these questions ma'am, i'm going to the car for a second. I forgot something." Dax said, before he headed out the door.

"Okay, no problem Mr. Truitt." Nurse Rebecca said with a smile before reverting her questions to Mia.

An hour later, Mia held up the black and white sonogram photos as she and Dax walked outside to the truck.

"My little sweet pea." Mia said, examining the pictures. "Let me drive home babe, I want to stop by my grandmom's before we go home."

"Aight. I almost left your mothafucking ass in there though for real babe. Bitch gone ask me if I do drugs. Damn right I do drugs bitch, fuck she talking bout." Dax said, as he climbed into the passenger side of the truck.

Mia ignored him, still focused on the images. After a few moments, she looked over at him and decided to lighten the mood after she recognized the frustration on his face.

"Chill out babe, we're having a baby." She said, handing him one of the pictures. "Let me sing a song just for you hubby, hold up." Mia said picking up her phone after starting the truck.

Dax watched Mia as he waited for her to pick a song.

"I must not have been paying attention," Mia screeched after selecting Monica's *"Love all over me".*

Dax immediately bust out laughing at her horrible singing as she pulled away out of the parking lot.

"Come on babe sing it with me yo," Mia said before she continued to sing.

"Ohhh, I got your lovee all over mee." Dax sang, joining in before they both busted out laughing.

"No, I gotta another one, just listen to the chorus. This is how I feel about us." Mia said, picking up her phone after they stopped at a stop sign.

Mia chose Dru Hill's *"You are Everything,"* and instantly began to sing it to him as she drove. The song resonated with Mia for various reasons. He was apologizing for the mistakes he made in the past, causing her hurt and sadness. When deep down she was everything to him and he just wanted to be her only love. It was exactly how she felt about Dax, he and Malakai were her entire life. But the song also brought Reese to her mind once again, making her regret everything she'd done to him. What started out as a feeble attempt to get back at Dax turned into something more. She knew that she ultimately crushed Reese, regardless of how nonchalant he tried to act around her. They had shared a lot of special moments. That guilt would be with her forever, she decided that she would never use another man for her own selfish motives.

"What you know about this babe?" Mia asked, blocking Reese from her thoughts.

"I do know this song lil mama he's trying to get his girl back," Dax said, concentrating on the rearview mirror. "Hold up babe, I think this is that bitch ass nigga Davis behind you, but don't pull over yet." Dax said turning down the music and digging inside of his pockets for his last Percocet, after noticing the cop lights behind he and Mia. He was grateful that he left his gun at home.

"We're good now, go ahead and pull over." Dax said, breathing a sigh of relief, after swallowing the pill and drinking his sprite.

"Okay." Mia said, putting on her signal to get into the right lane.

"Afternoon, license and registration ma'am." Officer Davis said after walking up to Mia's window.

"Get the registration for me babe." Mia said pointing to the glove box.

"What did you pull her over for though? She wasn't speeding." Dax said, bending down to see officer Davis through the driver side window.

"She stopped past the white line at the stop sign, a few blocks back." Officer Davis smacking on a piece of gum.

"We're good babe, give it to me." Mia said, softly tapping Dax's arm with her fingers.

"This bitch ass nigga man." Dax said, as Mia handed Officer Davis the documents.

"Alright just give me a second to run this through the system and I'll be right back." Davis said before heading back to his police cruiser.

"This nigga gonna say you stopped passed the line." Dax scuffed.

"He just wanted to get under your skin. They know our truck." Mia said, watching the cop through her rearview mirror.

"I just gave you a warning, you guys are free to go." Officer Davis said after returning to Mia, "And Mr. Truitt watch yourself." He said before smiling, handing Mia her documents and walking back to his car.

"Bitch ass nigga." Dax said once again, as he stuffed the papers back inside the glove box. "I'm not coming to any more doctor's appointments Mia."

Mia just shook her head, because what the fuck did the doctors appointment have to do with getting pulled over. This was how it was in a small town the cops knew everybody by name. They knew ,their vehicles and where they lived; that was how it had always been. *He can ride around with Spook all day and night but he couldn't come with me to a fucking doctors appointment.* She thought getting madder by the second. *Ain't no way I left a peaceful relationship for this.* She decided to bite her tongue and just turn the volume up on another song.

"And you can drop me off over my cousin Kea's, I got something to do." Dax said.

Mia cut her eye at Dax before she sucked her teeth and rolled her eyes.

"Why the fuck do you have to get an attitude everytime I tell you I got to leave? I make my money in the streets! What you forgot? You want a mothafucker to just sit in the house with your ass all day, broke!" Dax snapped, looking over at her as she drove. "I've been this way since you met me and I ain't changing."

"You can get a regular job my nigga." Mia said.

"Bitch I aint no regular nigga. The fuck! You want a regular nigga call Reese bitch ass." Dax said.

"Shit, don't give me any ideas." Mia said, underneath her breath.

"What the fuck you say? Say it again, I ain't hear you!" Dax yelled, turning to Mia.

Mia ignored Dax and switched her playlist to drill music. She decided to drive a little faster to get him to his destination before he got under her skin any further. She floored the gas pedal and began weaving in and out of traffic as she headed towards the Eastside. She didn't know Kea that well personally but she knew she had multiple female friends that frequented the house regularly. So the fact that he'd rather spend the majority of his time over there versus at home with her made her question what the fuck went on over there.

"Man what are you doing!? Slow the fuck down bitch!?" Dax barked, as Mia's driving caused him to sway side to side.

"Ayo watch how the fuck you talk to me." Mia said, pointing at Dax while increasing her speed even more.

"Matter fact, since i'm a bitch. I ain't taking you nowhere." She continued, as she drove furiously as she rerouted their destination and headed to their house instead.

“Stupid bitch man, and you wonder why a nigga don’t stay home.” Dax said, gathering his belongings before removing his seat belt, as he held on to his door handle ready to hop out as soon as she stopped.

Mia could feel the tears beginning to build up as she came to a stop sign and slowed down but accelerated as soon as Dax cracked his door open. She made a sharp right turn running over the curve, in the process. She didn’t care if she messed up the truck or if he fell out, when she was mad her anger always got the best of her. All reasoning went out of the window along with her common sense.

“Woahh! Man what the fuck are you doing!? This is why I don’t like to be around you for long periods of time! You can't even control your emotions yo.” Dax yelled.

“Nah you really a disrespectful mafucka and it’s unnecessary.” Mia said, blinded by the tears of rage that fell from her eyes. Every single time he caught an attitude he got disrespectful out of his mouth and after being with Reese she realized there was more to life, but she just wanted Dax.

Noticing the traffic stuck at a red light up ahead, Dax grabbed his belongings and quickly hopped out of the car as soon as she slammed on the breaks.

Mia watched him, dip off down a side street to her right and floored the gas as soon as the light turned green and the car in front of her moved on. She busted a sharp right and spotted Dax jogging through the grass of the well-manicured homes.

Dax figured she’d chase him down like she

always did but he was sure she wouldn't jump the curb to get to him.

Mia turned her wheel slightly toward the curb and floored it. The large tires on the SUV easily drove up onto the sidewalk like speedbumps. Dax dashed through somebody's backyard after he saw Mia gaining on him as she cut across the front yards, tearing their grass apart.

He shook his head and chuckled after he heard the truck bounce off the sidewalk before she skirted off in the opposite direction.

Later that day, Dax and Nearee sat at Kea's kitchen table.

"Sheeshhh." Nearee smiled, closing her eyes and bending her neck from side to side before she reached up and stretched her arms into the air, exposing her snake shaped belly ring.

"You feeling it now huh?" Dax said, leaning back in his seat and rubbing up and down his arm. The molly and weed had them both feeling relaxed and open. He closed his eyes and leaned his head back as he felt waves of pleasure throughout his own body.

"This shit is the best feeling hands down. Especially... when you're with your person." Nearee said, dropping her arms before she reached for her lime green weed grinder.

"Mia don't even know I be fucking with this shit." Dax admitted, solemnly as if he hadn't just put her through the ringer just a couple hours prior.

"For real Dax?" Nearee said, pouring the weed into

the blunt.

"For real." He said, nodding.

"You wack for that. It's the best sex, and she would love it after she tried it. I don't see how people don't fuck with it." Nearee told him, as she looked down at the blunt, rotating it as she examined it.

"Nah she be on some bullshit man. You know since her mom was on drugs she don't be fuckin with it like us. You see how long it took her to try weed." Dax said, sarcastically as he slouched in the chair.

"Shit we beefing anyway, that bitch tried to kill me earlier." Dax said, in an nonchalant tone. "But fuck that shit. Who you fuck with now anyway Nearee, you still fuck with Cash?" Dax asked, shifting the focus to her.

"Damn, but I got me a nice little line up." Nearee laughed before she began to lick the blunt. "But speaking of Cash yo that just gave me an idea. He be mixing the molly with the weed." Nearee said.

"You want to try it?" She asked Dax.

"I'll try a little bit." Dax said, laughing at her.

"Alright bet. But like I was saying, I still fuck with Cash but his cheating ass don't know how to love nobody and I can't be faithful to his ass after everything he did." She said, as she concentrated on the weed and molly.

"Just because a nigga cheats don't mean he don't love you." Dax said, leaning onto the table.

"You sound just like him, but I ain't going for it. I'm going to continue to do me and have fun." She said, before she began to seal the blunt with her mouth.

"I definitely feel you on that." Dax said, it made perfect sense to him and he decided right then and there that instead of going home and dealing with Mia's craziness, he would head straight to Kizzy's to relax while receiving, in his opinion, the best fellatio in da' Bury.

Chapter 10

The mood at Mia's job was unusually somber as they all stood around the line preoccupied with their own thoughts. Mia's mind was in shambles, after Dax didn't bother to come home the night before. She didn't know why she was surprised, he would always use their fights as an excuse to stay away for days at a time but since she was pregnant she figured this time would be different. She had been counting on him to stay home with Malakai so when he didn't show up she had to scramble to make arrangements and get him dressed and ready in time but luckily her grandmom came through for them. In addition to all that she spent the majority of her night tossing and turning about Dax's whereabouts, so she was exhausted but she was glad to be back to work with her homies.

"Yo what's wrong with ya'll? Why ya'll so quiet?" Mia asked, as she dropped the blister packs while eyeing Alyssa, Lola and Chanel.

Chanel remained silent as she averted her gaze from Mia.

"Who you think you fooling Mia? Huh? Since that nigga came back into the picture you don't even look like yourself." Alyssa speculated, before giving Mia a once-over.

Mia knew she had thrown on anything when she was rushing that morning but she was still taken aback by Alyssa's response. She took a quick glimpse underneath her lab coat, she didn't feel like her hot pink old navy t-shirt and grey tights warranted Alyssa hostility.

Normally Lola would have Mia's back and snap on Alyssa when she felt like her opinion was wrong but this time she actually agreed with Alyssa's assessment. It was the bags and puffiness around Mia's eyes that revealed the misery that she was trying to conceal. She looked like she had been crying for three days straight but yet she came in the door with a forced smile. The fact that she hadn't took the time to style her edges, was another clear sign that Mia was off her game. She didn't belong in the work environment pregnant under the current circumstances with the virus. So Lola had tipped their boss off while Mia was away at the doctor yesterday. She knew that HR would call Mia upstairs any minute to send her home but after seeing Mia maybe she should have let her pregnancy reveal itself.

"Man i'm good. Your trippin'." Mia said, waving Alyssa off.

"Mia, H.R. call for you, upstairs." Lulu disclosed, unaware of Mia's condition.

"Okay…" Mia said, slowly as she tried to rack her brain about what the bosses could want with her upstairs.

"I take your place." Lulu said, grabbed a handful of the medicine packs in front of Mia as she stepped up into her spot.

"Let me holla at you for a second Mia." Ms. Pat said, lifting her chin to signal for Mia to approach her.

Now Mia was really confused, because the only time anyone would hear Ms. Pat's voice would be when she greeted everyone when they all first arrived in the morning. Ms. Pat speaking up grabbed everybody's attention, they all watched wanting to see what she would say.

"It's not my business Mia but I just want to tell you to be careful. Sometimes as women when we fall in love we tend to lose ourselves a little bit. I'm only saying this, because i've been there. We're always taking a risk when we choose to love men that are hot headed and in the street... especially when you're hot headed as well," she paused, and lightly leaned into Mia before she lowered her voice and continued. "Yeah, I've listened to your stories over the years Mia, you've been through enough." Ms. Pat said, in almost a whisper.

"I already know." Mia said, trying to sound cool, but really she was getting emotional. She sniffled and cleared her throat.

"I know you're a smart young lady but remember this, when you've had enough baby girl trust me, you will know. It'll be like a light switch being flipped in your brain." She said, pointing to her temple while looking Mia in the eyes.

Mia respond with the tiniest of smiles before turning to walk away. Ms. Pat's word echoed inside of her mind as she headed towards the exit, she didn't turn back and look because she knew she'd break down.

Alyssa watched Mia as she walked out but didn't say anything, she could only hope that she would marinate on the advice O.G. gave her. She couldn't help but feel sad witnessing her departure, little did she know it would be Mia's last time at the job.

Mia laid across her sofa as she listened to the grumbling and dripping sounds of thunder and heavy rain pour. The weather matched her mood entirely, she and Dax had gotten into it on Monday and here it was Tuesday night, and yet he hadn't called or returned. Hurt and resentment boiled inside of Mia, each time he ignored her calls and messages. She would never carry him the way he was unapologetically dragging on her. She grew bitter while reflecting on the hundreds of phone calls, during his season's away, that she would eagerly sit and wait by the phone for. Year after year, bid after bid. She would never miss his phone calls, she prided herself on being the one he could call for anything at any given time. He was always the number #1 priority in her life. What Dax wanted she made sure she made it happen with no questions asked. He made sure that everybody knew that his wife was his rider and his down ass bitch but now she was pregnant and she couldn't get him to send so much as a *fuck you*, or *kiss my ass*. She reached her limit as she went to quietly check on Malakai who was sleeping in his bed. After silently closing his door she headed into her bedroom, threw on anything and opened her nightstand to find her rainbow pocket knife before slipping it into her purse. Since he wanted to play with her feelings like she was some kind of joke, she was fully prepared to show him just how funny she could truly be.

Dax and Spook were leaving a lick as they cruised through the rain with the windshield wipers on full speed.

"You better slow the fuck down nigga, before we fuck around and hydroplane into some shit." Dax said, leaning forward in his seat as they both struggled to see the lines on the road.

"Nigga, do you know who you riding with? I got this." Spook said, as he gripped the steering with both hands. He was talking shit, but truthfully he was thinking the same thing.

"We're close to Dre's you trying to go over there or do you want to go back over Kea's?" Dax asked him.

"Knowing Dre' he's probably laid up in some pussy." Spook said, before they both laughed.

Mia's first stop was Spook and Mercedes. She pulled in front of their door, not even bothering to park. After hopping out she banged on the glass screen door until Mercedes appeared with an attitude.

"What's up Mia?" Mercedes asked, with a puzzled look on her face. She was wondering why Mia would be out in a whole storm banging like the police.

"Is Dax here?" Mia asked, figuring he wasn't when she realized Spook's car was missing.

"Nah, they left a couple hours ago." Mercedes said, she still didn't understand why Mia was in the rain, looking crazy.

"Okay." Mia said, walking away and pulling off.

She immediately headed back to the eastside and it was just her luck that she spotted Spook's car pulling up to Kea's right in front of her. She pulled up behind the dodge and hopped out after grabbing her knife and sliding it into her back pocket.

"So this is what we're doing?" Mia yelled, as she approached Dax after he climbed out of the passenger side.

"Chill Mia, I haven't been doing shit. I just wanted to give you a couple days to get your mind right before I came back." He said, slightly hunched over as the cold rain trickled over his head and shoulders.

"So you thought, ignoring my calls and texts for days was going to make me calm down? Are you fucking dumb?" Mia shouted, shoving him in the chest. The sight of his handsome mug, enraged her. She forgot all about being pregnant after getting a whiff of a mixture of soap and cologne. She instantly swung on him, with all her might trying to box his head off to let out her frustrations.

"Chill out! Look at how you react to shit, don't nobody want to come home to that bullshit." Dax said, grabbing ahold of her wrist as they stood tussling, both drenched in the rain.

Mia didn't hear a thing he was saying as she relentlessly tried to break free of his grip. She imagined him between somebody else's legs every night, as she laid at home in their bed home alone, pregnant and miserable. "I should fucking kill you out here." She gritted, seeing red. She twisted her whole body and yanked her wrist free from his hold and promptly pulled out her knife, lunging at Dax with the 4-inch blade.

"Woahhh! You fucking crazy!" Dax yelled, after dodging Mia's attack and running to the other side of Spook's car.

Spook watched from Kea's porch as they played ring around the rosy a few times before Mia stopped to catch her breath. As she stood bent over, with her hand on her knees she realized how ridiculous she was behaving. She knew her family, friends and coworkers were right. She couldn't force him to act right. After getting her breathing under control, Mia removed her wedding ring, tossed it into a stream flowing along the side of the road. She looked down at the spot where her ring once sat on her finger, before calmly walking back to her truck.

"I'm done." She said, out of breath as she climbed into the truck and pulled off.

An hour later, Mia stood over the tub in a tangerine colored tank top and purple underwear as she poured an entire bottle of bleach over Dax's favorite jeans, hoodies and sweatpants. She lightly chuckled to herself as she watched the bleach turn his expensive garments into an ugly version of tie-dye designs. He wouldn't continue to lay up with bitches in clothes that she had bought him. Her hair was still wet, sticking to her face as she wiped her tears, before laughing out loud to herself. She knew how much pride he took in his appearance and wardrobe and couldn't wait to see his reaction. She grabbed her phone off the sink before taking the pictures. She poked her lips out, as she silently debated on whether she should post it to her facebook story or just send it directly to him. Choosing the latter, she swiped the hair out of her face and smiled after pressing send.

"Let them bum ass bitches buy your clothes." She said, leaning over the sink as she looked at her reflection in the mirror.

"Man what the fuck?!!" Dax blurted out, jumping to his feet after Mia's picture came through his imessages. He walked over to Spook and revealed what Mia had done.

Spook's eyebrows shot up, as he grimaced at the photo.

"Damn bro, but at least she didn't fuck with your shoes." He said, before handing the phone back to him.

"What are you gone do though?" Spook asked.

"I got something for her ass. Just wait." Dax said, sitting back down before staring off in space.

Chapter 11

Dax

After brewing from Mia destroying his clothes, Dax sat patiently one street over every morning waiting for her to leave so he could make his move. It took 2 days for her to come outside with Malakai in tow, after they climbed into the truck and pulled off. Dax directed Spook to pull up.

"Nigga what are you about to do?" Spook asked, after pulling up.

"I'm going to get the rest of my shit." Dax said, before climbing out.

After using his key to get in, Dax went straight into the kitchen and grabbed 2 large trash bags from underneath the kitchen sink and headed into the bedroom. He quickly emptied the remainder of his side of the closet and dresser drawers and made a few trips to the car with all of his shoe boxes. After he got all of his belongings, hc doubled back and returned to their bedroom. Since Mia wanted to play dirty he decided to take her small jewelry box that held 2 of her gold necklaces that he knew she loved and dumped them into his pockets. He got down on his knees and lifted the bed skirt and pulled three shoe boxes from underneath the bed, before toting them to Spook's car.

Spook simply shook his head as Dax placed the stack of boxes on the backseat but Dax still wasn't finished. He went back inside and unplugged the living room and Mia's bedroom t.v. the smaller t.v. fit on the floor of the backseat with no problem but he struggled to squeeze the 55-inch living room t.v. into the car. After removing his trash bag of clothes and throwing it in the trunk he put the television over the seat at an angle and slammed the door. He ran back inside and looked around for a second, after concluding that he was satisfied and headed back to the car.

Back into the passenger seat, Dax looked over after Spook, "What? Bitch better read a fucking book or something. Shit, she likes reading anyway, she'll be aight."

As soon as Mia walked in the front door, with her grocery bags she noticed her t.v. missing.

"Now, i'm really gonna kill this nigga." She said, dropping the bags and heading to her bedroom to see what else was missing.

After realizing that Dax took her two necklaces that she wasn't wearing along with her bedroom t.v., she headed back out the door to look for him.

Dax purposely stood outside of a popular store on the Westside with a crowd of niggas, as he waited for Mia to pull up. Less than 20 minutes later she arrived with Malakai bouncing in the backseat before she slammed on the breaks and hopped out.

Mia didn't give a fuck that she was about to make

a scene as she went to her trunk to get the loose brick that she had pulled over to retrieve for the occasion. She grabbed the brick and slammed the trunk as she walked up to Dax leaning back as she approached him, she planned to pitch the brick at his head as if she were playing for a major league baseball team.

"Damn Dax, I heard ya' wife was crazy." One guy said, moving away from Dax.

"She ain't playing no games."

"Chill shorty, you got your son in the back." another guy said pointing toward the truck, but Mia's focus was Dax and Dax alone.

"Mia, I swear to god if you hit me with that brick-"

Mia aimed directly for Dax's face, her jaw clenched as she launched it as hard as she could. She was hoping to knock a few teeth from his mouth.

Dax ducked, barely eluding the brick by a millisecond. When he heard the sound of the impact the brick made as it slammed into the storefront wall, his mind instantly snapped. He forgot about Mia being pregnant as he ran up to her and scooped her up. He flipped her over his shoulder and dumped her on her head.

The sound of her own neck cracking on the asphalt only provoked Mia.

"Damnnnn!" Everybody said in unison, as they watched.

"Mom!" Malakai cried as he opened his backdoor to climb out.

The adrenaline pumping through Mia made her numb to any pain, as hopped to her feet.

"Stay right there, Kai. I'm good." She said, pointing to the truck before she ran up behind Dax.

"Yo go head!" Dax said, as he walked bent over trying to avoid the punches to the back of the head from Mia.

"Matter fact." Mia said, abruptly turning around and running over to the brick.

Dax looked back when Mia stopped swinging and noticed that she was doubling back to get the brick. He gripped the side of his pants to hold them up as he slightly ran to put distance between them.

Mia scooped up the brick, before pursuing him down the street.

"You running, like a bitch!" Mia said, out of breath after Dax picked up his speed.

"What the fuck is they on?"

"They always been like this."

"They wildin'." The guys in front of the stores commented as they watched the couple.

"Yo go the fuck home Mia. Like what are doing? You're pregnant and you got our son out here. You on some bullshit man." Dax said, not realizing that his personal bag of molly had fallen out of his pocket as he jogged backwards.

Noticing the bag of molly on the sidewalk, Mia quickened her pace and ran full speed towards him. Hoping to grab the bag before he noticed it. After scooping up the drugs Mia turned around to head back to Malakai and the truck.

After climbing back into the truck, Malakai wiped his eyes as Mia looked at him through the rearview mirror.

"I'm truly sorry Kai Kai." She said, in a soft tone. She knew that her angry moments with Dax were always her lowest parenting moments.

The next afternoon, Mia's body felt the effects of the tussle from the day before. Sore from head to toe, she waited until 3 in the afternoon to head to Alyssa and Lola's house. She knew that if Dax had taken the time to really pack her t.v.s up, then he didn't plan to return them. So in return she had his drugs but didn't know what exactly the blue crystals were or have an idea what to do with them but she knew Alyssa would know.

She pulled onto their block and noticed their shiny blue Chrysler 300 already in the driveway.

"Come on Kai." Mia said, before she climbed out herself.

They both walked up to the front step of the townhouse and knocked on the door. She hadn't called or texted her about any of it because she didn't want to hear her mouth over the phone.

"Mimi," Lola sang after she opened the front door.

"Hey Kai!" She said, pulling him into her arms and hugging him.

"Lolo! I missed ya'll! What were ya'll doing?

Where's Alyssa?" Mia asked, walking into the living room.

"She's in the room go head, Kai do you want to play the Lyssa's game." Lola asked, looking at Malakai as Mia headed up the stairs.

"Sis, I need your help." Mia said, after she saw Alyssa standing in front of her dresser preparing a blunt.

"What happened now?" Alyssa asked, looking at Mia through the mirror.

"What kind of drug is this?" Mia asked, pulling the clear baggy from her purse before walking it over to Alyssa.

"Damn, this is that good molly! Where the hell you get this?" Alyssa asked, snapping her head in Mia's direction.

"Well," Mia said, plopping down at the foot of their bed. "It's a long story but basically Dax came and took all t.v.'s except for Kai's and I went to fight him and he dropped that."

"Wait, wait, now hold the fuck up. He stole your televisions?" Alyssa said, holding her hand up.

"Um Yup," Mia said, pursing her lips and slowly nodding.

"Yo call the cops on his ass. Send his ass to jail!" Alyssa demanded, before picking up her phone. "If you won't I will."

"Call the cops for what Alyssa?" Mia shrieked, snatching Alyssa's phone. She didn't have a problem with police officers in general but she didn't want the law in her business. She wouldn't tell them shit and she damn sure wouldn't show up to a courthouse to help them throw her man away. Dax was most definitely on some bullshit but jail was the last place she wanted to see him.

"Alright, he's going to end up killing your ass, just watch!" Alyssa yelled, turning back around to finish rolling her weed.

"Never that sis." Mia said, standing up and putting her arm on Alyssa's shoulder.

"So should I flush the shit or what?" Mia asked.

"Hell no crazy ass, we can sell it to somebody this weekend so you can buy at least one new t.v." Alyssa said, looking down at the bag. She guessed that it was worth at least $300.

At 10:30 the next morning, Dax sat in Kizzy's bed with her plum colored weed tray in his lap as he sprinkled molly into the blunt of weed he was preparing. They had both woken up, anxious to repeat everything they had done the night before. He showed up at her door high and pissy drunk, still fuming over Mia making him lose his drugs. But after taking his anger and frustrations out on Kizzy's mouth, throat and pussy he was over it and ready to dead all the bullshit between him and Mia. He had been enjoying the fact that Kizzy seemed less talkative than he remembered, giving him adequate space and time to think. He didn't really want to conversate or be touched unless they were in the middle of fucking or if she was sucking his dick. He didn't want to romanticize their dealings in anyway or get her hopes up like he had mistakenly done in the past. Kizzy was sexy and a good time but that was it in his eyes. He decided that he would return Mia's necklaces, but after they got into a fight he sold her bedroom t.v. and her 3 pairs of sneakers for $70 a piece. Which made up for the money that he lost when he dropped the drugs. So he was no longer upset, he just hoped that Mia would be asleep or at least too tired to want to fight on him.

Kizzy had been studying Dax's every move since he had arrived the night before. She could tell that something was upsetting him when he arrived by the way he manhandled her while they were fucking. She knew that she had literally sucked every ounce of attitude out of him but he seemed like he had a lot on his mind. She figured it was about Mia, she heard that they had gotten into a fight on the westside the day before. But everyone knew how they got down, they'd fight one day and then post pictures on the internet the following day as if nothing had happened. They were just crazy for one another, but Kizzy could care less. It didn't matter that he loved Mia as long as he came through and dug her out like the previous night. Their city was so small that everybody was sharing their man with somebody whether they wanted to admit it or not. Hood niggas like Dax were well known and highly sought after, so she didn't mind being sister wives with Mia. Her feelings for him had never left from 2014, she loved everything about him. The way he dressed, his confidence in the way he carried himself, the way the hood respected him, his smile, the way he laughed, but most of all, the way he fucked her nice and rough. He was perfect, in fact the only thing she disliked when she looked at him were the tattoos of Mia's name that made her skin crawl, he had already married the bitch and gave her a baby. Why did he have to mark his skin up with her name too? She leaned back onto her pillow, burning a hole through the fancy cursive inscription of "*Mia*" on the side of his neck. She wondered if she had his baby would he tatt her name too?

Later that night, Mia laid in the bed watching one of her favorite shows, "*Naked and Afraid*" on the new 60-inch LG smart t.v. that she and Alyssa had picked up from the store earlier. The show was a challenge to see who could survive out in deserts, jungles or swamps with no food, clean water or even clothes. She got a kick out of the show and couldn't imagine ever being outside hungry and thirsty while mosquitoes, ants and shit bit all over her bare pussy lips. *"Hell naw,"* she thought, when they'd show the bug bite ridden asses of the participants after one night outdoors.

"She got a new t.v. fast as a bitch." Dax thought to himself as he stood in the doorway of their bedroom.

"The hell you watching now!?"

Mia almost jumped out of her skin, unaware that he had entered the house but quickly sucked her teeth and rolled her eyes at the sight of him. "Boy fuck you." Mia said, calmly before she laid back down, returning her attention to her show.

Seeing how calm she was scared Dax, he wondered if she had her knife under her pillow or some other type of weapon. He swiftly yanked the covers completely off of the bed, to see if she was hiding anything under the blanket.

Covered in only a cami and a pair of boyshorts, Dax noticed Mia's nipples instantly harden when the air hit them and although he had spent the majority of his time away getting satisfied by Kizzy, the sight of Mia still caused his dick to jump to attention. Any female could make him feel good and get his rocks off but being inside of his wife, gave him a different level of comfort and satisfaction.

Mia paused her t.v. show before she sat up in the bed and locked eyes with Dax. "Man what's up my nigga? If you want to talk than, speak!" Talking with her hands and shoulders with her head tilted.

Dax smiled at the sight of her, he could tell by her facial expressions and aggressive hand gestures that she was on her fake gangster tip. She was obviously still heated but he was confident that by the end of the night she'd return to her normal, tender and intimate nature. He missed his little mama.

Chapter 13

Late November

"Alright Mia, when I count to 3 I want you to give me one more push, as hard as you can okay?" Doctor Lindsey said, as she looked up from in between Mia's legs.

"You got it babe." Dax said, looking down at Mia as she squeezed his hand.

"I can't! My pussy is fucking ripping I can feel it!!!" Mia screamed, with tears and sweat rolling down her face.

"It's not, you can do it Mia, just one more time. 1, 2..."

"You got it little mama. You're the strongest woman I know." Dax said, encouraging her. He couldn't imagine her going through this at 13 but he was so glad that he was there to be there for her and witness it this time around. Seeing her give birth to their daughter gave him a new found respect for her, she was strong, he had to give it to her.

Mia sat slightly off the bed as if she were doing a sit up as she held her breath and pushed so hard, that it caused her to shake violently. She could literally taste the blood in her mouth after she bit down into her jaw but it felt like nothing compared to the ripping and burning sensation she was feeling in her vagina, as the baby passed through.

"Pusssshhh Mia!! There you go." Doctor Lindsey said.

"I got her, you did it Mia." Doctor Lindsey said.

Mia collapsed onto the bed, out of breath and exhausted.

"You did good babe," Dax said, pulling his mask down before he leaned over to kiss her on the forehead.

"Dad, do you want to cut the umbilical cord?" The nurse asked Dax.

Mia cried tears of joy, as she watched Dax cut the umbilical cord.

Later that afternoon, Mia cradled Teal closely to her chest, before she looked over at Dax who was sitting in a chair next to her hospital bed drooling. He had been nodding in and out of sleep from the moment they arrived at the hospital. She knew a perk high when she saw one but she still loved him with everything in her. She couldn't help but wonder if he still felt the same. They fought and made up repeatedly throughout her entire pregnancy. The more they fought, the longer he'd stay gone, sometimes for days at a time. She could admit that she was miserable during that time.

Despite it all, she was willing to give it one last shot. Looking down at Teal reminded Mia of all the good times she and Dax shared. All she wanted was to be a family.

"Babe." Mia asked, leaning over to nudge him.

"Yeah little mama." He said, stirring up from his sleep.

"Do you still want this?" Mia asked, nodding down at Teal. "Do you still want us?" She said, clearing her throat attempting to contain her tears. She turned away, avoiding eye contact as she continued.

"Do you remember in the visiting room during our very last visit, you said you were going to name the baby-"

"Destiny." Dax said, cutting Mia off.

"Yeah" Mia said slightly chuckling. "But it's like with everything we've been through together over the years, bids, visits, letters, phone calls, being forced to be away from each other. Just hoping, wishing and dreaming for times like this right here babe." Mia paused and looked over at Dax.

"You really think I would leave my hubby over some perks and molly?" Mia asked. She knew he had popped perks since she was younger but after repeatedly finding small open baggies of molly in his laundry, she figured he was dabbling in that too.

Dax was shocked that Mia knew more than she led on.

"I never judged you for that drug shit, you never tried to make me do it and that's all that matters to me. I love you and i'm still out here holding you down. But you left me by myself for the majority of this pregnancy, and this shit has been depressing. I was lonely as hell. I refuse to continue on like that period, so I need to know if you still want this." Mia said, finally looking Dax in the eyes.

Dax sighed, as he realized that he had been doing the opposite of everything he had promised her and that it was hurting her. He couldn't imagine walking away and letting another man take his place and love his family. He put the rail down on her bed and sat next to her and the baby. He looked at the mascara smudges around her eyes and her hair in a messy bun as she laid in the oversized hospital gown, she was still beautiful. He couldn't imagine letting her go.

"I'd rather do a million years in prison than lose my little mama," Dax said, softly grabbing her chin and turning her face to his. "I'll always love you and need you."

Relieved, Mia finally released the breath she had been holding in, letting out the flood of tears that she could no longer contain.

Dax pulled her and their newborn into his arms as her sobs pulled at his heart strings. "I'm sorry babe. I've been letting my troubles and addictions come in between us but all that is going to change babe. I got you. We're going to go out when you heal up and get back to how things used to be."

6 weeks later

Mia sat on the toilet cringing as she lightly dabbed a baby wipe across her recently healed, fourth degree perineum tear where the stitches had previously been.

"You aight babe?" Dax asked, walking into the bathroom.

"I'm good. It's healed for the most part." Mia said, instantly replacing her grimace with a quick smile.

"So that means I can finally get some of that good good?" Dax asked, as Mia pulled up her underwear, flushed the toilet and stood at the bathroom sink.

Dax got into position behind Mia, and lightly pressed his meat up against her juicy round peach. He had let Kizzy suck him dry one last time before he cut her off after promising Mia that he would change in the hospital. So he had actually went over a month with feeling the inside of anybody. "You miss it?" He whispered in her ear, as he wrapped his arm around her.

"Mmhmm." Mia moaned and bit her bottom lip, as she leaned into him, with a palm full of foamy champagne toast hand soap.

"How much longer babe?" Dax asked, as he released her to let her wash her hands.

"Friday babe, you said we were going to drink, and go out right?" She asked, turning to him. The lock down had been partially lifted after covid, opening the malls, bars, clubs, and restaurants to a half full capacity and Mia couldn't wait to pop out.

"Yep, we got to before you go back to work. We got to find something to wear though. Do you still want to go to the mall today?" He asked, looking her over.

"No, I go to the doctor at 2:00, so really we can just go Friday, after I go get my hair done." She said, as she dried her hands on a towel. She could not wait to finally get cute, hit the bar, and have fun.

That Friday, Mia stood at the entrance to the mall as she waited for Dax, who had run back to the truck after forgetting her mask. They had lucked up after Lola agreed to watch the kids so she and Dax could have a night out. Mia stood there with her fresh 26' inch black bone-straight wig, in a pair of levis and a sand colored PLT hoodie as she waited for Dax. She had on her waist trainer and she was ready to find something chill but banging to show off her postpartum body. Her hips had gotten wider and her ass had put on a pound or two. She looked good and she was well aware of it.

"Alright babe, let's go." Dax said, grabbing Mia's hand as they walked into the mall and through the food court.

As they stood in the first sneaker store Mia spotted an outfit on the men's side that she knew would compliment her curves and achieve the look she was going for. She went over to the rack and searched for the smallest size.

"You like this outfit, with these shoes babe?" Dax asked, walking over to her with a pair of red and black 1's, a pair of black jeans and a black hoodie with red graffiti.

Mia frowned and shook her head as she took the outfit from Dax. "Babe don't you already have an outfit just like that? And I thought you wanted us to match or coordinate? I'm wearing this and i'm going to get a pair of beef and broccoli's." Mia said, holding up her cucumber green nike sweatsuit.

“I did before you bleached my shit!” Dax reminded her in an irritated tone.

“Damn,” Mia chuckled, “my fault babe but you can’t wear red if I wear green anyway hubby. You trying to have us walking in there looking like a Christmas tree. I’ll help you, come on babe. You can do a beige, a brown or just this same shade of green as me.” Mia said, throwing her outfit over her shoulder before she grabbed his arm and headed towards the shoes.

“Can we get two double shots of fireball and two double shots of Henny.” Dax said, to the bartender as he and Mia sat down.

Courtney the longtime bartender nodded and quickly pulled out four tall shot glasses.

Mia smiled as she looked over at Dax, they had just arrived and she was in a good mood after they had started drinking at home before they showered and got dressed together. He ended up choosing the same green nike sweatsuit as Mia but paired his with fresh white low tops. He flashed Mia the same flawless smile that got her hooked the very first night she met him. The drinks and music had her in her zone while she stared at the side of his face, spellbound as the ripples in his hair shined, underneath the bar lights. In her eyes he was still the finest nigga in the city. She missed nights like this.

“Come closer hubby.” Mia said, looking down at the gap between their bar stools. She wanted to be close enough to lean on him and whisper in his ear.

Dax looked at Mia but didn't protest, he stood up and dragged his stool until it touched Mia's. He knew how overly affectionate she always became when she'd drank alcohol. He sat back down in his seat and put his arm around her neck.

"You good babe?" He asked her, as she leaned into him.

"I'm good, let's take these shots." Mia said, after Courtney slid their glasses in front of them.

Mia picked up one glass and Dax followed her lead and drank his shot.

Mia leaned over and gave Dax a trial of kisses from his neck to his cheek before she whispered, "I love you soo much babe."

"I love you more little mama." Dax said, pulling her closer. He turned his head and his lips brushed against hers after she looked up at him. They both knew that everyone around the bar was watching them but neither of them cared. They both closed their eyes, locked lips and let their tongues wrestle.

"Ya'll two could've stayed home and did this." Spook said, after he and Mercedes walked over to them.

Dax laughed after he recognized Spook's voice.

"The only couple I know that comes to the club to boo love." Spook continued.

"Man you know how that shit go." Dax said, as he got up to give Spook dap.

"It's packed in this bitch huh?" Spook said, looking around. The club was only supposed to be half full with everybody wearing masks and sitting 6 feet apart, instead it was completely jam packed with half the city popping out and no one wearing masks.

"Hell yeah, I was surprised to see everybody in this mothafucker." Dax said, as he and Spook looked over at the dance floor.

"Everybody like who? It ain't nothing in here *BUT* bitches." Mia said, rolling her eyes as she picked up her second shot glass. She scanned the female dominated room with her eyes, and caught a glimpse of Kizzy eyeballing them from the dance floor. The smirk on her face instantly fired Mia up. She couldn't stand that everytime she came to the club, there was sure to be at least one female in the building that Dax had smashed or at least gotten his dick sucked by. This was the reason she never half stepped when it was time to pop out. She was well aware that she was some pressure when she put that shit on, she swept her long weave behind her shoulder before she turned in her seat to face the dance floor.

"There go one of your whores right there." Mia said, pointing at Kizzy. Hoping to get a rise out of her. She hadn't forgotten how Kizzy broad casted to the whole city that she was fucking her man years ago. Seeing her had Mia wondering how they never came to blows but in her mind, tonight was as good a time as any.

"Here we go with the bullshit." Dax said, sitting

back down beside Mia. Any other nigga would probably panic if their wife ended up with the room with one of their side chicks but Dax was used to the circumstances in their small city. He wasn't worried about, Kizzy or any other female that he fucked. They all knew that Mia was his wife, so if they ever tried to blow his spot up in front of him, he'd smack the shit out of them and let Mia whoop their ass. The whole city knew this, that's why he wasn't sweating Kizzy.

"Ay bro, we'll meet you and Mercedes over there at a table." Dax said, turning to Spook.

"Aight nigga." Spook said, walking to the back of the club.

"Please don't show your ass in here tonight, little mama." Dax said, pulling Mia into his arms.

"Shit I'm cooling." Mia said, shrugging her shoulders before finally taking her eyes off Kizzy.

"Ay Courtney, can we get two more doubles a piece." Dax said, holding up two fingers in the air. "Let's just have a good time babe. These hoes know who I love. Who did I marry? And who do I have tatted all over me?" Dax said, putting his hand over his ear and leaning into Mia. "I can't hear you."

"These bitches don't give a damn about no marriage or no tattoo." Mia said, clapping her hands in his face as she talked.

"Yeah they do too, trust me. So, who do I have tatted on my neck and wrist!?" Dax yelled, still leaning into her. "Who!?"

"Me nigga damn!" Mia said, folding her arms.

"Alright then!" Dax said, sliding her shot glasses to her, "Fuck these bitches! Cheers to my mafucking wife." He yelled, clanking glasses with Mia causing the liquor to spill a little and the people near them turn and look at them.

"Alright babe chill!" Mia said laughing.

Dax watched Mia as she took her shot before pulling her in for a hug. Mia made eye contact with Kizzy as Dax hugged her, before looking her up and down with a smirk.

An hour and a half later, Dax sat with Mia, Spook and Mercedes at a table in the back of the club watching everybody as they came in.

"What's up Mia?" Someone said, after he entered the club and walked past them.

Mia turned in her seat to see who it was but didn't recognize him. He was a skinny, tall brown skin guy with thick glasses and acne covering his cheeks.

"Who the fuck is he?" Dax said pointing to the guy, with his face frowned up.

"I ain't never seen that nigga, a day in my life." Mia said, still observing the guy.

"Yeah, aight." Dax said sarcastically.

"Look at him babe, I'm dead ass!" Mia said, holding her hand on her chest.

"Aight, well let's go meet this mystery nigga. Come on." He said getting up and grabbing Mia's arm.

"Ayo." Dax said tapping the guy on his shoulder from behind as he held Mia by her arm, "how the fuck you know my wife?" Dax said pointing to Mia after the guy faced him.

"I- don't know her personally, we're just friends on the gram." He stuttered, before folding his lips.

"Well listen, don't walk in and speak to my mahfuckin' wife like you know her. You must not be from 'round here. Good thing I didn't shot first and ask questions later." Dax said, pulling his pants over his ethika boxers.

"Steve Urkel looking ass nigga." Dax continued, as he turned to walk away.

Spook laughed at Dax as he watched him from his seat.

Mia felt bad for the guy, who looked out of place as he pushed his glasses up onto his face.

"Come the fuck on Mia, and delete that lame ass nigga." Dax said, jerking on her arm as he pulled her away.

"Get off me!" Mia said, trying to snatch her arm away. "Embarrassing as hell!"

"Embarrassing my ass, you got these clown ass niggas speaking to you." Dax yelled yoking Mia up by hoodie.

Nearee walked up to Dax, and Mia after she heard the commotion from the other side of the bar.

"What's up cuz, ya'll good?" Nearee asked, looking from Mia to Dax.

"Yeah we good, he's trippin bout a fanned out stranger." Mia said, with her lip curled up.

"Nah you fuckin trippin'. Come on yo we out." Dax said, grabbing her wrist. He raised his hand in the air when he made eye contact with Spook and pointed towards the exit.

"We'll catch you later sis." Dax said, as he pulled Mia behind him.

Mia snatched away, "stop yanking me around! I can walk by myself." Mia pouted, marching ahead of him. She couldn't stand when he manhandled her in a public setting.

"Well come your ass on then." Dax said, walking closely behind her towards the doors.

After stopping to get food, Mia headed straight for her weed as she and Dax walked into the house.

"I already got one rolled." Dax said, as he noticed her getting ready to roll up. "And fix your face." He said, grabbing her chin to face him.

Mia fought back the smile that was coming on her face before she slapped his hand away.

"You're always embarrassing, I didn't know that

man." She said, before she put the blunt into her mouth. Dax sparked his lighter for her and smirked.

Chapter 14

After getting dressed that following afternoon, Dax headed to Spook's after spending the morning cleaning the house with Mia.

"Give me a kiss babe. I'll be back." Dax said, leaning down to Mia as she sat on the couch rocking Teal.

"We should put the tree up tonight with Kai and start wrapping the presents too." Mia said, after kissing him. Christmas was right around the corner, and although she had done the majority of the shopping already they had yet to get into the Christmas spirit and decorate.

"Alright, I won't be long." Dax said, putting his navy blue puffy vest over his long sleeve orange, white and blue plaid shirt.

"You think you cute too nigga. Make me pull up and fuck you up." Mia yelled, as Dax headed out of their room, down the hallway.

"Chill shorty!" Dax yelled, before locking the front door, closing it behind him.

As Dax pulled up to the projects, he spotted Dre,

Cash, Kion and Spook standing in a huddle with a few niggas from around the way rolling dice. Everyone was dressed in their hoodies, timbs and toboggans. Blunts and bottles were being passed around as if it was a summer block party and not the beginning of December. Dax got excited at the sight of the scenery, he quickly parked and hopped out, ready to take everybody's money.

“Yoooo.” Dax said, as he walked up to the circle.

“What’s good bro?” Spook said, dappin’ Dax up.

“We see wifey finally let ya ass out the house huh?” Cash said, with a smirk before he blew on the dice in his hand.

“Right it’s going on 4:00 you straight bro? She ain’t fuck you up after lastnight did she?” Spook cracked.

“Shut ya ass up nigga.” Dax said, looking at the black altima as it slowed down on the street. Already knowing who it was, he put his head down and just prayed she’d keep going.

“Mm mm mm.” He said, shaking his head as the car pulled into the parking lot heading straight in his direction.

Spook looked up to see who had Dax trippin, “aw shit here we go.” he said, causing everybody to look in the same direction.

“Oh so, that’s how you feel Dax?” Kizzy shouted, as she rolled up on them while rolling her window down.

Dax sighed before he walked over to her car to try

to diffuse the situation before it escalated.

"Man, what's up why are you out here yelling and making a scene like you lost ya' damn mind?" Dax asked, with his face frowned up as he looked down at her.

"Nigga you know why! You don't think I heard you in the club yelling, talking about fuck these bitches and all that corny ass shit!?" Kizzy yelled, still heated that he had the audacity to play her like that when her homegirls knew she was fucking him. He humiliated her in the worst way and she wasn't going to let it slide. She hopped out of her car and got in his face.

"Bitch you better go head. I'm telling you some good shit!" Dax said, turning and walking away from her. He wasn't about to sit and argue with her hoe ass.

"Or what nigga?" Kizzy said, running behind him. The sight of Mia's name on his neck, as she chased him infuriated her all the more. "You in the club parading a bitch that moved a whole nigga into your crib while you was in the slammer! Fuckin clown!" She said, lunging forward and digging her long nails into his neck. Clawing at the tattoo.

Instinctively Dax turned around and punched Kizzy in the mouth before he put his hands around her throat.

Kizzy's scream got caught up in her throat as she clawed at his tight grip around her neck. Dax squeezed tighter, as he contemplated choking the life out of her.

"Chill bro." Spook said, trying to get Dax off of her.

Dax looked into her bloodshot red eyes and held

onto her for a couple more seconds before he slung her with all his might, "It is fuck you bitch, when it comes to my wife." He continued as Kizzy stumbled backwards, coughing. Dax dabbed at his neck, feeling the blood on his fingers.

"Stupid ass bitch, she gone fuck ya stupid ass up watch."

Kizzy continued to cough as she headed back to her car. "Nigga fuck you, ain't nobody scared of that whore. You need to get a DNA test for that baby that ain't yours! You fuckin Goofy!" she said after she was safely back in her car before turning her music back on and pulling off.

"How bad is it nigga?" Dax asked Spook, lifting his chin in the air.

"All imma say is, don't go home tonight nigga." Spook said shaking his head.

"She's lucky you was here, I was ready to slap the shit out of that bitch with my gun." Dax said.

"Bitches be doing the most." Cash said, standing with his arms folded.

Mia sat in the bed as Teal slept wondering when Dax would be back. It was already going on 10 and he had yet to make his appearance. "*How late does he think we gone put the tree up.*" she thought.

She picked up her phone, to call him. After he didn't answer she texted, "Where are you at babe?"

"I'll be there soon little mama." He replied.

She noticed how he didn't answer the phone but quickly responded to her text message. She decided to take a nap, to pass the time until he got there so she could press the issue face to face.

"How the fuck am I supposed to go up there with my neck like this?" Dax asked Kea and Nearee as they all stood inside of Kea's bathroom examining the two deep claw marks cutting across the "*Mia*" tattoo on his neck.

"Well why the hell would you fuck with Kizzy again, of all people. I know niggas like fat asses but her ass is just to fucking big." Kea said, with her face screwed up before walking out.

"Don't nobody want no bitch wit no flat ass." Dax said. "And that bitch give good head." Dax admitted, as he dabbed his neck with toilet paper drenched in peroxide.

"I know one thing. You always got the bitches in a uproar everytime you fuck wit em. My lil cuz included. What do you be doing to them?" Nearee asked, standing next to him in the tiny bathroom.

Dax looked at Nearee through the reflection in the mirror. She looked deep in thought before she walked out and headed into the living room.

He grabbed three small band aids off the sink before he followed her.

"Can one of ya'll put these band-aids on for me, this shit still bleeding like a mafucker." He asked, looking from Kea to Nearee as they both sat on the couch.

"I gotchu." Nearee said, getting up.

He went to sit in the chair in the kitchen with Nearee close behind. Dax tilted his head to the side, after sitting down before Nearee took the bandaids and began to rip them open.

Standing to his left Dax looked down at Nearee's Off-white 4's. She hid her curves in a pair of baggy army fatigue pants and an oversized cream-colored shirt that said, "*Essentials*" tied in a knot exposing her stomach.

"You got that shit on sis." Dax said, face to face with her snake shaped belly ring. From the outside looking in you would think Nearee was a tomboy. She dressed like one, she had all the kicks, she rarely got her nails done and her perfume of choice was marijuana.

"Don't I always?" Nearee said with a slight laugh. "Plus, i'm waiting for Cash to pull up. He was supposed to been here." She said, applying the last band-aid.

"You ready to go face the music Dax? Or ya'll trying to turn up? Spook is on the way here." Kea asked, walking into the kitchen with a bottle of Hennessy.

"Shit we might as well." Dax said, getting up from the chair, stretching. He knew whenever he went home, shit would hit the fan.

After three hours, a fifth of Hennessy, four blunts in rotation and Kea's fried chicken, Spook and Kea disappeared into her bedroom. Leaving Nearee and Dax sitting across from each other on the couches.

"I can't believe this mothafucka ain't show up for me, bro." Nearee said, as she slowly got up from the couch.

"I know Mia saying the same thing cussing my ass out but fuck it though sis, we keeping each other company." Dax slurred.

Nearee swayed from side to side as she walked towards the kitchen.

"Go your ass home bro. Where the fuck they put the bottle at?" She asked, dragging her feet.

"They took it in the room, but I got a little bit right here." Dax told her, lifting up the almost empty bottle of hennessy.

Reentering the living room Nearee plopped down onto Dax's lap. The two had hung around the same crowd for many years and nothing had ever transpired between them but now that she was sitting on Dax's lap he wished he had tried to hit sooner.

"Let me get that shit. Why you ain't go home yet?" Nearee asked, reaching for the bottle.

"Shit I'm here with you." Dax whispered into Nearee's ear.

"Whatchu tryna do?" He continued, handing her the bottle.

Nearee closed her eyes as she opened the bottle and put it to her lips.

"That's my little cousin Dax." She finally slurred.

"She'll never find out." Dax said, slightly lifting Nearee up to slide out from under her. There were more women that Mia didn't find out about than ones that she did. So he was confident that what he was saying was true.

Nearee didn't reply, she simply looked at Dax as she recapped the bottle and placed it next to her.

Noticing how unfazed Nearee seemed, Dax pulled out a small baggy of molly and poured some on his tongue before bending down towards Nearee. She leaned up and licked all the crystals from Dax's tongue without hesitating.

He poured more of the blue crystals on his tongue before getting down on his knees on the floor between her legs.

He felt Nearee finally relax and melt into the couch as he began a kissing trail down her stomach while trying to unbutton her pants.

"Lift up." Dax slurred through bloodshot eyes.

After she lifted, Dax swiftly pulled down her loose pants and Calvin Klein underwear. He wasted no time burying his face into her bald pussy.

Skipping the normally slow inception, Dax went straight for the finale as he swiped Nearee's clit with his thumb to remove the skin and expose her pearl, blowing on it and sucking on it.

It didn't take long for Nearee's back to arch as she bit down on her bottom lip trying to contain her moans.

She was in bliss as she felt the orgasm building up.

"Right-right there." She moaned out.

"Softer-" She said as she felt Dax picking up the pace with his tongue strokes.

"Mmmmm.." She moaned when the orgasm

released itself. She laid there with her eyes closed basking in the feeling. There was no better feeling than a molly-weed orgasm, it was always much more grand, intense and pleasurable. Mia didn't know what she was missing, Nearee didn't even want to have sex without that combo being in her system.

Dax wasted no time sliding his meat into Nearee's soppy, dripping twat as she laid there with her legs gapped open.

Done with trying to please her, he drilled away like a rabbit in heat as waves of pleasure rushed through his entire body.

Nearee had little to no time to enjoy the strokes after Dax collapsed onto her which was fine by her.

Mia woke up to the faint cooing sounds of Teal next to her in the bed and looked over at the clock.

"5:37," she said under her breath. Dax still had yet to return but Mia decided to not even trip.

"Hey ma-ma, hi baby." Mia said in her high-pitched baby voice as she picked Teal up while propping her pillows up behind her to sit up in the bed. Teal tried to eat her fist, letting Mia know that she was ready to eat.

"My little baby is hungry huh ma-ma." She said, before she picked Teal up.

After feeding her and changing her diaper, they both fell back to sleep.

The sun was shining through the blinds by the

time Dax and Nearee woke up out of their coma like sleep.

Dax's pants and boxers were around his ankles while Nearee's pants, underwear, and shoes were on the floor next to the couch.

They both jumped up as they heard Kea's door rapidly creak open. "Oh shit!" Nearee whispered, quickly trying to get her foot into her panties, as Dax stuffed his dick into his boxers.

"It's too late. We seen ya'll when I walked Spook to the door, early this morning knocked out. Dick out, pussy out." Kea said, in a dry tone as she walked, she waved them off as she walked past the duo, her bedroom slippers flopping with every step.

"I'm fucking hung over." She continued, as she walked down the hall towards her bathroom.

Dax and Nearee looked at each other with their mouths open.

"Oh my fucking gosh." Nearee said, covering her mouth with her hand.

Dax's mind instantly went to Mia and the fact that he never went home. Instead of getting ready for the holidays with his family like he was supposed to be, here he was fucking his wife's first cousin. Normally he didn't give tricks head but the drugs had him freaked out. He was ready to do whatever lastnight to get his rocks off.

"We triflin as shit for that." She Nearee blurted out, interrupting Dax's train of thought.

Chapter 15

Three days went by with no word from Dax as Mia sat home with Malakai and Teal. Christmas was in less than two weeks and he had her down bad as she consistently blew up his phone and rode around the city everyday trying to find him but he was no where to be found. She didn't know if he was dead or alive as she constantly checked case search and watched the news to see if he had been arrested but so far nothing. She had even called the hospital a few times and he wasn't there either. Anytime she wasn't around the kids she was somewhere crying, thinking the worst, she couldn't imagine him not showing up of his own free will. She knew she was fucked up when she didn't have a appetite after smoking. He knew she was supposed to return to work that Monday and here it was Wednesday and he had yet to return. Hadn't checked on her and the kids or nothing. She knew she was risking losing her job, missing all those days and not even bothering to call in but work was the last thing on her mind when her husband was missing or possibly doing her dirty.

"*Where the fuck is he? It has to come out eventually. The city ain't but so big.*" Mia shook her head at her own thoughts as she laid on the couch watching cartoons with the kids.

"Hey Mia. You should really call mom. She's been asking about you and the new baby. She don't want you to know though lol."- The message from Cali read.

Mia missed her mom like hell. She hated that they hadn't spoken since their fight at Cali's housewarming. She hadn't even gotten to meet Teal, who was now almost 2 months old. She hated that Corrie had moved so far away. Georgia was a twelve hour drive from Maryland.

"I could pop up on my mom and leave this nigga right here." She said, thinking out loud.

Dax sat at Kea's kitchen table after taking a shower. He had been hiding out over there ever since everything went down with Kizzy and then Nearee. He was there the first day that Mia knocked on the door and got Kea to lie for him. Nearee being Mia's cousin had him feeling extra paranoid that everything would come out when she questioned him about the scratches on his neck. He drank all day, popping perks and molly. He missed Mia and the kids but he decided it would be best to just camp out there, at least until his scratches healed up completely. He knew he should've at least given Mia a heads up that he was okay, he knew she was probably worried but he didn't know what to say. He knew she would be furious with him when he made it home. There was no telling what she would do.

That evening Mia was at her breaking point after laying a sleeping Teal in her crib. Malakai was across the hall in his room playing his game as Mia sat on the edge of her bed trying to think of something to do that she hadn't already tried.

Calling Dax blocked had never worked in the past so she decided to download an app that would give her a different phone number.

After less than 10 minutes she had everything set up and called Dax's phone. When Dax picked up on the third ring Mia almost dropped the damn phone.

"Yo." Dax said.

"Yooo." Mia heard Dax repeat before she simply hung up in his ear.

"Ohhh, so it's like that!" Mia said, oh loud to herself.

"So you mean to tell me that it ain't nothing wrong with this nigga!?" Mia continued, before putting her hands on her hips and pacing the bedroom back and forth while looking at the phone. Normally she would call Egypt, Cali, Alyssa, Lola, Ballow or even Chanel. But she knew everybody was tired of hearing about Dax's trifling ways and in the back of their minds she knew they would simply think "told you so." She decided to just keep it to herself as she continued to pace the floor.

She shook her head as it began to dawn on her that he was hiding from her and ignoring the fuck out of her. Here it was almost Christmas and he chose to do this. It could only mean one thing in her eyes. He was cheating and shacking up with another bitch. She collapsed onto the bed, starring at the wall with her mouth agape.

"This how he do me though? Ain't checked on me, Kai, Teal for 4 fucking days? Okay. I got something for

him." She thought.

Shooting to her feet, Mia bolted towards the kitchen, she grabbed the entire box of trash bags from underneath the sink, before heading back into her bedroom.

"Now you lost me." She said out loud to no one in particular.

Dax sat at Kea's kitchen table with Spook where he had been all day, wondering who was playing on his phone with a Randallstown, MD phone number calling and hanging up.

"You look depressed like a mafucka nigga. Why don't you just go home D? It ain't that serious, just lie like you been doing." Spook said, looking at Dax.

"Trying to wait until the shit ain't as noticeable but now I know she is going to be waiting with a knife under her pillow." Dax muttered.

"So why not just call her? You want me to go over there with you and play bodyguard while you calm her down?" Spook laughed.

"She'll stab ya big ass too mafucka." Dax said. *"I'm going to just go home tomorrow. Fuck it."* He thought.

By Midnight, Mia had bagged up all of her and the kids clothes, christmas gifts and essential items. She had a little bit of money saved and decided she was going to leave Dax right in Salisbury and take her and her babies to Georgia to be with Corrie and Keegan. She packed the back of her truck to the ceiling as well as the front passenger seat. She had had enough of Dax's conniving ways. If he could say fuck her and their kids over a piece of pussy than he deserved everything he had coming to him and she wasn't about to stick around waiting for his undeserving ass. Less than 3 hours later she did one more walk through of the house to make sure she hadn't forgotten anything before they left. She would miss the shit out of her little abode. After all she was a homebody, and it was her very first place. She had hand picked every single thing in the residence from furniture to the decor. Heading into her bedroom one last time she picked up one of the prison pictures of her and Dax happy and smiling. She couldn't believe it had come to this but she knew if he didn't appreciate her by now he never would.

She let one tear fall before she pulled herself together, quickly wiping it.

"Come on Kai, you ready to see your grandma?" She said, picking up Teal before heading into Malakai's room.

Malakai nodded his head as he walked and wiped his eyes. She felt bad that she was uprooting them so suddenly but she figured they would all adjust quickly being with her mom.

"You can sleep in the car because it's going to be a long drive." Mia said, guiding him out with her hand on his back.

The dark deserted roads were a direct reflection of just how Mia felt during the drive to her moms, alone. She thought about how she had gotten to this moment in her life. Taking a 12-hour ride alone in the middle of the night with a 6-year-old and 2-month-old. When she was supposed to be happily married. Since it was so late she couldn't call anyone to keep her occupied and she realized that she hadn't even informed anyone of her impulsive decision. She knew her work crew would be mad, and that Egypt and Cali would be surprised and have a lot to say but all that mattered in the moment was leaving Dax and making him feel that shit. She decided to spend the 12 hours listening to all her favorite love songs to get all the crying out of her system. She scrolled through her extensive play list and chose Rihanna's "*Unapologetic*" album and clicked on number 8, before pressing play as she pulled out of her driveway for the last time.

Chapter 16

Georgia

After almost 12 hours, a 5-hour energy drink and multiple stops to feed mainly the baby, change her diaper and fill up the gas tank, Mia finally pulled up to the low-rise multifamily apartment complex. She recognized her mom's red car and decided to park her truck directly next to it. Looking in the back seat at a sleeping Teal and Malakai, she silently thanked God they made it safely without a hitch. She picked up her phone to finally call Corrie to surprise her.

"Mom..." Mia smiled, after she heard her answer and say hello, "look outside."

Mia saw the blinds crack open behind the window directly in front of where she was parked and then a minute later Corrie appeared from under the dark apartment entryway.

Mia ran up to her mom and hugged her. She was surprised at how Corrie squeezed her back. Normally Corrie wasn't the affectionate type but it had been almost a year since she saw Mia.

"It's about time I met my new grandbaby" Corrie said after her and Mia let go and looked at one another.

Seeing her mom hit Mia like a ton of bricks.

"It's alright, at least you're here now." Corrie said, wrapping her arm around her shoulder.

"I'm sorry mom, I should've been called." Mia said, crying.

"It's all good." Corrie said, patting her on the back. "I'm just glad ya'll are here now! Come on, I have an extra room here for you and everything! I had a feeling something would happen. I'll watch the baby now so you can take a shower and take a nap if you want. I also want to show you around a little bit. You're going to like it here, they have everything close by." Corrie said, opening the back truck door.

"Wake up Kai Kai." Corrie said, as she unstrapped Teal from her seat.

"Mom mom!" Malakai said, as he jumped up and ran around the car to Corrie. Mia watched them hug before Corrie took Teal and snuggled her close to her chest as she headed into the apartment.

Corrie had the place cozy with a humongous seven-piece chocolate brown sectional with a chaise and an ottoman. She had everyone's pictures scattered across the living room including one of Teal that Cali or Egypt must've sent to her when they came to the hospital. She had a realistic 7-foot pre-lit artificial Christmas tree decorated beautifully with red, silver, and white ornaments. *"It could've all been so simply, all he had to do was come back home and put the tree up and spend time with us. This is what family does."* Mia thought as she observed the various presents sitting under the tree. She shook her head at the thought.

"You okay Mia?" Corrie asked her.

"Yeah mom." Mia said, following her into the kitchen. Which was small but clean with stainless steel appliances and a table to seat four.

"It's cute in here mom." Mia said.

"Alright let me show you the rooms, come on." Corrie said, excited.

Mia followed Corrie into the spare bedroom, that she, Teal and Malakai would share, which only had a queen-sized bed with a white flowered sheet set and a 6-drawer dresser.

"I can put my t.v. up here mom and hook my game up?" Malakai asked, pointing to the dresser.

"Yep."

"Of course you can, Kai!" Corrie and Mia said simultaneously.

"This is perfect mom, I brought all of our blankets." Mia said, turning to face her mom.

"I just need to unpack the truck."

"And you look exhausted so you can take a shower in the bathroom in the hallway. My room is the last door to the left. Keegans is on the right. If you want to take a nap you can. Me, Teal and Kai Kai can hang out. Ain't that right?" Corrie said, lightly rocking Teal side to side.

"Alright bet it, big Corr. I'm about to unpack all those bags, take a shower and take me a nap." Mia said, dancing.

The next morning, Mia woke up in a slight panic

when she woke up to an empty bed. Jumping up she walked to Corrie's bedroom door and peeked inside, where she found her mom, Malakai and Teal fast asleep in her bed. She silently closed the door and tip toed back to her room. *"I must've been exhausted, nigga putting me through it."* She thought to herself.

She didn't realize how tired she was. What was supposed to be a nap had quickly turned into fourteen hours of sleep with no interruptions. Walking back inside the room she stepped through the narrow path surrounded by black trash bags. She appreciated the memory foam mattress as she climbed back into the bed. Looking at the mess around the room she couldn't believe her rash decision drove her six hundred and ninety-five miles away from her husband and her city but she was happy to be back with her mom.

Picking up her phone she couldn't resist the urge to check snapchat to see if she could spot Dax in anyone's story. Just like clockwork he was on Kea's story from the night before sitting around her kitchen table, along with Dre' Spook and her cousin Nearee. She could see that the small kitchen was filled with smoke as they listened to music, passed blunts and took shots together.

Mia brought the phone closer to her face, examining Dax as she replayed the story over and over and over. His eyes were hidden behind a blacked-out pair of shades, but Mia recognized that he had a fresh shape up and a crispy white tee. He seemed like he was chilling as usual with his smirk and his tranquil posture as he lifted his bottle in the air when he noticed the camera on him. His unperturbed, relaxed composer almost sent Mia through the roof as she felt heat rushing through her body as her heartbeat sped up.

"This nigga don't give no fuck huh?" Mia said, out loud before slinging the phone across the room, with it landing between the path of trash bags.

She thought about how she had sat home crying day in and day out the past several days worrying about him. Here she was 4 states away from the home she loved trying to prove a point to a nigga that clearly didn't give a damn. Right then and there she made a promise to herself that she wasn't going back. She planned to make him see once and for all that he lost a good one, for good. No matter how hard it would be or how bad it hurt, she had to make him stand on everything he had done.

She decided she would never lurk and go looking on social media to check on him from that point on. That shit gave her chest pains, she came to the conclusion that she couldn't handle knowing what the fuck he was doing in her absence. She had to move on point blank.

Laying on her back staring up at the ceiling she heard two taps on the door before it opened.

"I can't believe you're here." Keegan said, walking into the room smiling.

"Why is your phone on the floor?" She asked before picking it up.

"That shit must've fell right out the bed." Mia said, not wanting to get into the truth of the matter. She exhaled before standing up to hug her little sister. She hadn't realized how much she missed her family until that moment. Seeing Keegan made her realize she should have been going to see Cali more when she was still in Maryland.

"So what's your plan now?" Keegan asked, before they both sat on the bed.

"Girl, I don't even know. I just know I had to get the fuck." Mia said, honestly.

"I still need to block him on everything." She said, thinking out loud before sliding the phone out of Keegans grip. Unlocking it, she scrolled down to the name "*Hubby*" in her contacts before blocking him.

"Damn what did he do?" Keegan said, knowing it had to be bad for Mia to finally leave.

"He just didn't really want to be married so i'm going to grant his wish." Mia said, looking at Keegan.

"But how is it here? You like it? What have ya'll been doing?" Mia questioned, shifting the conversation not wanting to show her sister just how sick she was about it.

"There are a million things to do here! We've been eating out a lot. It is nothing like back home. Do you know we're only 30 minutes from Atlanta? Girl the malls! It's so lit you'll see." Keegan said.

Mia didn't respond, she knew it was going to be a drastic change from their small hometown life. In their city Atlanta was referred to as the black Mecca, something like the black version of Hollywood. Whereas their small town only had one mall, big cities like Atlanta had a plethora of Malls. She'd hear stories about the infamous Lenox mall where a celebrity could be spotted on any given day. She had never met a celebrity let alone seen one, so that idea alone was overwhelming to Mia but she was excited for the time being, for the distance between she and Dax giving her the space she needed to somewhat heal or at least get to the point where her chest didn't ache at the thought of him. Being in Georgia would give her the chance to go back to the drawing board, seeing how life would be with just her Malakai and Teal.

"Girl, I still can't believe you actually came." Keegan said, once again, snapping Mia out of her train of thought.

"You ain't the only one." Mia said, suddenly remembering that she still had to call Cali and all of her friends.

Later that day, after unpacking all of their things, Mia sat back down on the bed and decided to finally let everybody know what was going on. Corrie had taken Teal out into the Living room while Malakai sat in the room with Mia on the floor playing his game. Sitting on the edge of the bed she added Alyssa, Lola, Chanel and Ballow to one group chat and then text Cali and Egypt separately. They all had their own opinions about her marriage, so she had to approach them all slightly differently. Cali was the most supportive and nonjudgmental so she decided to text her first because she would be the easiest.

`Big sis, so look right, Dax didn't come home for 4 days straight. So guess where I am?... Girl with Mom! That nigga is done! Do you hear me!? I packed up everything and` just left. And I saw on snap that he is still outside chilling popping bottles and shit but it's cool he has the surprise of a lifetime waiting for him at home lol. But seriously this is some sad shit though, can't lie. And while I'm sitting here sending out these texts to everybody let me just say, thanks Cali for always having my back and not judging my decision to be with Dax and just letting me work this shit out on my own. You are one of the only ones! I love you big sis.

Hey bestfrannn, call me later. I packed up and left everything yesterday. I'm in Georgia with mom now. This is crazy.

Hey ya'll it's Mia lol, I just wanted to let everybody know that I packed me and the kids up and came to Stone Mountain with big Corr. Long story short I had to get away from Dax. I've been keeping my distance because I really just didn't want to hear the I told you so's. I had to come to this decision on my own, *cough, cough* Alyssa... But I love ya'll and miss ya'll already.

Cali: Aww! I know mom is so happy!! But ugh! He's such a dumbass. He doesn't deserve you sis, and I love you too always!

Egypt: Wait. What!? You drove all the way to Georgia? By yourself? I'm going to call you when I get off!

Lola: Oh my gosh Mimi. Are you okay? And we will miss you too.

Alyssa: You didn't have to do all that to leave that nigga! Fuck him! Reese would've moved back in with the quickness!

Ballow: Damn sis.

Chanel: You had to do what you had to do.

Satisfied with the messages Mia headed out of the room to find her mom and Teal.

"I just told everybody that I left." Mia said to Corrie after she spotted her on the couch holding the baby.

Corrie looked over at Mia as she plopped down on the couch.

"So you didn't even tell anybody you were leaving? What about your job? Did you give a two weeks notice?" Corrie asked.

"Nope," Mia said shrugging. "I didn't get a chance to mom. It was a spur of the moment type of thing."

"So what about your house? Did you tell the landlord you wanted to break your lease?"

"Dang no, I just had to get the hell on mom." Mia

said, looking at Teal, the reality of her rash decision was starting to sink in.

Corrie shook her head.

"You have to email your job and call the landlord now Mia. Tell him you were in an abusive relationship and had to leave the house for your own safety. How many months did you have left on the lease?" Corrie asked.

"I never signed a new lease because we were supposed to be moving when I was still with Reese." Mia said, getting up to retrieve Teal.

"Okay at least you didn't break your lease, that's good. So just call and tell him that and then still email your job because you never know when you might want to go back to a job. Do you plan to go back home?" Corrie inquired, wanting to know what really happened between her and Dax but not wanting to ask.

"Nope, not anytime soon Big Corr." Mia said, tilting her head at her mom. "Sitting home waiting for a man to come home just don't sit right with me." She said, knowing her mom all to well.

"So I guess my relationship with Reese was worth something after all right?" Mia continued. Reese had definitely opened her eyes to a different type of relationship that she hadn't known before, and if nothing else she would always appreciate him for that.

"You damn right. That's a good man! But Mia call the landlord and get dressed so I can show you around." Corrie said.

Almost two hours later, Mia was strapping Teal's car seat into Corrie's car so they could ride out.

"Take my picture real quick big Corr." Mia said as she closed the car door. Reaching her phone to Corrie she began to get into her pose. Her silk press was getting old but still straight enough to put her hair into a slick top knot bun and style her edges. Looking down at her black uggs, Levi's, oversized grey, long sleeve T-shirt and black under armor coat. She wasn't the flyest but that was besides the point as she posed with her middle finger up.

"Here we go with this shit." Corrie said, throwing her cigarette butt down and grabbing Mia's phone.

"You not gone smile Mia?" Corrie asked.

"Nah, big Corr." Mia said, she just needed to post her location.

Though she had blocked Dax from her phone and from all of her social media accounts, she knew her post would definitely be screenshotted by several people and sent around the city with a quickness.

"Let me see mom." Mia said, before Corrie placed her phone in her hand.

"Alright let's go." Corrie said as they climbed into the car and pulled out of the parking lot.

Mia's focus was on posting her pictures on social media as Corrie maneuvered through the huge parking lot of the apartment complex.

"Okay Mia so we live in Stone Mountain right now it's thirty minutes from Atlanta without traffic do you want to start there or do you want me to show you around the neighborhood." Corrie said.

Mia was busy studying her pictures, making sure everything was on point before hitting "post."

"Mia!" Corrie snapped.

"Chill big Corr, I had a little point to prove." Mia said, looking around and paying attention to the unfamiliar surroundings as they pulled out of their apartment complex. Directly outside of the gate of the apartment entrance she saw a corner store surrounded by nigga's fully emersed in drug deals. She didn't know what they were peddling but the store was clearly a fully operational open air drug market. She saw fiends coming and going, disappearing behind the store. The niggas didn't even try to look inconspicuous as they did their hand in hand transactions out in the open.

"Look at these niggas mom." Mia said, watching the interactions.

"Yeah they cool though, I get my cigarettes from there." Corrie said.

"What is this place?" she asked pointing to a building with more than thirty people waiting in line to get inside.

"I asked the same thing when I first came here," Corrie said laughing, "It's like that everyday. I ended up having to google it, basically they pay you to donate your blood. I know that like $100 or whatever they pay, comes in handy to those homeless people and it helps kids with Cancer. You want to help?" Corrie asked turning to Mia.

“Oh hell no Big Corr.” Mia said still looking at the line through the review mirror on her side. felt bad for the children with Cancer but she wasn’t that bad off.

“Alright but what do you want to see?” Corrie said, glancing over at Mia.

“I’m trying to see Atlanta.” Mia said, looking out her window.

Chapter 17

Dax woke up on Kea's couch and decided that today would be the day that he would go home and make things right. He picked up his newport box and opened the pack, only to find it empty. He stood up and dug inside the couch cushions, in search of his phone.

After finding it he took a deep breath deciding that it was finally time to face the music and call Mia.

"The number you have dialed is unavailable." Dax heard Mia's phone say for the third time in a row.

"Damn she blocked me." He said out loud, he expected as much. It had been 5 days since he answered the phone, texted her back or went home but the scratch on his neck was healed for the most part and he was more than ready to see his little mama. He decided to check her instagram, but quickly realized she had blocked him on there too.

"What the fuck." He said, pacing Kea's living room. After realizing he was blocked not only from texting and calling but from every single social media platform she used. Shaking his head Dax dialed *67 ahead of Mia's phone number, trying to reach her privately to see if she'd answer. He knew she would be mad but he didn't expect her to go to such extremes within less than a week. After calling her two more times he hung up and called Spook.

"Yooo." Dax said into the phone.

"Fuck you doing nigga?" He asked Spook. He decided to just head home since he couldn't reach her by phone but he prayed she was in more of a talking mood then a fighting mood since he wasn't able to check her temperature with a phone call.

Dax and Spook pulled up to the house and immediately knew something was amidst when they noticed a white cargo van in the yard.

"What the fuck." Dax said, hopping out of the car.

"Yo what's going on?" Dax asked the two white men who appeared to be maintenance men standing in the living room. They both had on black boots with dingy blue dickie button up shirts and greasy, paint stained khaki pants.

"Afternoon sir," the taller of the two maintenance men said, "you are?" he inquired.

"Don't worry about who the fuck I am nigga. What the hell is ya'll doing in here?" Dax barked.

"We were told that the leaseholder had abandoned the property and we are here to dispose of the furniture and everything else left behind." The maintenance man said while pointing around.

"We are actually waiting for two more of our guys and a dumpster that is on the way." The other man said, finally speaking up.

"A dumpster? Man, where the fuck is Mia?" Spook asked, walking in the door.

Dax couldn't believe what he was hearing. The first thing that came to his mind was that Mia dropped everything and took his kids to move in with Reese, leaving all their shit behind.

Pushing past the maintenance men, Dax went straight into their bedroom to see what Mia had taken with her. Going straight for the closet he swung the door open and instantly realized that she had taken absolutely everything from her side of the closet, including Teal's things. He then checked her dresser drawers and underneath the bed and became astonished that all of her and the baby's things had been completely cleared out. All of her shoe boxes were gone, jewelry, clothes, baby wash, lotions, perfumes, everything gone. There was no trace of Mia. She had stripped the bed clean, not even leaving a pillow. The sight of Teal's empty crib was enough to drive Dax mad. Catching a glimpse of all the pictures on the dresser of he and Mia at various prisons, infuriated Dax.

"Bitch gone leave some fucking pictures!" He yelled, before swiping all eight picture frames from the dresser. The glass frames exploded as they hit the wall.

The maintenance men still standing in the living room, looked over at Spook who had never left from the entryway.

"My mans ain't know his wife was leaving him." Spook said, after looking up and seeing them both staring at him.

Next Dax headed into Malakai's room and it was more of the same. His game, his clothes, shoes and t.v.

were all cleared out. *Okay, she wants to play like this.* He thought as he headed into the kitchen to retrieve the box of trash bags from underneath the sink.

"Yo! What the fuck!!" Dax said, kicking the cabinet door off the hinges when he realized the box was gone.

"We might have to call the police on this guy." The smaller of the two maintenance men whispered to the other.

"Ya'll niggas ain't gone do shit." Spook said, instantly heading toward the kitchen and bumping into the small maintenance guy, almost knocking him down.

"Yo come the fuck on D, you got these white mafuckers scared than a bitch. Just wrap your shit up in a sheet or a blanket fuck this shit." Spook said, headed into Malakai's room. He snatched the ninja turtle fitted sheet off the twin sized bed before throwing it to Dax.

The moment began to feel like a deja vu to Dax as he emptied out his side of the closet, packing up his things just as he had done 10 months ago when Mia had bleached his clothes. Heading to the car with Spook in tow, this time packing the trunk of the car felt disheartening. When he packed the car last time it was about getting back at Mia but this time the circumstances were different. Mia was gone and had abandoned him and their home knowing they were going to throw his stuff out and that he would no longer have a place to call home. Her decision and actions this time were irreversible and to him it meant she had completely washed her hands of him. He had really fucked up this time, and the feeling was almost unbearable.

Slamming the trunk close Dax got an idea as he pulled his phone out.

"I'm bout to call the landlord bro and see what that nigga talkin bout." Dax revealed to Spook, while googling the number.

After finding the rental office phone number Dax pressed the call button from google.

"Emily from Martin's Property Management speaking, how can I help you?" Dax heard someone say after the second ring.

"Hello, my name is Daxton I stay on — and my wife Mia Truitt wants to move out but i'm trying to see if there's anyway I can just keep the place in my name." Dax said.

"Yes of course Mr. Truitt, I would just need your 4 last paycheck stubs, 2 months of bank statements, you would need a clean criminal record, no evictions within the last 3 years and you'd have to have been on your job for at least one year." Emily explained.

Knowing he barely met even one of the qualifications the lady mentioned, Dax hung up on her.

Digging in his pocket he pulled out his last 3 percocets and popped them like candy swallowing them without a drink. Normally he'd take one perc 10 at a time but in that moment he felt like one just wouldn't cut it.

"Yo, check instagram and see if she blocked you on that shit. I gotta find out where this nigga Reese stay at." Dax said, opening the car door.

"She ain't with that nigga." Spook said, looking down at his phone as they both climbed into the car.

Spook handed Dax his phone.

Dax's heart dropped as he looked down at the picture of Mia holding up the middle finger, while posted up in Georgia.

Chapter 18

DAX

"Just take me over Kizzy's house bro." Dax said, as he and Spook pulled out of the driveway.

"You can stay with me and Mercedes bro." Spook looking over Dax. He could tell his nigga wasn't thinking clearly, after the latest blow Mia hit him with. Spook knew Mia was crazy but just up and packing up and leaving a nigga to go to a whole nother state was some next level lifetime movie network shit. He could tell she had Dax fucked up bout it but trying to go move in with Kizzy's thot ass was not the move. Dax was better off staying at his crib or Kea's like he had been doing. For all they knew Mia could come back, she was clearly unpredictable and Dax living with another bitch would just fuck everything up all over again.

"Yo you home." Dax texted Kizzy, ignoring Spook.

"Pull up and find out." Was Kizzy's response and that all Dax needed to see.

"I'm not moving in with the bitch, i'm going to take my stuff to Kea's but right now I gotta go over there to clear my head." Dax said.

Kizzy was elated when she saw Dax pull up in front of her house. She had quickly ran to the bathroom and gave herself a bird bath in the sink after he called. The whole city was talking about how Mia had left him and was posted up in Georgia saying fuck him. Three of her homegirls had called her, each delivering the same news. And Kizzy was ecstatic that she was the one he chose to run to in his time of need.

"Take all that shit off." Dax said, not even bothering to speak as he walked past her straight to her bedroom.

Kizzy quickly complied in her bedroom, stripping butterball naked before standing and waiting for his next command.

"Lay down." Dax said, digging in his pocket for his molly.

Kizzy laid down on her back and propped up onto her elbows watching Dax as he poured the blue flakes onto his tongue.

"D." Kizzy said, sticking her own abnormally long tongue out. Signaling to him that she wanted some without doing too much talking. She knew him enough to know that he wasn't in the mood for any talking.

Dax dropped his pants and removed them and his sneakers simultaneously before climbing on top of Kizzy.

Kizzy leaned her head back as Dax poured the blue magic onto her tongue.

The drugs barely got a chance to dissolve before

she felt Dax slid inside of her and grab her throat harder than he ever had before.

Dax gave no fucks about how Kizzy felt as he squeezed her throat with both hands and pound into her guts, thinking of Mia leaving him.

Kizzy tried to hold her breath, hoping it would be a quick one, unable to breath anyway. But with her smoker lungs she couldn't hold her breath long at all, causing her to claw at Dax's hands like she had outside in the projects less than a week ago.

Dax had his eyes closed as his climax was building up. In the moment he didn't give a fuck if Kizzy's ass died, he wasn't letting go until he bust. Drilling harder he felt his volcano erupting and he finally released his grip on her neck and swiftly pulled out and discharged a heavy load onto her stomach.

Kizzy gasped and grabbed her throat, before coughing and sobbing.

Turning over onto his back Dax rolled over and collapsed next to her before closing his eyes.

Mia

Riding through mid-town Atlanta sight-seeing had Mia in awe at everything she was seeing. The skyscrapers, sidewalks packed with people walking around handling business, designer stores, Marta train stations were things you just didn't see in her tiny city. Baltimore was the closest she had come to knowing about true city living but though she was born in that city she still knew very little about it. Going across the Chesapeake bridge to chill with Cali on the weekends didn't help the situation. Baltimore city was still a foreign territory to Mia. All she knew was small town living. Consequently, the new environment was overwhelming her. She knew her decision to up and jump ship was a rash decision but a necessary one to leave Dax. So although she was beginning to feel like a fish out of water, she knew she couldn't go back home so she planned to force herself to stick it out.

"Girl they don't have foodlion, acme, giant none of them." Mia said, to Egypt while on facetime as she walked through the door behind Malakai.

"Dang, so what do they have?" Egypt asked.

"Girl we were just in a grocery store called Kroger, I can't." Mia said, laughing as she sat Teal's car seat down on the couch.

"Girl look at Teal." Mia said, as she unstrapped

the buckles in Teal's carseat.

"What is my girl doing?" Egypt asked, looking at her computer.

"You're not even looking." Mia said, holding the camera over Teal.

"I'm sorry girl, too much homework is due." Egypt said, finally looking towards the phone.

"Dang, it's been a minute since I had homework." Mia said.

"I know you need to get back in school. Maybe you can sign up while you're there and away from Dax." Egypt said.

"Yeah, maybe." Mia said, she did miss school, but she didn't know how she would juggle schoolwork and a new baby.

Egypt didn't reply as she redirected her focus on her computer.

"Alright well we're about to probably watch Christmas movies, so I'll text you." Mia said, walking down the hall into their bedroom.

"Alright just text me." Egypt said, distracted.

"Okay, I will." Mia said, before pressing the red end button.

Mia laid her phone down on the dresser before she began to rummage through the drawer with her right hand as she held Teal in her left arm, looking for pajamas. She heard her phone vibrate before she could find anything. She looked down at the phone and noticed a text from an unsaved number. As soon as she picked up the phone and read the first line, she knew the person behind the number was Dax.

Mia I know I broke a lot of my promises. I should've came home I should've answered the phone. I know I fucked up but how could you just up and leave a nigga high and dry? I need you babe, I need my wife, I need my little mama. Can you please just come back… I miss you. I miss our kids and I promise i'll try harder. I know I need to leave the perks alone, the molly, all this shit. But I can't do it without my lil mama, you know this. I'll go get help if you come back. Just give me one more chance. It's supposed to be me and you against the world remember? Don't give up on me when I need you the most.

Mia instantly felt her throat tighten as the lump in her threaten to accompany tears. She cleared her throat as she began to rock Teal in her arms. She swayed side to side as she reread Dax's message from start to finish. *Could he mean it this time?* She wondered, even though she knew better. Deep down everything inside of her wanted to drop everything and scream, "I'm on my way!" Leaping to his aide, but instead she denied her urges and fought back her tears and feelings. She had to stick to her initial plan and gut feeling. He would never change as he had had proven time and time again. Nothing she did was ever going to be enough to get him to do right. Come home, that's all she asked of him. Since he put any and everyone before her and the kids, she was no longer putting him first. Without replying, she locked the phone before placing it back down onto the dresser. Mia was done.

Dax

Dax's eyes were glued to his phone as stood in Kizzy's kitchen window, waiting for Spook to pull up.

He had expected for Mia to text him right back, but 20 minutes had already passed so he figured she was ignoring him. The molly normally made Dax feel jovial through most any situation but the current state of he and Mia's marriage had him in mental space that not even Kizzy's throat could fix. He stood in place scratching his stomach underneath his shirt when Spook finally pulled up.

He headed straight for the door without bothering to say bye to Kizzy who he assumed was in the shower by the sound of the water running.

"What's up bro?" Dax said, as he climbed into Spook's car.

"Shit. You good nigga?" Spook said, looking at Dax.

"Shit I'm good but I'm not understanding why the fuck she ain't texting me back or nothing. That nigga Reese is probably up there with her bro I'm trying to tell you. I know her. She wouldn't just ignore me." Dax ranted.

"How many times did you text her? She probably

still mad, give her bout a week. It's been less than two days nigga. She probably just trying to prove a little weak-ass point." Spook said, purposely skipping over the mention of Reese's name because truthfully, he had the same thought. He didn't put nothing passed pretty bitches like Mia. She had already shown that she could and would move the fuck on. And whether Dax wanted to admit it or not he was still fucking up, dragging on her, doing the same shit he been doing for years. Maybe she was fed up, you never knew with bitches these days.

"She wouldn't just ignore a nigga though." Dax said, leaning back in his seat.

"You trying to take a trip?" Dax said, with a smirk.

"Fuck no nigga, give it some time!" Spook said.

"Give it some time my ass, I might get a little rental no bullshit because in this frame of mind that I'm in I'm going to end up back on the white bus going back up the road." Dax said, before turning his attention to his phone.

A nigga don't got nothing to lose without his family.

Helloooooooo??

You really gone make me take this ride huh?

Dax looked down at the three text messages he sent and shook his head. With the texting app he couldn't tell if his messages were being delivered or not.

"Let me see your phone Spook." Dax said.

"Here." Spook said, placing his phone face down on the armrest before Dax picked it up.

Dax dialed Mia number and called her. He listened to the phone ring five times before it went to voicemail.

"You think you so slick, just gone leave a nigga high and dry. Ignoring my messages, blocked me on everything so I can't get to you. What about my kids bitch? You can't keep my kids from me. What if Kai wants to talk to his dad. Unblock me and come the fuck back. We took vows. It's til death you stupid bitch but don't worry about it. Tell that nigga I'll be up there." Dax said before ending the call.

"You is straight trippin out bro." Spook looked over at Dax with horizontal wrinkles in his forehead.

Dax knew he should of kept his message nice to get her back home but he became infuriated thinking of Reese in Georgia with his wife and kids playing house while she ignored him.

Chapter 19

Mia

"You are not even paying attention to the movie Mia." Corrie said, interrupting Mia's train of thought.

"I am mom." Mia said, playing it off.

"Oh yeah? So what's going on in the movie than?" Corrie asked, with her lips twisted to the side.

"The lady beeped the horn at the man so now he's chasing her and stalking her mom, I'm telling you I'm watching it." Mia said. She was watching it enough to know that but really her mind was elsewhere.

Even though she had made up her mind that she wasn't going back with Dax, she couldn't keep her mind off him. She had decided earlier to block the number he had texted her from, but she received the voicemail he left her. He sounded disturbed and deranged, ranting about the kids and thinking she had come way down to Georgia to be with Reese. She couldn't help but analyze everything he said. Was she keeping the kids away from him going to hurt them or bother them? She rationalized that the answer was no because when he would voluntarily go on his disappearing acts, not only would he go missing he would never check on her or the kids. And he didn't care about having a place to stay when she was there, couldn't pay him to stay home. He treated their home like a fucking storage facility and changing station. He was home to get dressed, sleep, shit, fuck and shower. He is a fucking clown, Mia thought to herself. She was tempted to unblock him to cuss him out but decided against it. The kids were good and even though she was still sad she was fine at the end of the day. When the man on the movie ran over a store clerk trying to help the lady he was stalking Mia decided to snap out of her trance and pay attention since the movie seemed like it was good.

Dax

Dax felt like he was truly going insane as he sat at Kea's with the normal crew. Dre', Spook, Kion and Kea sat at the kitchen table as Dax stood against the kitchen counter staring down at his phone. He hadn't put his phone down it seemed since he realized Mia left. He constantly checked his messages thinking she'd finally reply.

"Damn Dax you good bro?" Kea asked.

Dax looked up from his phone and noticed all eyes on him, "What the fuck ya'll think? Ask me no stupid ass shit."

He said walking out of the kitchen, he headed towards the front door as Nearee walked through the door.

"Hey D, I heard about that shit with Mia. She didn't leave because of what we did, did she?" Nearee asked, in a low tone.

"Nah, she don't know about that but come here." He said, grabbing her forearm and guiding her back out of the front door.

Nearee followed Dax wondered what he would say.

"There's no way she could of found out about the shit that happened between us unless Kea or Spook told her. You think they would?" Dax asked, looking down at Nearee.

"Hell no!" Nearee said, with a frown.

"You know we all keep each other's secrets, come on now." Nearee said, tapping Dax.

"I'm just asking because something ain't right." Dax said, glancing back at the door.

"You tripping Dax, my cuz been with you since she was a teenager. You don't think she could just be fed up? You been cheating from day 1 and now with me of all people." Nearee said, she knew how grimy they both had been that night.

"I ain't trying to hear that bullshit! Either she's with another nigga or somebody in this mothafucker rattin! Point blank." Dax said.

Nearee shook her head and walked back into the house.

Mia

The next day Mia was in Sugarloaf Mills mall shopping for Christmas presents for Corrie, Keegan and Justin. Malakai walked next to her as she pushed Teal's stroller, struggling to juggle the bags from various stores. The mall was gigantic compared to their hometown mall and Mia was in bliss as she

zipped through the stores she had once only heard of.

"Kai can you hold these two bags for me?" Mia asked Malakai as they walked out of the adidas store.

"Yeah mom!" Malakai said, taking the bags from his mom.

Mia looked at Malakai who was dressed in a red nike tech sweatsuit with a pair of crispy white airs. She had curled his hair with the sponge the barber gave her but he would soon need a shapeup. Which made her think of how she didn't even know where she would be going to get his cut.

"You look cute little son." Mia said, before looking down at Teal, who was beginning to get fussy.

"Ya'll hungry? Let's find the food court." Mia said, looking from side to side, not knowing which direction to even go in. She needed to find the food court before Teal's whimpers turned into her full-blown screaming cry.

"Ummm." Mia said, biting on her bottom lip as she decided to ask someone. She looked around and tapped the closet person to her on the shoulder.

"Excuse me?" Mia said. "Hi, sorry do you know which way the food court is?" She asked after the short chubby man turned to face her.

"Yeah, its downstairs. Do you need help? It's that way." The man said, pointing behind Mia while looking her up and down.

“I’m okay but thank you!” Mia said, turning the stroller completely around.

“The elevator is to the left!” She heard the man say behind her.

“Thanks,” Mia shouted over her shoulder. “Let’s hurry up Kai.” Mia said, putting some pep in her step.

Work Crew

Reese, Alyssa, Lola, Ballow and Chanel sat around the table in the lunchroom eating and looking at their phones.

"Shit really ain't been the same without Mia here." Alyssa said, looking at the empty chair Mia normally sat in across from her.

"I can't believe she really is in the A. She is about to be living it up. My cousin moved down there. She said it's cheap as fuck and fun as a bitch. Niggas everywhere." Chanel said, thinking of all the fun she would have down there.

"Them niggas down there be as gay as me!" Alyssa said.

"Mia moved and ya'll ain't tell me?" Reese said, sitting up straight in his seat.

"Dang Reese, we figured you was good. It's been a year now." Lola said.

"Why she move?" Reese asked, ignoring Lola's comment.

"She finally got tired of that nigga." Alyssa said.

"Thank God." Ballow said, continuing to scroll through I.G.

Reese got up and left the table walking out in the

hallway.

He pushed the elevator button and pulled out his phone.

`Mia, what's up pretty. I hope you're doing good. I'm just hearing about you moving away. That's crazy that I had to hear it from them but I guess you think I'm still mad right? Well, I'm letting you know now that I'm not. If you need anything or just want to talk hit me up anytime and tell my man Kai I said what's up.`

Since Reese hadn't spoken to Mia in awhile he didn't know if she would respond or if she changed her number, but he hoped she would. Even though he had moved on he would gladly rekindle things with Mia if she was willing to.

Mia

Mia sat in Atlanta traffic strolling through her social media timelines. The traffic was bumper to bumper and nothing like she had ever seen before.

"I ain't never gone get used to this shit." Mia said, looking through her review mirror at a sleeping Malakai and Teal.

When a message came through from Reese it gave her the much-needed distraction she needed. A smile quickly spread across her face. She hadn't spoken to him since the last time they talked in the hallway at work. She could hear his voice as she read his message, she missed his infectious laugh and ridiculous jokes and even though she wanted very much to talk to him. She knew she would only be using him as a distraction from Dax and she vowed that she would never do that again so with that in mind she decided not to reply, leaving the message on read.

Dax

Dax walked into the bar with Spook, Mercedes, Dre, and Kion and headed straight for the bar.

"What can I do you for?" Courtney asked Dax stopping directly across from him.

"Let me get my regular." Dax said, patting both pockets in his sweatpants.

"Two double shots of henny." Courtney said, quickly putting two shot glasses down from the shelf and pouring the liquor into both glasses.

Dax counted three twenty's and quickly came to the realization that he was broke. He didn't make much of a profit off of the blue magic like he was supposed to. He took too much of it for his own habit, but he didn't give a fuck. If he was broke he would just have to resort back to getting money the ski-mask way.

"Thanks yo." Dax said, slapping two 20's on the bar before picking up both glasses and walking away.

He headed back towards Spook and the guys until Chief Keef's *"3hunna,"* began to play through the speakers.

Any Chief Keef song instantly made him think of Mia and how she'd point her index and ring fingers like a gun as she rapped along. He headed outside and pulled out a baggy that only had one pill left along with his box of Newport's. He swallowed a perc 30 and grabbed a cigarette out the box putting it between his lips. He stood on the sidewalk outside the club, patting his pockets for his lighter.

"Fuck man." Dax said.

"You good bro?" Kion said, coming out behind him.

"Fuck you think nigga." Dax said, with the unlit cigarette bouncing between his lips.

Kion put his hands up and turned around, heading back inside.

"Punk mothafucker." Dax said, lighting his cigarette.

"Yooo." Dax said, to a group of females walking away from the club.

The group of girls looked back at Dax but kept walking.

"Fuck ya'll." Dax said.

"Yo, whatchu on D? You been cussing us out all day nigga." Spook said, laughing.

"Fuck that shit nigga, it's time for us to get back on that, again." Dax said, referring to robbing.

"Sayless." Spook said, looking around.

Chapter 20

Christmas Morning

"Mommy, wake up!" Malakai said, shaking Mia out of her sleep.

Mia turned away and pulled the cover over her head.

"Mommy! It's Christmas!" he said.

"It's still dark outside Kai, Santa ain't even had a chance to come yet." Mia said.

"Yes he did mom come look." Malakai said.

Mia reluctantly rolled onto her back and sat up, she looked over at a sleeping Teal and decided to get it over with.

"Alright let's brush our teeth. Did you wake mom?" Mia asked, standing to her feet.

"I'm in the kitchen." Corrie said.

"What about Keegan and Justin?" Mia said, walking into the kitchen to Corrie making pancakes, eggs and bacon.

"Do you have scrapple mom mom?" Malakai asked Corrie.

"Nope we haven't found any scrapple in any of the stores here yet Kai sorry." Corrie said, knowing it was his favorite.

"It's okay mom, come on Kai let's brush our teeth, it's time to open presents!" Mia said, giving Malakai a slight push as she did the Dougie behind him. She knew how excited he was about to be about his gifts.

Mia peeped her head into the room to check on Teal making sure she wasn't close to the edge and that there were no blankets or pillows around her that could cover her face and suffocate her. That was one of her biggest fears but since she was safe and sound asleep. Mia went to join Malakai in the bathroom where he grabbed his spiderman electric toothbrush and she grabbed her pink one.

"We gotta get the Christmas music jumping." She said, dancing to the music in her head.

Malakai started dancing too as he brushed his teeth.

"Let's go Kai, get it Kai. Okay, yeah!" She said, dancing and hyping him up.

They both continued to bounce as they brushed their teeth side by side at the conjoined his and hers sinks.

After opening all their presents and eating breakfast, Mia sat on the couch with Malakai and Teal as Keegan took pictures of them in the matching Christmas pajamas she bought from the mall a couple weeks back.

"Come on mom." Mia said, waving Corrie over. She had gotten two mom sets instead of the "daddy" set. She thought she would be sadder spending Christmas without Dax but she was happy with her family and it was getting easier as each day went by. Corrie sat next to Malakai and put her arm around him as Mia held Teal up to show her off in her tiny pajama set. Everyone was all smiles and happy.

"Alright, let me see Keegan." Mia said, reaching her hand out for her phone.

"They cute." Keegan said, giving Mia her phone.

"Yes, I can't wait to upload these but mom, I still got one more gift for you." Mia said to Corrie.

She quickly went to the room and grabbed a small box.

"Here mom." Mia said, before hugging Corrie. She wanted to make up for the lost time and show her how happy she was to be back with her.

"What is it?" Corrie asked smiling.

She quickly ripped the Christmas paper off of the box revealing a brand-new apple watch.

Corrie had been wanting an apple watch since they first came out and she saw her coworkers with them. She hugged Mia and the two embraced for several seconds.

"Now we matching big corr." Mia said, holding up her wrist after they released each other.

Dax

"Why did you stop fuckin wit Sosa again?" Dax asked, turning to face Nearee in the back seat.

"That nigga was lowkey dirty, he would have on the most expensive jewelry and clothes but I don't think he took showers everyday." Nearee said, moving her bang out of her face.

"You ain't tell him that did you? Does he still want to fuck with you?" Spook asked.

"I never told him, I just stopped answering his calls." Nearee said.

"Alright cool, so this is the plan, all you have to do is lure him to the hotel room Nearee. Start texting him today like you are ready to start linking up and doing whatever ya'll used to do. Aight?" Dax said.

"Me and Spook will be hiding in the bathroom, standing behind the shower curtain. You just gotta get him to strip down and you can come up with a code word that'll let us know to come out that mafucker."

"Don't ya'll think he'll get suspicious for me to just text him out the blue." Nearee asked.

"Nah ask that nigga for some bread or tell him you need your hair done." Spook said.

"Alright." Nearee said, pulling out her phone.

"His soft ass ain't do shit about me taking his molly. We should just run up in his shit." Dax said, glancing over at Spook.

"That nigga moved to Delmar for a reason, he knew what he was doing." Spook said, cutting his eye at Dax.

"You been on some wild shit lately D, you know got damn well niggas is going down fucking around in Delaware." Spook said, shaking his head.

Mia sat on Keegan and Justin's bed as they sparked the blunt and put it in rotation, she hadn't smoked since she got to Georgia and she had to admit she missed it.

She took a hard pull when Keegan passed her the blunt and immediately felt all her stress melt away after she exhaled.

"Man, I might as well go all in," she said, heading out into the hallway. Since it was a Friday night she decided to turn up.

"You good big Corr? Or should I say, am I good?" She said, with her hand on her chest, walking towards Corrie who was of course holding Teal.

"Go head I'm off tomorrow." Corrie said, waving Mia off.

Mia stroked her hand across Teal's curly bush before walking to her room. She snatched her small bottle of fireball out of her purse before returning to Keegan's room.

"Here sis." Keegan said, again giving Mia the

blunt.

Mia took a pull from the blunt before she cracked open her bottle and sat back down. She leaned over, reaching the blunt to Justin before she took the bottle to the head and began chugging.

“Damnnnn!” Keegan said.

“Chill shorty,” Mia said, recapping the bottle.

“I think it’s time for me to get a job, I don’t want to leave Teal but I will if mom will watch her and Kai at night.” Mia said, she had spent the majority of her stash on Christmas.

“It’s hella jobs out this bitch Mia.” Justin said.

“People from all over too, it’s girls at my job from fucking New Orleans, Florida shit one girl is right from Baltimore.” Keegan said.

“It’s lit.” Mia said, closing her eyes. She hadn’t drank or smoked in weeks and it was hitting her.

“Let me go lay the fuck down.” Mia said, standing up.

“Dang sis, already!?” Keegan shrieked.

“Girl!” Mia said, heading out of the room.

She walked into the room and was glad that Malakai had moved his playstation into the living room on Christmas.

She put her airpods in her ears and began to play love songs as she laid on the bed staring at the ceiling.

She instantly began to think about Dax, and wished she could just call him but even inebriated she knew she needed to just leave things how they were. She wanted a normal relationship, which made her think of Reese. She knew she didn't have to be single if she didn't want to but she also wanted something real. The fact that she could up and leave Reese the way she had let her know that something was missing in their relationship. She loved Reese but she wasn't in love with Reese and she wanted to be head over heels in love with someone. She figured just needed to give herself time to get over Dax first.

Dax

Dax and Spook arrived at the days inn hotel room to set the plan into motion three hours early. They wanted to already be inside before Nearee told him she wanted him to meet her there so he wouldn't have a chance to scope the place out early and see them coming.

"Damn." Dax said, looking Nearee up and down, after she opened the door wearing a basic grey jogger pant set with a pair of yeezys, a baseball cap and some oversized shades.

"Ya'll are we really about to do this shit?" Nearee asked, after she stepped in and removed her glasses.

"Whatchu mean?" Spook asked.

"We ain't gone hurt him though right?" Nearee asked.

"This nigga is toilet tissue soft Nearee, it'll go smooth." Dax said, before pouring some molly on his tongue.

"Chill on that shit D, you been eating it like its candy. We still need to be on point." Spook said, looking at Dax.

"That was the last of it mafucka. I hope this nigga got some on him so I take it." Dax said, pulling his gun out of his waist band, placing it on the dresser.

"Ight text him Nearee. Put the lingerie shit on and send his a pic or video what ever you do." Spook said, before sitting in the chair next to the desk.

It didn't take long for Sosa to knock on the door. Dax and Spook were in place in the bathroom.

Sosa walked in wearing a pair of Amiri jeans with a black amiri sweater and a pair of balenciaga sneakers. He looked out of place in the cheap hotel room as Nearee looked at all 5 of his chains glistening under the ambient lights. The pleasant smell of his Versace Eros cologne engulfed the small room overpowering the smell inside the stale space.

"Wassup Ree. We not staying here. Get dressed." Sosa said, closing the door, looking around the musty room.

"Nope I'm already wet for you Daddy." Nearee said, nervously.

She could feel herself beginning to sweat as she watched him frown.

"I'm ain't fucking in no motel Ree. You of all people should know. Wasn't it you at the Waldorf out D.C. wit me?" Sosa said, with his eyebrows furrowed.

This dirty ass nigga got some nerve. Dax thought, deeply inhaling the smell of bleach.

"Yeah, you already know but we can leave afterwards come on." Nearee said, grabbing his hand before walking backwards toward the bed.

"Fuck no Ree, look at the blankets in this mothafucka!" Sosa said, pointing to the brown and purple and yellow floral pattern comforter.

Nearee lightly chuckled, unsure of what to say.

Dax stood impatiently inside the shower.

"I wouldn't even take a piss in this bathroom shawty. You coming or not. I'll be in the car." Sosa said, heading towards the door.

"Fuck this shit." Dax said under his breath stepping out of the shower.

"Nigga sit ya bitch ass down." He said, busting out the bathroom with his gun pointed to Sosa.

Sosa could feel his heart drop to his feet, looking at Dax and Spook. He was surprised that Nearee would do him like that as his eyes shifted from Nearee to Spook and Dax's guns.

"Let's make this shit quick, whatever you got give it here. Chains, rings, money-"

"Drugs!" Dax said, cutting Spook off.

"I ain't got shit but some weed." Sosa said, scrambling to clasp his chains behind his back.

"Help this nigga Nearee." Spook said, pointing to his chains.

Nearee stood frozen off to the side.

"What the fuck you got on you? Got to have something." Dax said, patting Sosa's pockets.

"What's this?" Dax asked, before rummaging through his front pocket and pulling out a fat knot of money.

"Give me these got damn chains, nigga don't move." Spook said, stepping behind him before he started unclasping each chain.

"The rings too." Spook said, snatching the rings.

"Get down on your knees." Dax said, directing Sosa with the gun.

"I can get ya'll way more money if you let me go." Sosa said, with his hands up and he got down on one knee.

"Nigga fuck that." Dax said, raising his gun to Sosa's forehead.

Pop!

"Yo! What the fuck D!" Spook said, after he jumped to push Dax's arm causing Dax to miss the shot.

Spook quickly backhanded Sosa with his gun, knocking him unconscious.

"Yo that was never apart of the plan! Let's go!" Spook said, looking over at Dax.

Dax shrugged as he slipped the roll of money in his pocket. His nonchalant composer baffled Spook, shooting him was not a part of the plan and he and Dax always followed the plan to a T.

Spook watched Nearee dart towards the desk, struggling to gather all her belongings. He looked around the room and decided it would be best to just jet as well. He and Dax made sure to wear latex gloves from the moment they arrived but Nearee had touched everything.

"The cops are going to come up here because of the gunshot wipe whatever you think you touched Nearee just in case." Spook commanded.

"Fuck that let's go." Dax said, "they can't tie her to this mothafucker. Come the fuck on and cover ya'll faces when before we step out, cameras in the parking lot."

Dax pulled his nike ski-mask over his face, as Nearee slipped her sweatsuit on overtop of the satin teddy set she was wearing. She threw her shades and hat back on but also wrapped an oversized black knitted scarf around her face. Spook pulled his ski-mask down, before snatching the door open. The trio ran towards the crackhead rental they came in.

Chapter 21

Mia pulled up to the Walmart on Memorial Drive bumping Boosie's "*No Juice*," with Corrie, Keegan, Malakai and Teal in the passenger and back seat.

"Cold nights, real talk. Nigga they tellin lies, Nigga what block you off?!" Mia used her hands as she rapped along, turning into a parking spot at the same time.

"I can't with Mia's playlist. If it ain't Pop smoke it's some old ass song." Keegan said, climbing out of the car after Mia put the truck in park and turned it off.

"Nigga don't even know you, no juice, no juice." Mia sang more of the lyrics walking up behind Keegan, laughing.

"I got the baby." Keegan said, walking to the other side of the truck to Corrie and Teal.

Mia looked down at her outfit as Malakai jumped out of the truck. She had washed her hair and was feeling herself in her white hoodie and khaki's.

"What are we eating tonight ya'll? We might as well get that now too." Mia said, opening the trunk to get Teal's stroller.

"I thought you were trying to go to the mall after

this so we can find something to wear for new year's?" Keegan asked looking at Mia.

Mia agreed to go out with Justin and Keegan when she was drinking but sober she wasn't interested. "We can," Mia said.

"Alright bet. It'll be fun." Keegan said, as they headed towards the store.

Dax

"Salisbury police department and Maryland State police are reaching out to anybody who may have information on who these three suspects could be, after a robbery took place lastnight at the Day inn motel."

Dax looked at the photo taken from the hotel's video surveillance of him, Spook and Nearee running to the car the night before. Since they were asking for tips he knew they had no clue who they were at the moment which was a good thing. As long as it stayed that way he was good. He didn't even know what possessed him to try to shoot Sosa in the head. He knew that wasn't apart of the plan but realizing that he didn't have any percs or molly on him made Dax snap for a split second. He hadn't heard from Nearee or Spook since they dropped him off, which was a good thing for the time being.

Mia

Later that night Mia Laid across her bed on her stomach on facetime with Cali.

"I can't believe you're pregnant." Mia said.

"Me either girl, Zay been running around buying the baby everything already we don't even know what it is yet." Cali said.

"Even Black bought the baby a pink northface." Cali said, shaking her head.

"What if it's a girl?" Mia asked.

"That's what I said but they don't care." Cali said, shaking her head.

"They tripping," Mia said, thinking of the night she met Black.

"What's up with him though Cali?" Mia asked curiously.

"He asked me the same thing that night you and mom was fighting, but girl trust me you don't even want to get involved with him with the babymom he has." Cali said.

"Nah I was just asking, I'm way down here Cali what am I going to do with him!?" Mia asked.

"Girl that nigga be all over, if I told him you asked

for him he would be on his way." Cali said laughing. "He drives all the way to Florida all the time."

"Dang maybe you should tell him then, I'm bored as hell I'm trying to go to Florida." Mia said, propping her chin onto her fist.

Cali shook her head and chuckled.

"Nah I'm just playing but let me go sis, I hear Teal fussing." Mia said, getting up from the bed.

"I can't wait to see you though!"

"I know I can't either. Bye sis." Cali said.

"Bye." Mia said, smiling.

Chapter 22

"Dax wake up!" Kea said, shaking his shoulder.

"Huh," Dax said, stirring awake. He looked down at the open bottle of Vodka in his hand before looking around the room. Feeling his body aching as he sat up and stretched, he struggled to remember what happened the night before as looked around for the top to the bottle.

"Here," Kea said, reaching him the red cap that was on the arm of the sofa. "Look at the fucking news bro."

Dax looked at Kea as she pointed the remote towards the television, turning up the volume. He gasped when he saw him and Spook's pictures on the television.

"What the fuck!" Dax said, scooting to the edge of the couch.

"Police have identified two of the suspects from yesterday's robbery as 25-year-old Jarvous Spencer and 24-year-old Daxton Truitt. Today Law enforcement officers are on the lookout for the duo who both have lengthy criminal records, including assault along with previous 1st degree robbery charges. They are both considered armed and dangerous. Police are asking anyone who may have information on identifying the 3rd suspect or information on the whereabouts of the two known suspects to contact the local police department today."

With his fingers interlocked on top of his head, Dax stood to his feet and began pacing the living room, struggling to figure out how the cops figured out their identity in less than 24 hours.

Kea watched as Dax paced the floor, talking to himself before he began to pat at his pockets. He pulled out a zip lock bag of what looked like pills along with a lighter and a soft pack of newports. He headed towards the front door putting a cigarette between his lips, before turning on his heels and heading to the back door.

"I'm going to smoke out the back since them bitches looking for me." He said throwing his hands up.

Kea shook her head and wondered if she should send Mia the news clip but decided against it since they hadn't spoken since the time Mia came looking for Dax and she lied to her.

Mia

Mia laid in bed with headphones on listening to music while Teal and Malakai slept next to her. She searched for jobs hiring nearby and clicked on a bartending job as a message came through from Egypt.

"Im glad you got away from him, the cops are looking for him for armed robbery in a hotel."

Egypt's message said, along with a link.

""Police have identified two of the suspects from yesterday's robbery as 25-year-old Jarvous Spencer and 24-year-old Daxton Truitt. Today Law enforcement officers are on the lookout for the duo who both have lengthy criminal records..." Mia could feel her heart racing as she jumped up from the bed as soon as the pictures of Dax and Spook popped up on her phone.

"They are both considered armed and dangerous... She instantly pictured the arrogant smirk on Officer Davis' face. He wouldn't stop until he found Dax. *What if he catches him and they have a shootout... or he goes to prison forever!!!"* Mia thought as she snatched opened the drawer and pulled all of her clothes out throwing them onto the bed.

"Bags, I need trash bags." She thought running to the kitchen.

"I have to go Keegan!" She said, running past her

in the hallway.

"What? Leave where?" Keegan asked.

"I have to help Dax, here look." Mia said, running to get her phone with the box of trash bags.

Keegan was on her heels as she turned around replaying the news clip.

"Well how are you going to help him? You gone hide him from the police?" Keegan asked, with a frown.

"I don't know but all this bullshit bout me running here leaving him is over with. I should've never left this nigga." Mia said, pulling out one of the trash bags before flapping it in the air attempting to open it.

The noise startled Teal who woke up screaming, who in turn woke up Malakai.

Mia picked Teal up and rocked her back and forth.

"I can't just leave him. This is crazy." Mia said, looking down at Teal.

"Mom is going to be so upset if you leave." Keegan said, still shaking her head.

"I have to help him." Mia said, "can you hold her, I'll make a bottle. I got to." She said reaching Teal to her sister.

As she packed she thought of how upset her mom would be when she returned home from work and discovered her and the kids disappearance, so she decided to send her a text.

I know you won't understand mom but I'm about to go again. I have to go help Dax. He got himself into some more trouble and I feel like they will bury him under the jail if they catch him. So, I feel like he needs me like I can't just leave him hanging mom I'm all he's got but if I could stay I would. I love you and me and the kids will be back.

Mia couldn't help the tears that were dripping all over her phone as she sent that message. She knew that leaving would crush Corrie but she felt like the situation was out of her hands. Avoiding and dumping Dax was no longer an option.

Remembering that she was almost broke, Mia went over to her purse and retrieved her wallet.

"$60 to my name." She said, sitting on the bed. She knew she had a half a tank in her truck but she would need at least $50 more to make it back home. She could only think of one place that would give her money the same day, even though she had mocked the people standing in line less than a month before it was now her turn to stand in line.

Two hours later Mia walked out of the plasma center with a cotton ball covered by a band-aid. She stopped on the sidewalk and pulled down the sleeve on her hoodie before looking both ways to cross the parking lot. Once inside her car, she pulled out her phone, went to her contacts, scrolled down to the name hubby and unblocked Dax.

"I'm on my way." Was all she said in the text.

Dax

Dax was just about to smash his phone as Mia's name came across the top of the screen on his phone.

He instantly felt a little bit of the weight lift off his shoulders knowing she was coming back for him.

It wouldn't stop the cops from looking for him but his little mama would finally be back by his side. It was a little after noon so by midnight his wife would be back in their city.

"I'll meet you where we had our first kiss at midnight." He said, before he cracked the phone with Kea's hammer. When he heard a horn honk he pulled his black hoodie over his head and pulled the strings tight before tying it.

He peeked out the blinds and saw Kizzy sitting in her car before heading out to her. He looked left, right, and then left again. Scanning the street for anything suspicious in case she was setting him up. Not seeing anything out of place Dax climbed into the passenger seat thankful for her dark tint. He reclined the seat back as far as it would go, "Go head," he said.

He felt bad for a second being with Kizzy since Mia was now on the way but he brushed the feeling off quickly, since he needed her to go into Walmart for him to get him a burner phone and he needed to hide out at her house. He was paranoid that the police could easy track him to Kea's. Kizzy's house was the better option but once Mia got back it was dead. He smiled to himself as he looked out the window, his wife was coming back.

Midnight

Dax heard nothing but the crickets as he sat on Pearline's steps waiting for Mia. He had Kizzy drop him off on the corner 20 minutes early so they wouldn't have a chance to run into each other. He removed his hoodie from his head before sitting on the front step. He wasn't to worried about the police running down on him because of the way the house sat on the street. He would be able to see them coming from every angle possible. He pulled out a cig and relaxed, feeling relieved that Mia was actually returning. It had been almost four weeks since Mia left, and he couldn't wait to reunite with his family.

For Mia the ride back to her city was nothing like the drive leaving out. She was in high spirits as she blasted every love song she knew. Singing along with her music, she was exhausted but the anticipation of knowing Dax would be waiting gave her an unexplainable boost of energy. With eleven hours down and less than one more to go, she eagerly floored the gas as she crossed the Virgina line into Maryland. There wasn't a cloud in sight by the time she reached the Eastern Shore the full moon was directly in front of her illuminating her path like a lantern in the dark.

When Mia finally pulled up to Pearline's and

spotted Dax sitting on the step, her stomach did a somersault, and she knew the butterfly flutters wouldn't be too far behind. She pulled into the driveway and leaped out of the driver's seat leaving the door open. She jumped into his arms, just as she had when he walked through the prison gates in 2020. She noticed immediately that Dax had lost a significant amount of weight as he gripped her behind lifting her up and spun her around. Instantly breaking down in that moment all that mattered to Mia was being there for Dax, his cheating and disappearing acts had become irrelevant. She planned to do everything she could to keep him away from the cops and take care of he and the kids well being. She had always thought no moment would ever top the day of his release but something about being away from him voluntarily, hit Mia's soul differently. Dax laughed as Mia squeezed the life out of his neck, his little mama was back.

"Don't ever do that to me again, I was going crazy. You really left me and that was fucked up. It felt like I was never going to see you again." Dax revealed.

Mia didn't respond, she closed her eyes as she inhaled and silently told herself she wouldn't abandon him again.

Thirty minutes later, after checking into a hotel Mia went to retrieve Dax, Malakai and Teal from the truck.

"Keep your hood on and your head down." Mia said, as she threw the strap on Teal's diaper bag over her head.

"Aight little mama." Dax said, laughing as he climbed out of the car.

"Come on Kai Kai." Dax said, opening the backdoor for Kai.

"Daddy?" Malakai said, rubbing his eyes.

"That's right, son son. I missed ya'll." Dax said laughing as Malakai leaped up and wrapped his arms around Dax.

"Come here." Dax said, lifting him up to hug him. Mia felt a tinge of guilt as she watched Dax and Malakai's interaction. Though she never meant to be the reason they separated she realized that she was in fact the one who caused it. Deciding not to carry the car seat, Mia removed Teal from her straps and held her close as they entered the hotel. After the keycard gave them the green light to enter, Mia went over to the two queen sized beds, placing Teal in the center of the bed.

"She got bigger babe." Dax said, standing over Teal as she slept.

"That's fucked up you went and took my kids away from me like that." Dax continued as Mia created a pillow fort around Teal.

Mia looked up at Dax but remained silent as she removed Teal's coat and checked her diaper.

Dax walked to the other side of the bed with Malakai after he laid at the bottom of the bed. Mia went to retrieve Teal's diaper bag from the desk by the door, to change her before after turning on cartoons for Malakai.

"Lay right here Kai." Dax said, patting the bed

next to Teal. After tucking Malakai in, Dax and Mia headed to the bathroom. In the bathroom they immediately started the shower. They remained silent, basking in the presence of one another as they both undressed. Smiles spread across their faces as they periodically glanced at one another. Once Dax removed his shirt Mia's thoughts were confirmed, he was at the smallest weight she'd ever seen him. She sighed and moved closer to him, reaching her arms out to hug him. Dax pulled Mia into his arms and kissed her forehead and cheek.

"Come on." He said, guiding Mia towards the shower.

After they stepped in the shower together, Mia stood behind Dax and just wrapped her arms around him, relishing in the moment. Dax placed his hands over top of Mia's before turning to face her. He gently motioned for her to turn around. Cupping and lifting her cheeks after she did. After finding her opening he slipped him meat inside and instantly breathed a sigh of relief after the feeling the snug, vacuum sealed tightness he was used to.

After they both delicately washed up and rinsed off, they dried each other with the white hotel towels.

After coming out of the bathroom Mia checked on Teal and Malakai, who were both still sleeping peacefully. Mia went over to her pink duffle bag and dug through it. She pulled out a tan oversized t-shirt and dropped her towel. After putting on the shirt they climbed into the bed.

Dax held Mia from behind.

"Do you know you lost a lot of weight?" Mia asked Dax before she turned over and looked into his eyes.

"Hell yeah, I was fucked up." Dax admitted, thinking about how he was moving after Mia left him. Silence filled the room as they both realized they were miserable without each other. Things were easier for Mia since she had her family and the kids to keep her occupied. She hated to admit it, but Georgia had quickly begun to feel like home with her mom. Dax scooted closer to Mia before he pulled her head closer to him and kissed her forehead.

"I'm sorry." Mia said, feeling conflicted. She knew had good reason to leave but she would've never left had she known the outcome.

"I was going crazy in that house before I left babe. You just don't know. I was in stuck in there thinking you was playing house with somebody else while me and the kids sat home waiting for you to decorate the got damn tree." Mia said, shaking her head before pointing her thumb behind her.

"I definitely wasn't doing that. I was fucked up I been popping so many pills, I-"

"Look I told you in the hospital, we in this together it's like we went from you being on house arrest- us having fun, to you getting off the box and going right back to being on the bullshit. Now I'm not in school, I don't have my job, I became distant from all my friends, I don't have a babysitter, we don't have a place to live, and now you on the run from the police for a robbery and you're saying all this shit is because you wanted to pop pills?" Mia asked with her face screwed up.

"I'm sorry for breaking all of my promises little mama, you just don't understand. The pills fuck with your head and make you extra paranoid, I be feeling like people are after me and some more shit." Dax admitted.

"You got to stop popping them." Mia said, laying her head on the pillow.

"I will, now that you're back. We gone get it all back babe. Remember my Aunt Mary? She's watching kids now at her house. She can watch the kids. We gone go there tomorrow." Dax said, rolling onto his back and looking at the ceiling.

"I need to smoke." He said, before sitting up and looking for his pants.

"We can't smoke in here babe, this ain't the budget inn. They gone call the police but tell me what happened that night. What should we do about the police? Do you think we should just drive back to Georgia and hide out. Just start a new life." Mia said, looking into his eyes. Whatever he wanted to do she was down.

"Nah, if I can avoid Davis. I'm good." Dax said, falling back onto the pillow.

"Man this little ass town babe, how long you think you gone be able to do that. Ain't no way." Mia asked, thinking of all the times officer Davis has pulled Dax over.

Dax shrugged.

"You really want to keep looking over your

shoulder forever? Everytime you end up in the courtroom they sentence you to more years than the last time. You got lucky with that mistrial, but they are going to try to sit you down for a while this time." Mia said, thinking about the possibility of him being put away for good this time.

"I think we should just go." Mia continued.

"I would be looking over my shoulder regardless of where we are. But I rather stay where I know what the fuck is going on in my own hood. But no listen babe this is what happened, me and Spook were supposed to just rob this nigga and I swear I don't even know why the fuck I tried to kill the nigga. If I never shot the gun, it wouldn't be as big of a deal as it is right now." He said, purposefully leaving Nearee's name out of it. Her name hadn't hit the news yet, so Mia had no idea she was involved.

"Can't we plead insanity? I don't think you were in your right mind because of the drugs. I think we should just lay low, hide out and save up to get one of them Johnnie Cochran niggas." Mia said, popping up in the bed.

"You gone wake the baby up." Dax said, laughing before he pulled Mia into his arms. He cherished her and felt a wave of joy seeing how determined his wife was to have his back.

Mia pulled away and reached her hand out to Dax for dap, "Nah that's the plan babe, shake on it." She said, before she and Dax did their handshake. She was ready to do whatever she had to, to keep him safe and out of prison doing a life sentence. Dax pulled her back in his arms and placed a trial of kisses down her face and neck.

Chapter 23

"Wake up babe, we're at my Aunt Mary's." Dax said, to Mia after he opened the back door to get Teal out of her car seat. The excitement of being reunited had Dax and Mia up talking until the sun began to peak through the hotel blinds and it was just hitting her as she slept in the passenger seat.

"We should've took a nap." Mia said, stirring awake after Dax shut the truck off.

"Come on in here ya'll." Dax's Aunt said, standing in her doorway.

"Leave the rest of your happy meal in the car Kai, we're going to be quick." Mia said, turning to Malakai.

They all headed up to the front door after piling out of the car.

"Hey Aunt Mary!" Dax said, smiling as he walked up to her with open arms.

"Hey boy, I see you all on the news boy you better stay out them streets. You have a family now. How are you doing beautiful? It's nice to finally meet you. You're family." Aunt Mary said to Mia, after hugging Dax.

"Come on in ya'll." She said, before closing the door and grabbing Mia for a bear hug.

"Ya'll look exhausted both of you. You drove all this way dear? From where was it?" She asked.

"Georgia." Mia said, with a smile as she sat down on the couch next to Malakai.

"Georgia? By yourself. Shit you better than me. I can't be driving on no highways. I take the back roads." Aunt Mary said.

Mia laughed in return.

"But yeah, Aunt Mary we came because we will need a babysitter soon so we can get back on our feet." Dax said, as he pulled up his pants with one hand and held Teal in the other.

"Yeah you know that's no problem. I got ya'll. Right now, I just have a little boy that I watch on weekdays. He's around Malakai's age. Here's in the backroom playing the game. Do you want to meet him Malakai?" She asked.

"So, I know Malakai's name but what's the baby's name?" Aunt Mary asked.

"Teal." Dax and Mia said in unison.

"Let me hold her." Aunt Mary said, before Dax placed her in her arms.

"She'll be 3 months in a few days." Mia said.

"I got her, anytime." Aunt Mary said, while rocking Teal side to side.

"Do you all want me to watch them for tonight? So you can sleep? We are family I got them." She asked Dax and Mia.

Mia looked up at Dax.

"I'll ask Kai if he wants to stay." Mia said, getting up to walk towards the back room.

"Do you hear him back there already? He'll be fine. Just go get their things and bring it back here. Ya'll two can have a night to yourselves." Aunt Mary said, while rocking Teal side to side.

Seeing Dax heading towards the door made Mia laugh but she was hesitant to leave them.

"They will be good with Aunt Mary Mia, come on. We can go out." Dax said, holding the door open.

"You gone have to get used to leaving them with her and they have to get used to her so why not start now. Come on little mama." Dax said.

"Alright well, I need Aunt Mary's number." Mia said, pulling out her phone.

"You can get it from me." He said.

"Okay. Text me if anything goes wrong."

Mia was thinking about the kids as they drove down the street in silence.

"The kids are good little mama." Dax said, putting his hand on Mia's thigh.

"I guess I feel better now. I just need to find a quick little job. It's almost tax time. We really can just use that money to get a lawyer. I'll save my money for a place. We just have to lay low until then and we'll be good." Mia said, looking at the side of Dax's face as he drove.

Dax nodded, as he continued to drive.

"I'm dead serious babe, but yo' you need to get your waves back asap." She said, looking at his nappy bush and scruffy facial hair. She could tell he hadn't brushed his hear or had a shape up in weeks.

"Maybe you weren't cheating after all." She said, laughing.

"Hahaha." Dax said, cracking up before quickly stopping and giving Mia a blank stare. He was well aware of how rough he looked but when Mia was gone, he didn't give a damn.

Ten minutes later they pulled up to Spook's.

"You should start wearing these kind of masks instead of squeezing that tight ass ski-mask around your head." Mia said, handing Dax a fresh surgical mask.

Dax took the mask and put one of the loops behind his ear before hopping out of the truck. He cuffed the other one as he began to knock on the front door.

A few seconds later, Mercedes opened the door.

"What's up Dax. Spook ain't here." Mercedes said, leaning her head out of the door before looking both ways.

"Fuck you looking for?" Dax asked as he snapped his neck around to scan the parking lot as well.

"Seeing who you came with. Mia's back in town?" Mercedes asked, waving at Mia.

"Tell Spook I came." Dax said, heading back to the

truck. "Nosey bitch."

"Ay take me to the other side." Dax said, pointing to the other side of the parking lot.

Dax spotted Cash rolling dice and instantly hopped out.

Cash turned around and whipped out his joint.

"Oh shit Dax watch how you run up on me, almost clipped your shit." Cash said, taking his hand off of the small gun he had inside his coat pocket.

"Yeah, alright nigga. What you on though? I know you got some of that on you." Dax said.

"Some what? Jiggas, Yerky's, Hard? I can't tell with you. I been hearing about you out here tweaking nigga. You better chill." Cash said.

"Hard? Stop fucking playing with me mafucka." Dax said, pulling up his pants.

"Yeah alright," Cash said, folding his arms as he looked at Dax.

"Nigga do you got that or not. You playing." Dax said, clinching his jaws.

"Nigga dead ass I do not know which one you want? Molly's or Percs?" Cash yelled.

"Both!" Dax said, pulling out the roll of money.

Cash pulled out a fat orange prescription bottle and a zip lock baggy full of the regular molly he had been used to in the pill form.

"How much you-"

"All of it." Dax said, cutting him off as he counted

out a little less than half of the money in the roll.

Dax stuffed the bottle and baggy into his hoodie after the exchange before heading back to the car.

“Alright let’s go to the liquor store and the barbershop. We’re going to have a good night.” Dax said, doing his little dance after getting back inside the car.

Later that night, Mia and Dax woke up to his burner phone ringing. It was Spook.

“Yoooo,” Dax said, after opening the flip phone.

“Ya’ll coming out to the club tonight it’s supposed to be packed. We should be good as long as we leave before the bullshit pop off.” Spook said, into the phone.

“Yeah, damn I ain’t even know it was this late.” Dax said, squinting his eyes as he looked at the time. “I’m glad you hit me. We would’ve slept the whole night away and I got that on me too.” Dax said, referring to the money.

“Aight, I’ll see ya’ll out there.” Spook said before ending the call.

“Wake up lil’ mama. Let’s start drinking. We’re going out!” Dax said, shaking Mia’s hip as she laid on her side.

“No, the fuck we not. The police are looking for you. They might send an undercover in that joint.” Mia said, sitting up.

Dax threw the covers off his legs before he

retrieved Mia's party bucket of fireball.

"Come on with the scary shit babe. Let's turn up! You're back and the kids are with Aunt Mary. We lit." He said, opening the bucket.

"Scary or smart?" Mia said, pointing to her temple. "But alright let's get an order to go before we drink so I don't get sick! And let's smoke in the car!" Mia said, dancing at the thought.

"We can smoke right now." Dax said, as he joined Mia dancing.

"I told you yo, we can not smoke in here!" Mia said, climbing out the bed.

"Alright, let's go then." Dax said.

Mia was feeling her drinks as she sat in the passenger seat with a chicken wonton taco in one hand and her bottle in the other. The truck was full of weed smoke as they rode down route 13 and Mia was in complete bliss. Drinks, food, and music while riding was one of her favorite things to do. With the kids especially Teal, it had been awhile since she had a chance to do it.

"You ready to pull up to the club?" Dax asked, turning onto Columbia drive off of route 13.

Mia looked down at her mint green 2-piece ribbed outfit. She paired it with a beige puffy vest with a beige NY yankee's baseball cap and was feeling herself. After her shower she did her hair, styled her edges and put on some fluffy mink strip lashes.

"Fasure hubby." She said, sitting up in her seat, pulling down the sun visor to look in the mirror. She pulled her watermelon VS lip gloss out of her purse before applying it and rolling her lips together.

"Your wife is cute as fuck." Mia said, looking in the mirror. She readjusted her hat before slamming the mirror shut.

The entire street was lined with parked cars on both sides. Dax rode pass the building and made a u-turn in the street. He made sure to see if any cops were parked anywhere in a cut lurking, after confirming that was coast was clear he parked on the grass of a nearby business and hopped out.

Mia climbed out slowly still clutching her bottle as Dax walked around the truck to meet her.

"Leave the bottle babe, we'll get shots." He said, taking the bottle from her and putting it on her seat.

He grabbed her hand and guided her towards the club before they both spotted Spook standing in a crowd in front of the door.

"My mothafuckin nigga." Spook said, holding his hand out as Dax walked up to him.

Dax let go of Mia's hand as he and Spook gave each other dap before leaning into each other.

"My nigga." Dax said, after they let go and headed

inside the club.

As they walked through the first door, Mia noticed that the security guards didn't even have the metal detector plugged in. Mia pulled Dax's hand to get his attention. Mia waited for their eyes to lock before looking in the direction of the metal detector knowing Dax would follow her eyes. He peeped and gave Mia a slight head nod as they walked into the second door entering the club.

Dax caught Mia's drift but he wasn't worried about shit. If anything he was happy he didn't have to pay to get his own pole in the club.

The whole city was in attendance as everybody stood jam packed shoulder to shoulder inside the building. Even the outdoor smoking area, that would normally be empty on the fall and winter nights was completely packed as people stood on and around the picnic tables.

"Damnnn." Mia said, as Dax slowly made his way through the crowd pulling Mia along as he stopped every now and then to give people dap.

The Dj had the building going up as he blasted Von and Durk's, *"All these Niggas,"* Mia observed everyone rapping along as she headed to the bar behind Dax.

Dax watched as Spook continued towards the dj who was on stage talking on the mic.

"If you're having a good night in this

mothafucka let me hear ya'll make some noise!" The Dj said into his mic over the music, before Spook stepped up onto the stage and removed the mic from it's stand.

Spook was feeling the drinks and the music as he got on the stage rapping along with Von into the mic. He didn't know how much longer he's be out on the streets, so he planned to enjoy every minute of it.

Dax changed course and pulled Mia along as he headed to the stage.

"Fuck that, come up babe." Dax said, as he climbed up onto the stage too.

The drinks and weed had Mia in a fuck it zone as she joined Dax and Spook on the stage, even though they were both wanted criminals.

Dax took the mic from Spook, "we in this mafucka." He said, laughing as he looked over at Mia who was rapping along as well.

Dax pulled Mia into his arms before they hugged and stumbled on the stage almost falling before laughing and kissing. Spook shook his head as he looked at the couple.

A fight from the outside smoking area broke out and began to spill into the club.

Pop, pop, pop!

The gunshots from outside went off.

"Come on ya'll," Spook said, to Mia and Dax.

Dax pulled Mia by her hand out of the club. Some people were running out the door along with them but most ducked down on the club floor while still trying to see what else would pop off.

There was pandemonium in the parking lot as everybody was running to their cars and pulling off.

"I'll call you tomorrow bro, here!" Dax said, as he dug in his pocket.

Mia spotted Nearee as she ran across the street with Kea in tow.

"Damn cuz you ain't speaking now!?" Mia yelled, holding her hands in the air.

"We was just trying to get the fuck out of here before the police pull up." Nearee yelled, before jumping in passenger seat of the car.

What the hell? Mia thought, normally Nearee was always on some overprotective big cousin shit.

"Ya'll ain't speaking to ya'll sis? Kea didn't speak either. Ain't they ya'll besties?" Mia asked, looking from Dax to Spook.

"Aight bro," Spook said, giving Dax dap after Dax gave him the money.

"Ya'll quiet but when I was in Georgia ya'll was together everyday on snap! And Kea is your cousin right? So let me guess you fucked Nearee?" Mia asked, getting in Dax's face.

"Come on before the cops come." Dax said, walking away. He dug in his pockets looking for molly before climbing into the car.

Mia jumped into the car but remained silent as she deciphered if her accusations could be true. She watched Dax pop something into his mouth as she thought about him and Nearee together. She noticed the claw mark that were now scars running through the tattoo of her name and shook her head. Somebody was mad about him having her name tattooed on his neck. Was it Nearee? Nearee was one of the prettiest girls in the city so it wouldn't be a long shot. Dax had been hanging around her for years. For all she knew, they could had been fucking all along. Nearee was a hoe everybody knew it but Mia just assumed that she always respected that she and Mia were cousins and that Dax was hers. She folded her arms and looked out the window, as they headed back to the hotel.

Back in the room Mia took a big swig from her bottle as she walked over to Dax as he took his clothes off.

"What happened to your neck? The tattoo. Who did that?" Mia asked, pointing to his neck with her bottle.

When Dax didn't respond Mia huffed, before walking backwards. She sat down on the window seat across from Dax. She squinted her eyes as she looked at him and waited for him to say something. His silence had her blood boiling.

Dax looked down at his jeans on the floor as he sat on the edge of the bed.

"Don't tell me you really fucked my cousin. Man do you know what I did just to get back to this fucking city to be with you and be here for you!?" Mia said, before she opened her bottle and took another swig.

Dax didn't know what to say after he lifted his head to look at Mia. He thought about the night he had with Nearee. They were both high and drunk out of their minds. That shit didn't count.

"I didn't." Dax finally said.

"You fucking did!" Mia yelled, again pointing her bottle.

"Look, I've done everything I really can to show you I love you and that I'm here for you. Think about that shit!" Mia yelled.

"I held shit down my nigga." Mia said, standing up. "Never missed a fucking visit, never cheated, I really waited, you came straight home and shitted on me immediately. Had another girl pregnant! Okay cool," she continued as she talked with her hands, "I take you back, you still cheating, shit crazy for real so I move on, finally!! I moved the fuck on and I was happy! But no you pop out and I just had to give you another chance! And you still cheating!! Nigga you don't deserve me." Mia said, looking at Dax in disgust. "Shit truth be told I was good in Georgia. I didn't have to come back." Mia shrugged, shooting Dax a smug look.

Even though everything Mia was saying was true it infuriated Dax. *How dare this bitch say she was happy with another nigga. So she really did have him in Georgia with her?*

Dax rubbed her hands across his waves before digging in his pocket for a perc or more molly. He pulled out the baggie with molly and poured some in his hand, before quickly throwing in into his mouth, hoping it would have a calming effect.

He looked over at Mia, as he thought about his next move. Maybe she will understand if she just tries the molly. Every girl he fucked with recently, did his drugs with him. He picked the baggie back up and poured a nice amount into his hand before standing up and walking towards Mia.

Mia looked at the bewildered look in Dax's eyes as he approached her with the drugs in the palm of his hand and knew he had lost his fucking mind.

"Try this lil' mama, all that shit you talking will be irrelevant you will be so happy you-"

Mia slapped Dax's hand so hard the drugs flew out of his hand, sprinkling across the hotel carpet.

"You're acting like a fucking crackhead nigga, you know I don't-"

Whoop!

Before he could catch his self-Dax smacked the shit out of Mia for wasting his drugs and then talking shit on top of it.

Holding the side of her jaw, Mia became enraged at the audacity of him for hitting her because she didn't want to do drugs with him.

"A crackhead?" Dax said, as he paced the floor.

He wants to hit people do he? Mia thought instantly jumping up to grab her bag that held her rainbow pocketknife.

Realizing what she was doing Dax lunged at Mia grabbing her hair, he quickly let go when he felt a sharp pain in the palm of his hand.

"Bitch you stabbed me!" Dax yelled, looking down at his hand leaking blood. He quickly grabbed his phone off the bed and called Spook.

"Hurry up and pull up to the hotel off route 50 bro, across from Denny's. She stabbed me my shit leaking." Dax said, before hanging up.

He went to his bag and pulled out his glock, with a trial of blood following him.

"You don't even know how easy it would be for me to end all this shit right here do you?" Dax said, holding the gun, he shook his head as stuffed everything back into the bag with one hand.

Mia's intoxicated state didn't allow her the common sense to have fear in her current situation.

"Do what you feel my nigga." She said, pointing the knife at him, "you slapped me on some junkie shit!"

Dax looked at her and clenched his jaw as he struggled to put his pants on with one hand.

"You don't know how lucky you are girl. If it wasn't for my kids you'd be dead. Fucking bitch gone stab me." Dax said, as he put his shoes on.

He put his jacket on with no shirt, grabbed his bag and went out the door.

Mia knew the cops would probably be there at any second so she looked around the room before getting up and gathering her stuff as well.

By the time she made it to the car she knew she was too intoxicated to drive. She wrapped her arms around her steering wheel and put her head down as she contemplated her next move.

Chapter 24

Mia

The truck was still running when Mia woke up the next morning still laying on the steering wheel.

"Ay fuckin yo." She said, looking around. She sat back in the seat and put her head back. She had a pounding headache as she thought about the situation at hand. Once again trying to be with Dax had her between a rock and a hard place. Here she was back in her city with a half a tank of gas, no money, and no where to stay with her two kids. This might have been the worst situation thus far. The only good thing was Mrs. Mary watching the kids.

"I just need a job." She said to herself before she backed out of the parking lot. Instead of saving up to help Dax in any way, she would just save up for herself and the kids.

She pulled up to Aunt Mary's in less than 10 minutes.

She got of the truck and walked up to the door, listening before knocking. The first face Mia saw was Teal's as soon as the door swung open.

"My baby!" Mia squealed, as she scooped Teal up from Aunt Mary's arms.

"Hey Aunt Mary, how was it? Were the kids good? Did they cry?" Mia asked, as she walked in and sat in the same spot on the couch that she had the day prior.

"Good morning these kids were good and happy with me but you look like you had a long night. And where is that nephew of mine?" Aunt Mary said, with a side eyed look.

"It's a long story but basically, I'm going to have to get me and the kids out of this situation by myself. Is that okay will you still watch them?" Mia asked, tears threatening to erupt.

Aunt Mary looked at the bruise on the right side of Mia's face and the smudged mascara under her eyes and knew something bad must've happened with her and Daxton.

"Of course I will ya'll are family." Aunt Mary said, "come look at Malakai in the back room still sleep."

"Okay and can I brush my teeth and wash my face? I might need them to stay so I can find a job quick fast."

"Of course."

Mia sat in her truck once again fighting tears, she hated leaving her kids. She knew things were easier in Georgia with Corrie and she missed her mom but she loved her own city, so she decided that even though she originally came back to be with Dax she was just going to stay and thug it out to get herself back on her feet in her own city.

Since she didn't mind driving she decided to try her hand at being a taxi driver. She backed out of the driveway and headed to Lake street on the westside to a popular cab company everybody used since she was younger.

She put her truck in park and looked up at the Bailey's Taxi sign before hoping out and heading into the tiny office building.

Inside the office was nothing but a gumball machine next to a bench and a desk with one man sitting behind it with a radio and an old school landline telephone.

"Hi, my name is Mia, are you guys hiring?" She asked the man.

"Nah we aren't hiring but you look familiar, do I know you from somewhere?" The man behind the desk asked.

Mia shrugged, not in the mood for small talk after he said they weren't hiring.

"Who's your mom?" He continued,

"Corrie." Mia said, over her shoulder and she headed back towards the door to leave.

"Corrie Smith?" He asked, sitting up in his seat.

"Yeah." Mia said, with one hand on the doorhandle.

"Man, I knew you looked familiar. I grew up with your mom on Wicomico street. You were one mean ass little girl when you were little." The man said laughing, "So look right, this is what I'm going to do for you, we are completely full on the dayshift. They fight over calls and everything. Are you willing to work a late shift at night? It's slow during the week but Thursday through

Sunday you can really make it up." He said, looking up at Mia.

"I'll work any shift right now." Mia said, perking up.

"We do 12-hour shifts so it would be 3:30pm-3:30am. Can you do that?" He asked.

"Yeah, I'll do it. What's your name?" Mia said, walking back to the desk as she observed at the older man. She didn't remember ever meeting him, he was slightly chubby with a short salt and pepper afro with a matching beard.

"Are you busy now I can put you in a car with one of our drivers now so you can see how it is, if you want? But my name is Gary." The man said.

"I don't need to see it, can I start asap? Because I really need the money." Mia admitted thinking about where she would even sleep when she was finished.

When Gary stood up Mia was surprised at how tall he was as she watched him get a clipboard and an application before reaching it to her.

"You can't start until to get a taxicab license. To get one you have to pay for your fingerprints and background check. And you have to get a drug test and physical. But for now fill this out. I'm going to hire you but you still have to complete the application." He said.

"How long will it take to get all that back?" Mia asked.

"A week at the most." Gary said.

As Mia sat down and filled out the application she thought about where she would stay while she waited the week. All of her family members in the city, she either didn't have a relationship with or their homes were already full of people. This was especially true of her grandmom Pearline's house. Her cousins and Uncle had every room occupied. She knew she could call Chanel, Lola, Alyssa, Ballow and even Reese but she didn't want to explain why she was back in the first place or what had happened. She knew she could drive the 2 and a half hours to Cali's or Egypt's as well. Taking the trip to Baltimore would have been preferable if she had gas money and didn't have to do all the running around the city for the taxi license.

After filling out the application, she realized she didn't have the money to do anything. She would need money to hold her over to take care of the kids, stay in a hotel, buy food, the taxi license and pay for the fingerprints. She didn't have a choice but to break down and call her mom for help.

An hour later, Mia pulled up to the cheapest motel in the city with the money Corrie sent for a week's stay. She had never stayed at the motel and for good reason. It looked like something out of a horror movie as she looked out of her windshield at the place. The single level U shape building made her think of the movie Vacancy and the show she loved Bates motel. She knew it was not somewhere she would want herself or her kids laying their heads, but it was only temporary she had to keep telling herself. She pulled her hat down low over her eyes as she headed into the motel office.

The office smelled like a giant musty ashtray as soon as Mia walked in.

"Can I help you?" The short Turkish man asked.

"I need a room for a week." Mia said, still looking down as if she was hiding her face.

"You? Here?" The man asked with a confused look.

"Yes me." Mia said, finally lifting her head to look the man in his face.

The man was surprised that the young lady was all alone and requesting to stay at his motel, which was normally only occupied by prostitutes, drug addicts and seasonal Spanish workers. He saw the light bruise on her face and felt sorry for her. He decided to give her one of the rooms, that he considered the safest, closest to the highway and streetlights.

"Okay, $125 please." The man said.

Mia slid her bank card onto the counter and headed back out of the door after he slid it back with the key and room number.

"Thank you." She said.

She headed straight across the street to the family dollar for cleaning products before picking up the kids and heading back to the room.

Thirty minutes later Mia was pulling back into the parking lot of the hotel with Malakai and Teal in the backseat.

"He gave me room 1, ugh! Everybody in the city will see my car. I need to hide it." She thought to herself.

She pulled to the back of the parking lot instead of parking near her own door. Occupants of the other rooms sat on milk crates outside of their doors smoking cigarettes and drinking beers. Mia stood out like a sore thumb as she climbed out of the truck.

"Hola, linda mamá."

"Phwwwhht." Someone whistled.

Mia heard multiple cat calls as she unstrapped Teal's car seat. She covered Teal with a blanket before pulling her close to her chest and grabbing Malakai's hand as they walked down the outside corridor towards their room door. Mia retrieved the key from her vest pocket as she stood in front of the door. She cringed after she opened the door and walked inside. Malakai looked up at her after she sighed. The room looked like something out of the 1960's as she looked around. The dark green carpet had white stains and several burn marks from what looked like cigarette or ashes. The single queen-sized bed was covered with a cheap, microfiber, paper-thin navy-blue blanket along with two straggly pillows. There were two wooden night stands on both sides of the bed, one holding a lamp and the other a small cheap LED alarm clock. There was a single brown table sitting in front of the bed holding a big back RCA television. A small black fridge sat underneath the table. Mia exhaled as she stepped over to the bed, pulling the comforter back to examine the sheets.

Ain't no mothafuckin way! She thought to herself as she saw light brown stains on the cream-colored sheets. She looked up at the ceiling a saw the chipped paint and figured the roof probably leaked straight onto the bed.

"Ugh," She said, with a frowned but quickly straightened her face when she remembered Malakai was watching her every move. When the pair locked eyes Mia smiled.

"Should we go back to the hotel with Daddy?" Malakai asked, with his little eyebrows raised.

"No, I am going to clean this place up and we will only be here for a little while. Okay?" Mia said.

"Okay." Malakai said.

"Okay, hold your sister, but don't put her on the bed yet Kai. I'm just going to run to the car to get our blankets, snacks, bags and cleaning stuff." Mia said, handing Teal to Malakai.

I can't do this shit. Mia thought as she jogged to the truck, to retrieve their things. She contemplated on if maybe she should just go and take the kids back to Corrie's. She struggled to carry everything, wanting to take one trip from the truck to the room.

"Do you need a hand, mamacita?" A short Spanish guy asked, as he stood at his room door holding a coors lite.

"I got it thanks." Mia said, before slamming the truck and juggling everything under her arms.

She dropped everything to the floor after reentering the room.

"Thank you Kai Kai!" Mia said to Malakai before taking Teal back into her arms.

"Okay, let me get it together." Mia said, looking around.

Dax

Dax knocked four times and waited; he looked both ways down the street as he stood on the unfamiliar porch.

Nearee came to the door with a dark pink bonnet, in a pair of black spandex tights and a grey belly shirt.

"Come on." She said, waving him in.

Dax followed Nearee up the narrow steps, his eyes glued to her ass as she led the way. He sat in a pink and black gaming chair that sat across from her bed as she closed the door. He watched Nearee as she sat on her bed. Silent filled the room.

"Can I smoke in here?" Dax asked her.

"Yeah but sit right here and blow it out of the window." She said, pointing to a spot at the foot of her bed, next to the screenless open window.

"Aight. So what do you want to talk about?" Dax asked, looking back at her as he relit a half-smoked J.

"Just seeing what's up, I feel like you and Spook are the only two people who know I was there with ya'll that night. And I've been wondering what happened the other night after the club. Did Mia ask about us?" Nearee asked, in a low tone.

"I tried to deny it but she knows. It is what it

is though, she probably already back in Georgia as we speak. She stabbed me bout that shit." Dax said, holding up his left hand, to show Nearee his sloppily wrapped hand.

"Damn. You got any molly?" she said, sitting down next to him.

"Hmmp." Dax said, reaching the blunt to her, before he pulled out his ziplock bag, that held his stash of molly and pill bottle.

"Can I get a perc too?" Nearee asked, as she exhaled the smoke.

"Here." Dax said, laying back on her bed. Nearee had a colorful tapestry with a black girl smoking weed in a forest full of mushrooms on her ceiling, over her bed.

"We might as well be together Nearee, at least until this shit dies down." Dax said, putting his good hand behind his head.

"You ain't worried about Mia?" Nearee asked.

"Come here." Dax said, taking his gun out of his pants and placing it on the window seal. He lightly grabbed Nearee's arm before pulling her onto his lap. He looked her in her eyes and asked, "are you?"

Chapter 25

Mia

Over an hour had passed, by the time Mia felt like the room was fit to live in. She had removed all the bedding and replaced it with her own. She bleached down the entire bathroom floor, toilet, sink and shower and used a febreze linen and sky scented plug in to make the place feel more like home.

Mia waited until Teal was fast asleep, before she climbed into the tiny walk-in shower still cringing as she stepped her foot inside. No matter how much comet she used or bleached she sprayed it still felt unsanitary. *Fuck this, I might have to get me some flip flops and use them like jailhouse shower shoes.* She thought but she was glad she bought her own, rags and soap. Her mind drifted off to Dax as she lathered her body. The fact that their initial fight was about whether or not he fucked her cousin was crazy. Here she was donating blood like a jackass to get back to him, whole time he's fucking her family. She shook her head at the thought. She would never forgive him for her current predicament. It would be something different if he had been with her and the kids in the roach motel. But he was nowhere to be found as usual and for that she didn't have anymore chances to give him. She was getting older, it was time to grow up. So she decided that as soon as she got on her feet she would file for a divorce. Tomorrow she would drop the kids off to handle her business to obtain the taxi license and from there she'd wait to hear when she could start. She just had to stack her money and apply to as many places as possible.

"Tap, tap, tap!"

Three light taps on the door, interrupted Mia's thoughts in the shower and since she hadn't told a soul where she was she wondered who it could be. She turned off the water and wrapped her pink fluffy towel around herself. Stepping onto her clothes versus the dingy yellow bathroom tiles.

"Hold up!" She said, as she opened the bathroom door. She slipped into her bedroom slippers as she headed towards the door.

"Who is it?" She asked, trying to determine if she needed her trusty rainbow pocketknife.

"Who is it mommy?" Malakai asked.

Mia held her hand up to shush him, as she retrieved her blade thinking that it could be one of the perverts living out there.

"Open the door Mia." The person said.

"Reese?" Mia said, with a frown.

"Yes." She heard him say.

She looked around the stale room and was mortified. *How the fuck did he find me?* She thought.

"Yo, just open the door." Reese said.

Mia reluctantly snatched the door open, Reese stood flashing a smile as he held pizza, wings, his ipad, and fireball.

Mia felt the color flushing from her face, as shame and embarrassment began to flood her. She covered her face and shook her head as he walked inside.

"Well, it smells good in here." Reese admitted.

"Poopy head!" Malakai screeched, startling Teal, who woke up crying.

Reese and Malakai hugged, as Mia went to pick Teal up.

"Who is that Malakai? Is that your baby sister?" Reese asked Malakai.

Malakai nodded as he watched Reese.

"Let me hold her." Reese said, putting everything down on the bed.

"You want some pizza Kai?" Reese asked, as he took Teal into his arms. He couldn't help but wish she was his baby as he looked down at her.

"How did you know I was here?" Mia finally spoke.

"I peeped your truck. I was riding down 13." He said, looking at Mia. "I went straight home, changed and called the pizza in."

"What if I wasn't alone?" Mia asked, with her eyebrows raised not wanting to say Dax's name out loud.

"That was a chance I was willing to take. But since my instincts were right, just let me be here for ya'll Mia."

He said, as he rocked Teal from side to side.

Mia didn't respond, normally she'd be worried about being loyal to Dax and worried about whether he would pop up and catch them but after everything. She truly didn't give a fuck. She went back into the bathroom to put on her pajamas.

"I brought the ps5 Kai, you want me to go to the car to get it?" Reese asked.

Malakai looked at the old tv and didn't answer, causing Reese to laugh.

By midnight, Reese was the last one woke as he held Mia who was fast asleep along with Teal and Malakai.

He put on a brave face for Mia so she wouldn't feel embarrassed, but truth be told the motel was no place for Mia, the baby and Kai to be staying. Especially alone. Anyone of the men lingering around could get drunk and break down the old ass wooden door and rape Mia or anything else. He would try to convince her to come home with him in the morning but knowing her she'd say no. So, he planned to stay there with her for as long as she was there. Whether she liked it or not.

That morning, Mia woke up to the subtle piano sounds of her alarm letting her know it was time for her to get up. She struggled to roll over in place and was surprised to Reese wide awake and peering directly at her. She could tell he hadn't slept a wink by the bags underneath his eyes.

"You never went to sleep did you?" Mia asked him.

"Nah, not really. I missed you pretty." Reese admitted, lifting his hand to stroke her face.

"Reese-" Mia attempted to say as she turned her head away.

"Don't even say it. Just let me be there for you. You and the kids do not have to stay in a place like this." Reese said, looking around the room.

"I have more than enough space, I'm not saying we have to put a title on anything or even that we have to sleep in the same room. There's 3 other bedrooms." Reese continued.

Mia looked down and couldn't help but think of how she so easily dismissed him when Dax came home. After everything Reese had done for her. She dwelled on how good he had been to her and how quickly she discarded him and for this reason she felt like she didn't deserve his help.

"I have to do this on my own. I need this shithole for motivation." Mia said, referring to the motel. "And honestly, I don't feel like I deserve your help at all. I don't want to use you in my time of need." Mia admitted. Reese had it going on in comparison to Dax. He was definitely a safe space for her but she just couldn't put her finger on what was missing.

"Use me." Reese said, interrupting her thoughts.

Mia sighed, she didn't understand why he still felt responsible for her wellbeing, but she would never move into his house and give him false hope. When she knew deep down she didn't want to be with him.

"For real Mia, I don't care what we been through,

this ain't no place for ya'll."

Mia avoided eye contact, not knowing how to respond.

Reese took her hand into his, realizing that he would not be able to get her to change her mind.

"You are still stubborn." He said shaking his head. "It's not safe here." Reese said.

Mia reached across Reese to grab her purse off the nightstand, she unzipped her bag and retrieved her rainbow pocketknife. She looked down at knife and noticed the dry blood on the blade and smirked to herself.

"Now you know, I'm a gangsta. We good." She said, before folding her arms while looking at Reese.

Dax

Dax looked over at Nearee as she slept next to the wall. He sat up before reaching down for his pants that laid on the floor next to him. After picked them up he dug in his pocket pulling out a Newport, along with his favorite prescription bottle. The silence from the bottle when he shook it instantly put a frown on his face, he held the bottle up in the light towards his face, confirming his fears when he realized that the Percocet bottle was empty.

How many did we take? He thought looking back at Nearee who was still fast asleep.

Bitch probably high off my shit right now. He thought shaking his head. Before he began to slip his legs into his pants. He had to go find some more. He dug in his pocket again after he stood up and found that he some molly left in the baggy but he could do without the molly it was the percs that he had to have. Mentally but physically too. It couldn't have been more than 6 hours that he had been sleep. Normally as soon as he opened his eyes in the morning the first thing he did was swallow a pill. He wouldn't take a piss or brush his teeth without that in his system first. He silently blamed Nearee as he bent down to get the heel of his foot into his Jordan 5's. Maybe Mia not doing drugs was a good thing after all. Nearee's pill habit was just as bad as Dax's if not worst. He was almost certain she had some tucked somewhere but he didn't have the energy to figure it out as he walked out of the room. He made a mental note to hide his stash from her ass from that point on. He slightly jogged down the steps and out of the front door. He knew he probably smelled as bad as he looked. He didn't take a shower or even bother to wash the crust out of his eyes. He didn't even have a ride lined up to get to where he was trying to go. The only thing on his mind was avoiding the hot flashes, chills, diarrhea and vomiting that came when he went to long without a percocet.

Chapter 26

Mia

A week later, Mia stood at Aunt Mary's door after knocking with Malakai and Teal in tow.

"Hey Babies!" Aunt Mary said, after she snatched the door open.

"Hey Aunt Mary!" Mia said, smiling before she turned to look down at Malakai.

Mary took Teal who was asleep in the carseat and walked towards the couch, leaving Mia and Malakai alone.

"Alright Kai, I have to go so I can get us a nice place to stay right?" she said, before she leaned down to hug him.

"Yeah mom, so we can get out of that hotel." Malakai said, in a matter-of-fact tone.

"Yep we will not be there long, I promise. Watch after your baby sister for me and let me know if any of these kids try to mess with ya'll, i'll turn this place upside down." Mia said, leaning down and whispering into his ear. Malakai laughed before he gave his mom a fist bump and walked inside.

"Thanks again, Aunt Mary." Mia said.

"I got them baby." Aunt Mary reassured.

Mia parked her truck and cringed as she looked at the crew of workers standing in the parking lot. She hated the first day of work and she hated being the new girl. She checked her hair and rolled her lip-gloss into her lips before climbing out of the car. The conversations went from loud to quiet as she walked up and the scene made her think of her first day at Cadista, walking past Alyssa, Lola, Chanel and Ballow. Alyssa had called her LB after she walked past, causing Mia to laugh and instantly breaking the ice. She couldn't wait to see them again.

"You the new girl for the 3-3 shift?" A heavyset guy with cornrows asked.

"That's me." Mia said, looking him over.

"Oh okay, I'm Quan. We all on the 4a.m. to 4p.m. shift but shit you bout to make that bread on that shift, especially tonight." He said.

"That's the plan, nice meeting you though." Mia said, before walking into the office.

After Gary assigned Mia to a vehicle and gave her the keys, he sent her on her way. The best way to learn was through experience he told her.

Mia recognized the car as a 2007 crown victoria. The whole fleet of cars were the same with different colors and nothing but the company name and number on the driver and passenger doors. She had been assigned to Cab number 6. Once she hopped in the car and turned on her two-way radio she was on the way to her first customer immediately.

"Base to cab 6." Mia heard Gary's voice emanating through the radio speaker.

Mia struggled to remove the mic from the radio clip and laughed to herself, *I'm going to have to get used to this.*

"Cab 6." Mia said, with the mic nearly touching her lips.

"You have a couple at food lion on Nanicoke road going to waterside apartments." She heard Gary say.

"Okay bet." Mia said, into the mic.

"Nah, just say 10-4." Gary said, Mia could hear him stifling his laughter.

"Oh shit, 10-4." Mia said, in the mic. *They're going right down to street,* she thought.

She pulled up at the grocery store within 5 minutes and spotted the couple standing with a cart full of groceries.

She pulled in front of them and popped the trunk, "ya'll need help?" Mia asked after she rolled her window down.

"Nah we got it shorty." The male told her. The couple looked a little older than Mia and looked like they both smoked a pound of weed before shopping.

The couple simultaneously climbed into the backseat, one entering on each side of the car with the female behind Mia. They rode in silence causing Mia to turn the music up on the radio. She was glad they were going a few blocks around the corner.

"We live in the back to the left." She heard the girl say behind her.

"Alright bet." Mia said, whipping into the apartment complexes parking lot, eager to get her next customer.

"Cab 6, are you clear?" Mia heard Gary ask as the couple climbed out of the car.

"Almost," Mia said, as she popped her trunk.

"Next you have several customers at 423 Patrick avenue going to 900 South Division." Gary said.

"Alright 10-4." Mia said, as she watched her review mirror and waited for the trunk to slam.

The male came up to the passenger window and passed Mia a 10-dollar bill. She took it wondered how much the ride itself costed.

"Good looking." She told the man.

She made a right on Parsons road as she headed towards Jersey road towards her next call.

Mia observed the street as she pulled up to the house, she beeped the horn twice when she found the house she was looking for. She watched as 4 Mexican men walked out of the front door, each carrying 24 pack boxes of Corona's. They all looked like they just got off work, wearing muddy boots and pants. She sighed hoping they wouldn't be on the same shit the Mexican men would be on, from her side of town. They'd whistle and offer money to her and her friends even as young teenagers.

"Hola Mami." One of the men climbed into the front seat. The other three men climbed into the back seat, placing their beers on their laps.

"What's up ya'll?" Mia said, before pulling off. She shook her head as the men started talking in Spanish, no doubt talking about her.

"Mami you drive alone? You don't have a man?" The one in the front asked Mia, while holding up his ring finger and pointing to it.

"Nah, Divorce." Mia said, looking over at him as she drove.

He began to speak in Spanish again, as if he was translating to the men in the back.

"Aye, ya'll English, okay? Ya'll know English?" Mia asked looking in her review at one of the men in the back.

"You want a beer? We have plenty." He spoke up and asked clearly.

"Oh! So ya'll talking that shit in your language but know English?" Mia said, laughing to herself.

"You want beer?" The guy next to her asked this time.

"I don't drink and drive." Mia told them.

"Where's your man." He continued.

"He ain't here right now. Where ya'll going with all this beer? A party?" Mia asked attempting to keep the questioning on them.

"Yeah, we party it's Friday." One said, before they started speaking in Spanish again. Mia couldn't get them to their destination any faster.

It took less than 15 minutes for Mia to pull up to where they requested, she watched as the man in front seat dug into his pants pocket and pulled out a small knot of cash. Mia pulled out her phone as she waited him to hand her the money. He peeled off a 20 and a 10 handing it to Mia.

"Thank you, ya'll have a good night." Mia said.

One of the men slipped another twenty dollar bill up to Mia, "A tip." He said, before climbing out of the car.

"Thank you." She said, slightly confused because the first guy had already tipped.

"Gracias Mami." The one in the passenger said, as he climbed out. "He likes you." He said shrugging his shoulders, before he closed the door.

"Fifty dollars for a 15-minute ride, not bad." Mia said out loud to herself.

"Cab 6 is clear." She said into the radio.

Dax

A little after midnight, Dax was feeling the two perc 30's he had previously swallowed when he first arrived at the VFW with Nearee and Spook.

"Where everybody at?" Nearee said, looking around the practically empty building.

Dax turned to see who was all in attendance, aside from a few old heads scattered around the room the place was dead.

"Probably all the rain keeping everybody in." Spook chimed in after looking up from his phone. The duo had already been on the way to pick up Nearee when it started raining like cats and dogs outside.

"It's cold as a bitch out there too." Nearee agreed.

"Ya'll trying to go get Kea and we can all just go back to my house?" Nearee asked, since they were all to paranoid to chill over Kea's.

"We can." Spook said, looking from Nearee to Dax.

"Hold up," Dax said, before putting his arm around Nearee's shoulders, "let me get a double shot of Henny."

"Chill bro." Nearee said, with a slight chuckle as

she removed his arm.

"Fuck around and have Mia whoop both of ya'll asses in here." Spook said, looking over his shoulder at the entrance before turning his gaze to Dax's loosely wrapped hand.

"Nah bro, I think she could tell I was ready to kill her dumb ass this time." Dax said, as he recollected on the scene in the hotel room. He silently thanked God that he hadn't pulled the trigger on his wife, because for a few seconds he really considered it. He could still imagine the look in her eyes after she stabbed him and he grabbed the gun. There wasn't a doubt in his mind that she wouldn't have hesitated had the shoe been on the other foot with her being the one holding the gun.

"Crazy bitch." Dax said to himself, as he picked up his glass and swallowed the double shot in one big gulp.

By midnight, Mia had been driving for more than 6 hours and she felt like a pro had she zipped through the city streets. She was glad she had decided to stay in her own city. The boy Quan hadn't lied when he said it would be a busy night and as the knot in Mia's bra got bigger, she wouldn't have it any other way. She began to have fun meeting new people and running into familiar faces while making money, she started relaxing and blasting her music between customers.

She turned her music down as she pulled up to a small house on record street on the eastside.

"Nah turn that shit up." Someone said, as they

opened the passenger side door, before sliding in.

"Shit you came out of nowhere." Mia said, looking around the street to see if anybody else was outside.

"They got Ms. King driving the cabs hmm." The guy said as he closed his door, and locked eyes with Mia.

Mia leaned back into her door, looking at the mystery man with a frown. She examined him but didn't recognize him. He was the same caramel complexion as she was with a tiny red broken heart tattoo under his right eye and two tear drops under the other eye. She could tell her was nicely built underneath his brown and green plaid button up shirt. He had his brown fitted cap to the back, with jeans and a pair of beef and broccoli Timbs. The smell of his cologne mixed with marijuana smoke had the entire cab lit up.

"How you know me?" Mia finally asked, as she turned away and shifted the car back to drive.

"I don't know you, know you, I just know of you." The guy said.

"Oh okay," Mia said, it was common for gossip to travel around the town so that was nothing new. "What's your name?"

"Ransom." He said, before he pulled out his ringing phone.

"And I know ya name because I know all your peoples." He said, sliding the phone back in his pocket.

"Your mom Corrie knows me, ask her bout me. I know your aunt Leena, your sister Cali, all ya'll." He said, looking over at Mia.

"Ms. King, Ms. King, you were always my favorite, ya little ass. Every time I would hear stories about you, you were on that gangsta shit." Ransom said, laughing.

"Ayo." Mia shook her head, she couldn't help but laugh at the last line.

"So you're going down Nanicoke road right?" Mia asked him.

"Yeah, but I'm not staying I'm running in and out and I know this is going to take up like a hour of your time but I gotchu." He said, pulling out a wad of cash.

That was all Mia needed to see and hear. He could've told her to drive him across the bay bridge and she would have as long as he was paying. That's what she was driving for.

By the end of Mia's shift, Ransom was still in Mia's cab, after making several stops all across town, he was finally getting dropped off.

"Alright so what's your cab number, so I can request you for tomorrow." He said, leaning down into the door after he stepped out.

"Six." Mia said, with a sigh, it was after 3a.m. and she was exhausted and ready to go to sleep.

"Say less." He said, peeling off three 50's and two 20-dollar bills before handing them to Mia and closing the door.

Mia counted what he had gave her and was surprised by how much he paid. He had went to several places but it wouldn't even had cost him half of what he gave her. She liked Ransom he kept her laughing and he was looking out, she exhaled a sigh of relief as she pulled away. She rode in silence to the gas station.

It had indeed been a successful night but reality hit her like a ton a bricks as she headed back to the only place she had to lay her head. She dreaded the thought of going back to the roach motel and for a second she contemplated taking her money and buying a better room at a hotel that was more to her liking but that would only take from her newly acquired stash and push her further back from her goal because if she could she'd be at the Hampton in a heartbeat. But at that rate she would never be able to save. So she decided that it would be best to thug it out. After getting the gas she headed back to base to swap cars, pick up the kids from Aunt Mary's and call it a night.

Chapter 27

Mia

The next afternoon after dropping the kids off Mia walked into the office and was greeted by Gary.

"What's up Mia, I hope you are ready for tonight because tonight is the real money maker." He said, removing his Newport from his mouth as Mia approached his desk.

"I thought yesterday was the money maker?" Mia said confused.

"Friday's are cool but on Saturday's everybody goes out to the bars to get drunk which means they all need rides home and there's normally a lot of extra tipping." Gary said.

The way the cigarette dangled between his lips as he talked from the side of his mouth reminded Mia of Dax as she watched him.

"And I don't know what you were doing in that cab yesterday but keep it up because you had several customers requesting cab 6. I told them you don't come in until the afternoon shift but you have one person waiting for you to come in." He said, looking through his papers. "Yeah somebody on Record street, they said they would wait for you." He said, looking up from his papers.

Ransom. Mia thought.

"Thanks Gary." Mia said. As he put his cigarette out in a small white ashtray on his desk.

Gary handed Mia the keys to the same car she had from the previous night and waved as she headed out.

Mia pulled up to where she had dropped Ransom off less than 12 hours before and gave her horn two slight taps.

She tried not to stare as she peeped his outfit after he slid out the door a couple minutes later wearing a pair of blue and grey 3's with a grey Jordan jogging sweatsuit, and the matching blue and grey Chicago bulls' baseball cap.

"M beezy!" Ransom said, after he hopped into the passenger seat and began to rub his hands together.

Mia chuckled at the newly acquired nickname.

"What's up Mr. Ransom." Mia said, looking at him as his cologne invaded her nostrils. "What is your real name?"

"Why do you want to know my government?" Ransom asked, turned his fitted cap to the back.

"You know mine!" Mia said, with a frown as she pulled off. "We spent all that time riding together lastnight and I don't even know your name."

"You do know my name, Ms. King. I have 3 stops to make today." Ransom said, before leaning his seat all the way back.

"Ayo. I'm not complaining or anything but why don't you have a car?" Mia asked, looking him up and down. She knew he had the money for a vehicle.

"Who said I don't have a car?" Ransom asked with a scowl.

Mia was confused as she looked at Ransom.

"You know what, I ain't asking you nothing else." Mia said, turning up the radio.

The pair rode in silent the whole trip making subtle glances at one another. Ransom told her where to go and Mia ignored him after she caught him eyeing her as she drove and vibed to her music.

Ransom peeled off a hundred-dollar bill and a fifty after he arrived at his final destination. He climbed out of the car and leaned down and looked at Mia.

"Rashaad Ms. King, my government is Rashaad." Ransom said.

"Rashaad what?" Mia asked.

"Rashaad Banks." He said, before closing the door.

By 11:30pm Mia could see the difference between her Friday shift versus the Saturday shift almost every passenger she had picked up had been heavily intoxicated and practically handing her all the money in their pockets as they paid her.

Mia pulled up to Prince Street on the southside, which was a diverse area of working-class people. She pulled in front of the house and an older man who looked to be in his early 60's came strolling out of the front door wearing a baseball cap that said, "Vietnam Veteran" on it.

"How are you doing young lady?" He said, as he climbed into the backseat.

"I'm good, how are you?" Mia asked, turning around to look at him.

"I'm doing lovely, I go meet my friends every Saturday night over on North Park Drive." He said, as he shut his door.

Mia never heard of the street he was referring to and decided to put it into her phone gps.

"It's not far, right around the corner. But young lady I have to tell you, I've never seen you driving before and I hope you are being careful. A young female driving alone, this late, might not be the best idea. When I have encountered females driving the night shift they usually have a brother or a male friend riding with them in the passenger." The man advised.

"Thank you, but I'm okay. This is just a temporary little hustle." Mia said, looking over her shoulder at the man.

"Are you in school?" He asked.

"I stopped going with Covid when everything got shut down but I'm going back soon." Mia said.

"Yeah, you do that, because this ain't no place for a woman. Carrying cash too hmmp!" The man continued.

"Get you a little taser." He said, pointing to Mia.

Mia was happy when they arrived at his destination, he was nice but he repeated himself multiple times and Mia understood the first time.

"Alright, young lady remember what I told you now. I'm Leroy by the way." The man said as he opened his door to climb out.

"Alright Mr. Leroy I gotchu, and I do have a blade in my bag." Mia said.

"Aw shit girl they illegal." Leroy said laughing, as he passed her a twenty. "Keep the change young lady."

Mia shrugged and he closed the door.

Her next stop was on Camden Avenue. When a bunch of girls headed towards her cab she wondered where they all thought they were going to fit. She counted at least 7 girls under her breath.

"Hello! Me and my friends want to stop at the cookout and then go back to our place." One of the girls leaned down to say to Mia.

"All of ya'll are not going to fit." Mia said, with her eyebrow raised.

"We do this all the time we always fit." Another said.

Mia shrugged, before they all squeezed into the backseat piling onto each others laps.

"Ya'll are tripping." Mia said, as she turned around in her seat to 6 girls packed in like a can of vienna sausages.

The main girl climbed in the front and looked at Mia.

"You're like really pretty." She said, turning to face Mia.

Mia looked over at the blonde-haired blue-eyed bomb shell, truth be told she was probably the same age as Mia or older. She had shoulder length hair with crimps and an American eagle sweater, white tee shirt, jeans and a pair of white chuck taylors with the laces tied tight as hell.

"Thanks, you are too." Mia said, they were her age but living completely different lives than her. Here they were living the college life leaving parties and having fun while she had 2 kids at home driving a cab to survive and living out of a motel. *Damn life is crazy.* Mia thought.

After taking the girls to get their food and pulling up to their vast house, her new friend who's name she found out was Taylor pulled out a crisp hundred-dollar bill handed it to Mia and waved good-bye.

"Cab 6 is clear." Mia said, into the radio.

She thought about how it would feel to live like those girls for a second but was snapped back into reality when she heard Gary's voice come through the radio.

"You have a customer at the green turtle in front of the mall. The daughter called but it's going to be a white male in his 50's that you pick up." Gary said.

"Okay cool." Mia said into the radio.

"I mean, 10-4." She still needed to get used to the radio lingo.

Mia pulled up to the green turtle to a white male with his arms folded wearing a green ralph lauren polo shirt with tan khaki's and some suede penny loafer's. The girl standing next to him, held his jacket in one hand and smiled and waved at Mia with the other as she pulled up.

"Hi, this is my dad can you take him to Arden Drive it's right down the highway, behind the state police barracks." She said to Mia.

Mia could see the Mercedes key fog she was holding and looked around the parking lot, she spotted a brand-new white Mercedes Benz AMG CLA45 Coupe sparkling under the moonlight in the corner of the parking lot.

"Yeah, I would take him home, but me and my friends are headed to Ocean city to a bonfire party and we are already pretty late." She said, when she noticed Mia looking at her dad's car.

"Yeah, it's fine I'll take him." Mia said.

"I'll call you tomorrow dad. Mom is waiting for you." The girl said, as she opened the back door for her dad.

"Alright, let's get you home." Mia said, looking over her shoulder after he climbed in and shut the door.

The man pulled out his iphone and didn't reply.

Mia decided to follow his lead and not say anything.

After a few moments of awkward silence Mia could feel his eyes burning a hole through the side of her head.

She turned to look at him and he tilted his head and exhaled.

"You know?" He said, "You're nice looking for a black girl."

Does he think that's a compliment? Mia thought.

She frowned her face at the thought and continued to drive.

"You smell nice and I bet you can cook. I love fried chicken." The guy said, closing his eyes.

"Ay yo." Mia said, under her breathe.

Mia turned right at the light in front of the police barracks and traveled down a road she had never actually been on. The homes were beautiful with huge yards and manicured grass. *I can't wait to get me one of these, I'm going to go register back in school asap.*

"I'm retired state police. 35 years." He said, interrupting Mia's thoughts.

Mia turned to look at him again and noticed he had scooted closer to her in the middle of the back seat.

"Let me know which house is yours." She said, after she made a right onto Arden Drive.

"It's the last house on the left, you will see a black Ford F-250 in the driveway." He said.

"Are you mixed? You have nice hair." He said, leaning in between the two seats.

Mia pulled up to his house and slammed on the breaks, causing him to jerk forward onto the middle console.

"You're home." Mia said, with the fakest smile she could muster. She turned to face him and got a better look at his face. He had the typical buzz cut with the short hair on the top and the faded sides, that reminded Mia of the majority of police officers or the average macho white guy. His facial hair was completely shaved off leaving only his silver eyebrows. He smelled like a mixture of aftershave and tequila.

He dug into his pocket and pulled out his tan leather wallet and removed a small stack of bills folded in half with a gold clip holder.

He looked at Mia and raised his eyebrows as he showed her the money. He had large bags sitting underneath his dark blue eyes.

"What the fuck you-" Mia attempted to say.

"You're one of the cute ones." He said, before grabbing Mia's shoulders and pulling her closer to him.

"A little kiss." He said, putting his large hand behind her head.

Mia was stuck with her mouth open until she saw him stick his tongue out as he pulled her face closer to his. She quickly shifted in her seat and thrushed her elbow into his chest as hard as she could.

"UGHH!" He said, instantly putting his left hand over his chest.

"Old ass gone give yourself a heart attack. Get the fuck on with that shit." Mia said, hoping he would get out before anything got out of hand.

"You black bitch! Thank your lucky stars I'm retired." He said through gritted teeth.

"Man, I don't give a fuck." Mia said, as she watched him unclip his money and grab a fifty-dollar bill. He crumbled it up in his hand and threw it at her before climbing out of the car and slamming the door, still holding his chest.

Mia grabbed the crinkled up bill and straightened it out. She watched him walk up to his cape cod style home. "This nigga crazy."

"Cab 6 is clear." Mia said, into the radio, before bussing a U-turn.

Leroy was right, I'm going to get me a taser from the flea market tomorrow.

Chapter 28

Dax

A few days later Spook, Dre and Kion were looking at Dax like he lost his fucking mind as he talked. They were sitting in the living room of Kion's new girlfriend's crib out in Pemberton apartments.

"Ya'll think I'm bullshittin but I'm trying to tell ya'll some good shit. I'm a freemason now, and I'm highly connected. They told me it's my job to cleanse the streets for all the real niggas." Dax said, as he held a notebook and a pen.

"This nigga man. Don't tell me you been smoking that K2 spice shit again nigga. It got you buggin in this mothafucka bro." Spook said.

"Nah I'm getting my list together now. This is some real shit." Dax said, looking at the blue gel pen and yellow writing pad he was holding.

Dre and Kion looked at each other.

"Come on bro we already never hear from these two nigga's right here." Spook said, pointing at Dre and Kion. "You scaring these niggas."

"Alright, ya'll think I'm playing. Just wait." Dax said, dropping the pad.

"D man why don't you ride in the cab with your wife. Everybody talking about how she damn near got attacked the other night driving in that bitch by herself." Dre said, changing the subject.

"Hell yeah, Mia think shit is sweet til one of these little niggas fuck around and rob her." Kion said.

"I think her being your wife is the only thing saving her." Dre said, looking at Dax.

"Yeah they saying sis got that bitch bussin though. Taking everybody money." Spook said.

"Why the fuck ya'll ain't been tell me? I probably would've been hopped in that bitch with her." Dax said.

"Don't get too cocky nigga, ya hand just now starting to heal. Ya'll two can't even be around each other without blows being thrown." Spook said, getting into his fighting stance, punching the air while laughing.

"You right, I ain't fucking with Mia." Dax said, examining the scabbed wound in the palm of his hand. "I got bigger shit to handle."

Mia sat in her cab parked at base as she waited for calls to come through the radio. It was a slow Wednesday and she had already been sitting for 45 minutes as she sat on the phone talking to her sister Cali.

"I'm telling you sis that nigga wanted some black coochie! And it was ridiculous because he was clearly racist!" Mia said into her phone.

"Yes!! Just like back in the days the slave owners couldn't keep their hands off them black girls." She continued.

"Based to Cab 6." Mia heard Gary's voice through the radio.

"Alright sis, well me and the kids will be up there soon to visit. I have over a thousand saved and I'm about to start putting in applications to apartments then we'll up there." Mia said.

"Alright I got to go." She said, she couldn't wait to see her sister.

"Cab 6." Mia said, after hanging up with Cali.

"It took you long enough, look your boyfriend is waiting on Lake street for you." Gary said, with a chuckle.

Mia knew he meant Ransom and she was actually happy he was calling, she felt safe riding with him plus she knew him being in her cab meant easy fast money. The situation in the cab with the ex-cop had Mia paranoid. She had went and bought a pink taser but it didn't really put her mind at ease. Riding with Ransom was when she felt the safest in the cab.

"10-4." Mia said, into her mic as she pulled out of the parking lot and down the street.

She spotted him standing outside of lake street park wearing all black.

"What are you doing stand out here looking like the grim reaper?" Mia asked, after she pulled up on him.

"Sometimes you got to be on that. But look I need

you to take me to Catherine street real quick and I'll call you back here in like 2 hours and ride with you for a while." He said, pulling the black ski mask down from his mouth.

Mia was disappointed he was getting in and out so fast on a slow day but she didn't tell him that.

"I gotchu." Mia said.

"Base to cab 6." Gary said, as Mia made a right onto west main street.

"Alright M Beezy. I'm going to call you." Ransom said, hopping out the cab without paying.

She started to say something but thought of all the times he over paid. He had paid her enough to get 100 free rides down the street.

"Cab 6." Mia said.

"You got a call to Pemberton manor apartments. They requested you specifically, but they didn't say where they were going." Gary said.

"Alright 10-4." Mia said.

Mia pulled in the apartment complex and passed the empty security guard booth at the entrance.

She drove slowly as she looked, the parking lot was mostly empty was she could see people smoking in groups on the steps inside of various buildings. She passed the pool and thought she was tripping when she spotted Dax to her left waving her down.

"Hoe my gosh." Mia said, out loud.

"If you called me, I ain't for no bullshit." Mia said, after she rolled her window down and watched Dax walk to the passenger side.

"Unlock the door." Dax said, as he pulled on the door handle.

Mia unlocked the door and inspected Dax from head to toe. He didn't look like his normal well-manicured self, he looked rough with his scruffy beard and black nike sweat pants with food stains on the front.

"So what's up?" Mia asked, looking over at him.

"What the hell you mean, what's up? I'm going to ride with you. I'm your husband." Dax said.

Boy please. Mia thought. *I'm two seconds from running to the courthouse to file them papers.*

"Cab 6 is clear." Mia spoke into the mic.

"You can pick up right around the corner on Marine Road." Gary said.

"10-4." Mia said.

"You sound like the police." Dax said, watching Mia.

Mia ignored him and turned the radio up.

"What the fuck you ignoring me for? You crazy I'm the one that got stabbed. I should be the mafucker mad." Dax said, lifting up his wounded hand.

"Let's not forget *what*, I stabbed you for." Mia said, cutting her eyes at him.

"I'm saying though, I'm here to help you out. Nigga's is ready to rob you, sounds like rape you and some more shit." He continued.

"Alright now you dragging it." Mia said, pulling the pink taser out of her door and flipping the switch to turn it on.

She pressed the button on the side making it come to life with lightening sounds of electricity causing Dax to jump back in his seat.

"You should know I ain't going like that." Mia said, with a smirk.

"Oh I know! Put that mothafucker away. Let me stay on your good side." Dax said, shaking his head. He knew she would use the taser on him if they got fighting and she was around it.

Mia put the taser back, before she busted a u-turn in the parking lot.

Dax watched Mia as she drove the taxicab, he couldn't help but feel complete admiration for his wife. A stranger would never be able to tell what she had been through by looking at her.

"My little mama." Dax said, closing his eyes. He was high and feeling good.

"I'm about to pick these people up. Don't be in here nodding off yo." Mia said, nudging Dax's elbow sitting on the center console.

"I'm good yo. Listen wifey, I haven't seen you in a couple weeks but listen, I'm plugged in to some deep shit now and you gone be straight. I just have to handle something." He said, as he straightened up in his seat.

Mia stopped in front of the house she was supposed to pick up at and watched as a lady with two small kids came out of the front door.

Mia looked at Dax and waited for him to elaborate on what he said but he never did, instead he pulled out a small notebook and began to write something that looked like a list.

An hour later Dax and Mia had picked up a few people but mostly rode in silence as Mia rapped her songs in between customers.

"Base to cab 6." Gary's voice came in.

"Cab 6." Mia said.

"Your favorite person is waiting back on Catherine Street." Gary said.

"10-4." Mia said, looking over at Dax who she knew would be waiting for an explanation.

"Who the fuck is your favorite person?" He said, glaring at her.

"A customer that has spent a lot of money that's who." Mia said, tilting her head. *While you were nowhere to be found,* she thought to herself.

As she pulled onto Catherine and honked the horn, she wondered what Ransom's reaction would be after seeing Dax but she figured it wouldn't be much because if he knew as much about her as he claimed, he had to know she was married to Dax.

Mia looked at Dax and hoped he wouldn't act a fool as Ransom approached the car.

"What's up wit it?" Ransom said, after he opened the passenger back door and slid inside.

"Ain't shit." Dax said, turning around to face Ransom.

"But yo' I'm hearing that you been this big spender in this cab but you know Mia's my wife?" Dax asked, nodding towards Mia.

Mia turned and looked at the two men as they had their exchange.

"Yeah, I know." Ransom said, pulling out a wad of cash from his pocket. "I'm just looking out."

"As long as you know nigga." Dax said, turning back around.

"I'm just going to meet somebody at that laundromat in Fruitland Mia, you can drop me off." Ransom said.

The trio rode in silence the entire ride there with Dax cutting his eyes at her every few minutes. Mia knew he was just waiting for Ransom to get out the car.

Ransom leaned forward in his seat and gave Mia four twenty's as she pulled up to the laundromat.

"Thanks." Mia said, taking the money.

Ransom winked at Mia after they made eye contact and hopped out of the car.

"That old ass nigga's trying to fuck you Mia. And you stupid feeding into it. Taking this nigga's money." Dax said, as soon as Ransom climbed into a blacked out QX-80 Infinity truck.

"Cab 6 is clear." Mia said, into the mic while looking at Dax.

"You can pick up at the apartments around the corner on Poplar Street." Gary said.

"10-4." Mia said, still watching Dax.

"Nah I really see what the fuck is going on. You want to drive cabs to find you a new man, huh? Fucking blowing my high." Dax said, pulling out a cig.

"You act like I gave him my number or I talk to him outside of work! Listen yo, I'm struggling living out of motels with our two kids and you ain't no help so call it what you want!!" Mia said, as she pulled out into the traffic on route 13.

"Matter fact, you don't have to ride in this mothafucker with me because I didn't ask you to! I'm good! You got in here yourself and now your mad because somebody is looking out and overpaying? Make it make sense! You should be thankful somebody is helping to get your wife and kids out the mothafucking motel, cuz you ain't!!" Mia yelled.

"Nah fuck all that! Remember how you used to hate Percy with a passion? Well, this nigga is Percy times 10. And he's married that was his wife in that truck! Out here giving money away." Dax said. *The nigga just wants to see if he can fuck my wife. Slick, sheisty mothafucker. I don't think it's to many bitches around the city that he hasn't fucked.* Dax thought. He and Ransom had a history of fucking with a lot of the same girls around the way, but he couldn't tell Mia that.

"But what you're not understanding is that, none of that has shit to do with me." Mia said, even though she was a little surprised that he was married. He never wore a wedding ring but like the pot calling the kettle black, neither did she.

"How much did he give you?" Dax asked, he needed the money to buy some more pills and possibly weed.

"Why?" Mia asked with a frown, he hadn't contributed a dollar or even stayed with her in the roach motel, so why was he counting her pockets.

"Because I'm trying to get some weed and percs that's why." He said, looking at her like she had three heads.

"Man what? Why would I," she said, as she steered the car with one hand and held her other hand over her chest, "give you the money I need to get me and the kids a place to stay, for some drugs?"

Dax was getting madder by the second as he thought about Ransom. He knew he had handed Mia at least $60 and that would've been enough to get him what he needed for the night. He wasn't asking for all of her savings, just the money she had just received from that nigga.

"Well look, after you drop these next people off. We need a figure a way to rob this nigga." Dax said, looking at Mia with a straight face.

"You are fucking crazy." Mia said, with a frown.

"Either give me the money or we're going to go get all that." Dax said. "I needs that!"

Mia shook her head at Dax's crazy mentality, there was no fucking way she would go rob the main mothafucker that was helping her more than he even probably knew. Fuck no.

"I'm about to drop you off." Mia said, shaking her head.

"Give me the money." Dax said.

"Nope." Mia said, shaking her head.

Dax was done talking to Mia. He reached over as she attempted to make the turn onto Poplar Street and reached into the front of her shirt, in search of her folded up money that she slipped in her bra.

"Yo, let it the fuck go!" Mia yelled, steering the car with her thighs, as she tried to grab Dax's hand and grab the taser at the same time.

"POW!"

Not wanting her to get ahold of the taser Dax cocked back and knocked Mia's brains loose so violently that blood began to slowly pour from her right ear. She grabbed her head with both hands causing herself to completely lose control of the car. The taxi veered off to the left and slammed into the ditch on the side of the road.

Mia and Dax both jerked forward when the cab came to an intense holt into the gutter.

"You stupid ass bitch." Dax said, snatching the money with one hand as he opened his door with the other. He had to ram his shoulder into the door multiple times for it to open.

"Leaving your dumb ass right here." He continued.

Mia's head felt like it was about to explode, the sharp throbbing pain radiating from her ear indicated that this was the hardest he had ever hit her. She opened her eyes and grimaced after she saw the blood covering the palm of her right hand.

His voice sounded muffled as if she was

underwater, but she could still hear him cussing at her as he took her money and climbed out of the passenger seat. After all the bad things he had done to Mia over the years, leaving her in a vehicle that was stuck in a ditch after possibly busting one of her eardrums all over some money took the cake. She closed her eyes as she tried to shake off the pain in her head and eardrum.

"Word of advice Mia, any nigga that would get you to risk your freedom, smuggling drugs into prisons for years! For their benefit, never gave a fuck about you or the child you could potentially be taken away from."

She shook her head at the thought. Reese was right, Dax truly didn't give a fuck about her and it took her all this time to realize it.

She opened her eyes and looked for her phone to call Gary. She hoped this situation wouldn't cause her to be fired.

It didn't take long for Gary to pull up with a tow truck behind him.

"You good Mia?" Gary asked, after he got out of his car.

"I'm cool." Mia said, sitting stationary in a daze.

Gary signaled for the tow truck driver to go ahead and pull the car out of the ditch.

After attaching the hook to the tow hitch the car was pulled out in less than sixty seconds. Gary gave a thumbs up to the driver and he jumped out and unhooked the car.

"There's a flat tire but other than that this ain't shit, you're good Mia." Gary said to her after she got out the car.

"Your ear is blooding girl, are you okay?" He asked her when he saw the blood running down her cheek from her ear.

"I'm okay Gary but I just need to go." Mia said.

Gary didn't know what had transpired but he knew she had to be upset to not finish her shift.

"It's okay, you can take that cab back to base and go ahead home." He told her, pointing to the cab he pulled up in.

Mia decided to not pick the kids up that night as she pulled up to the motel. She knew she would not be able to keep up her usual happy facade in front of Malakai and she didn't want him to see her crying and a mess.

Calling Reese crossed her mind as she walked through the door but she knew she only wanting him to be there for her comfort. He always cheered her up but he deserved to be more than just a shoulder to cry on, so instead she grabbed her bottle of fire ball and her small JBL speaker from the table and went into the bathroom. She picked up her phone and pressed shuffle on her apple music before she picked up the dollar flip flops she bought from old navy. She took a big swig from her bottle before she bit the tag off of her new shower shoes and turned on the shower before she went and stood in front of the mirror. Durk's lyrics from his old 2X album was talking that shit as she stood in the mirror staring carefully at her own reflection. *"Been there when nobody was there, it was dark too."* She turned her back on the mirror and leaned on the sink as the tears began to fall.

Chapter 29

Mia woke up in the motel bed alone and starred up at the nasty brown stain on the ceiling. *"I know you're a smart young lady but remember this, when you've had enough baby girl trust me, you will know. It'll be like a light switch being flipped in your brain."* Mrs. Pat was talking some real shit, and she hated it took so long for her to finally wake up but that switch she spoke about had officially been flipped. It was time to focus on herself and move forward. She couldn't even remember what being single felt like but in her mind, it was time to find out. Mia sat up in the bed and grabbed her phone. She went straight to her recent call log and dialed Gary.

"Hey Gary, I'm not coming in today. I have a lot to handle." Mia said.

"I understand Mia." Gary said, on the other end of the phone.

"I appreciate it Gary." Mia said, before she hung up. She got up from the bed and connect her phone to the Bluetooth, she selected Nicki Minaj's remix to Welcome to the Party before heading into the bathroom and grabbing her toothbrush. She looked at herself in the mirror as she rapped along and brushed her teeth.

Music always put her in a better mood, and Nicki Minaj had a way of reminding her that she was that bitch.

"This nigga got me fucked up." Mia said, pointing to herself in the mirror after spitting into the sink. She turned the music up on full blast and knew it was going to be a good day.

Dax rode in the passenger seat with Spook, Dre and Kion. He was watching his review mirror as they pulled out of Jersey heights.

"I'm telling ya'll, when we pulled out of the driveway, this white car pulled out too." Dax said, watching the car in the mirror.

Spook looked in his mirror and saw Dre and Kion frowning and shaking their heads.

"Chill bro, that's an old ass man." Spook said, slowing down to get a good look at the car as it rolled up on them.

"What the fuck are you breaking for nigga, I'm telling you!" Dax yelled, grabbing Spooks coat arm while still watching the car.

"Nigga I swear this looks like them cartel niggas bro!"

"In a Buick?" Spook asked, causing Dre and Kion to fall out laughing. *Unfuckin-believeable*, Spook thought.

"Ya'll niggas going to be some dead niggas. Keep on thinking shit is a game out here." Dax said.

Spook stopped at the stop sign, before making a

left turn. He watched in his review mirror and saw the white Buick make a right turn in the opposite direction.

"See bro, the nigga went that way." Spook said, looking over Dax and nodding in the direction of the car behind them.

"You can take me back to P block." Kion said.

Spook was still looking over at Dax.

"Bro, I think it's time to chill with the percs. We both on the run and you ain't gone make it out here this paranoid." Spook told him, he had noticed that Dax hadn't been his normal self for awhile but now he was to the point where he didn't care about his appearance and hygiene for a few days at a time. He was losing it.

"I'm a grown ass man nigga." Dax said, getting offended, "the fuck you think you talking to? Ain't gone make it? Nigga if I don't make it, it's because one of ya'll niggas ratted." Dax said, sitting up in his seat and looking at each of them in the car.

"I taught ya'll niggas everything you know and I ain't gone make it?" Dax asked.

"Look there they go again, ya'll niggas keep sleeping gone fuck around and die!" Dax said, looking in the review mirror as a white dodge charger approached.

That's a completely different car, Spook thought.

"Them cartel niggas on me because I didn't handle that." Dax said, pulling out the notepad he had been carrying for two days in the inside pocket of his coat.

It was after noon by the time Mia made it the community college to reapply. She had already been to the courthouse to pick up divorce papers. Instead of the delaying the process, she decided to fill the packet out in the car so she could just be done with it. She also went to print out her bank statements before going to apply for several apartments around the city. She had put on her loose-fitting Kappa sweatsuit with her black uggs and a black faux fur ankle length coat. She was feeling good and decided she wanted to celebrate the day. She headed back to the hotel, to pack up anything of value before she went to the office.

"Khan my man." Mia said, with a smile as she walked into the motel office. After being at the motel for a couple weeks, they became acquainted and learned each other's names.

"Mia." Khan said, as she approached the desk.

"Khan, so I'm about to go to see my family for a day or two. I took the majority of our stuff out, but can you keep the room for me?" Mia asked, him as she placed her pink nike gym bag down.

"Of course, the room is paid for." Khan said with a shrug.

"Thank you, see you when I get back. Hopefully I'll be out of here real soon." Mia said, as she picked up her bag and headed for the door. She turned around and used her back to open the door and saw Khan hold up both of his hands, crossing his middle and index fingers.

"Fingers crossed." Khan said, as Mia walked out.

Mia headed to her truck and put the rest of her belongings in the trunk. She just had to fill up her tank and just had to go pick up the kids from Aunt Mary's house.

Two and a half hours later, Mia pulled up to Cali's house on Washington Boulevard on the southside of Baltimore.

"Come on Kai Kai." She said, as she hopped out and grabbed her coat. She opened the back door to unstrap Teal who was fast asleep, before the three of them headed to the front door.

Tap, tap, tap

Mia screamed when Cali opened the door with a huge belly protruding through her silk pajamas.

"Oh my gosh!" Cali yelled, "Ya'll are here!!!"

Cali and Mia hugged, squishing Teal in the process.

"Awww look at my niece!" Cali said, after she finally let Mia go.

"Hey Aunt Cali." Malakai said, as he covered his grin.

"Heyyy Kai!" She said, before she bent down to hug Malakai. She took the baby from Mia after she let him go.

"Girl let us in, it's cold as fuck." Mia said, pushing past her to get inside.

Mia walked into the living room, Cali had a jumbo navy-blue suede sectional with a grey, tan and blue area rug, along with various matching portraits and vases.

"Nah, this is fly. You know blue is my shit. Me and my hubby Pop Smoke." Mia said, laughing.

"Malakai do you want to play the game upstairs, Zay is up there playing." Cali said, before Malakai bolted towards the steps.

"What's all this noise down here?" Zay came down with Black behind him.

"What's up Zay! I know sis is pregnant but I need somebody to go to the liquor store with me. I just filed for my divorce, and I came to turn up." Mia said, looking from Cali to Zay.

Zay turned and looked at Black before they both laughed and Black stepped forward.

"I gotchu Slim." Black said. "It's one right next door on the corner, we can go there or we can go to King's liquors they got a drive through."

"Ya'll have a liquor store with a drive through?" Mia said, with her eyebrows raised.

Black laughed at her and looked back at Zay.

"What?" Mia asked, putting her hand on her hip.

"Nothing really you just sound country as hell, just like your sister." Black said, nodding towards Cali.

"These niggas won't let that country shit go." Cali said, as she rocked Teal from side to side.

"Alright well, I ain't know the liquor store was right there. I can go by myself for real." Mia said, pulling her coat up onto her shoulders.

"Nah, let's go to King's they cheaper anyway."

Black said, heading to the back door.

Mia looked at Zay and squinted her eyes, as she walked past him.

"You good Mia, that's my mans." Zay said, laughing.

"Ya'll look just alike." Mia heard him say to Cali as she headed towards the door.

"Cali my keys are on the couch, ya'll get Teal's diaper bag." Mia said, as she headed out the door and saw Black's Acura TLX parked directly behind Zay BMW X5 in the alley.

Mia looked out the window after she climbed into the passenger seat. She really didn't know what to say, the last time she saw Black was over a year ago at the housewarming when she was crying and carrying on.

"What do ya'll be listening to, on that side of the bridge?" Black asked as he pulled up to a red light and scrolled through the music in his phone.

"We listen to the same stuff ya'll listen to." Mia said, with a frown.

"You act like it's a whole nother world." She continued.

"Nah it definitely is, I used to work over there." Black said laughing.

Mia looked out the window at the young boys trying to make money by cleaning people's windshields at the redlights and all the trash lining the streets. They had junkies on the corners leaning and nodding out.

"You might be a little bit right. Ya city wild." Mia

said, still looking out the window.

"This ain't my city." Black said, looking over at her.

"What? So where are you from?" Mia asked, confused.

"I was born in DC but technically I'm from Riverdale. We moved to Baltimore when I was in high school." Black said. "Where you from? Or should I say where were you born?" He asked.

Mia paused and laughed before she looked over at him.

"I was born here." She blurted out.

"In Baltimore?" Black asked, puzzled.

"Yeah." Mia said, she studied the side of his face as he drove, his accent and velvety chocolate skin was intriguing to Mia. She looked at his large hands as one gripped the steering wheel and the other gripped his phone, his fingernails were clean. She couldn't stand when niggas had black dirty fingernails, she would've been ready to get out the car but nah, he was clean. His car was clean and he smelled too good. She looked down at her own phone, she knew she would more than likely start talking big shit to him after she started drinking.

"Oh, so this is your city." Black said, nodding his head.

"Nah, I'm from the bury." Mia said.

"Nah this ya' city." Black said, looking over at Mia as she started laughing.

"Just play your music, let me hear what ya'll listen

to in Riverdale." Mia said.

Black smiled as he shook his head and picked his phone back up. Mia looked out the window as they took an exit onto 695 while I Am Northeast's "*Swerve*," began to play through the speakers.

"Let's go inside, I don't drink like that but I'm going to celebrate with you since Cali pregnant." Black said, as he pulling into the parking lot.

"Alright bet." Mia said, laughing as she removed her seat belt.

Mia got a good look at Black as he held the door open for her. She had to look up at him so he was at least 6 foot easy, he had on a pair of crispy white and black Jordan 5's, and a pair of black G-star raw jeans with the matching hoodie. He was her type to a T, clean, dark and handsome.

He smiled at Mia when their eyes meet. She laughed knowing he saw her checking him out.

"Chill yo." Mia said, laughing as she walked into the door.

It was definitely going to be harder than she thought to just focus on herself and remain single.

By 10 p.m. Mia was absolutely lit, Teal was asleep in the spare room and Malakai was upstairs on the game.

"We gotta run somewhere real quick." Zay told Cali, as she and Mia sat on the couch catching up.

"Ya'll want italiano's down the street? The food is good." Black asked Cali and Mia.

“For sure.” Cali said, laughing. “Let me get the mild wings with the fries.”

“Aight, we just going to get a bunch of stuff. Pizza for Malakai too.” Black said.

“The food is good Mia.” Cali said to Mia after Zay and Black went out the back door.

Mia was feeling good and decided now would be a good time to fill everybody in on what had been going on.

She propped her phone up and decided to do one big group chat on facetime.

She dialed Egypt, Alyssa, Lola, Chanel, Ballow and even Corrie and Keegan all in one. She applied her lip gloss as she waited for them to pick up.

“Mimi!” Lola yelled.

“Lb!!” Alyssa said.

“Sisss!” Ballow said.

“Now I know she must be lit.” Corrie said.

“Sister girl!” Keegan said.

“Are you in Baltimore!? I know not.” Egypt said, when she answered before hanging up abruptly.

“Egypt is crazy but no listen ya’ll!” Mia said, slurring.

“She’s fucked up.” Corrie said, watching Mia.

“She is litt mom. She filed for divorce today though so, so be it.” Cali said, chiming in.

“Yooo!” Lola said.

"Ayyee!!" Chanel said.

"About mothafuckin time!" Corrie said.

"Let's go!" Ballow said.

Everybody began hooting and hollering at once.

Mia fell out laughing as she watched and listened to everyone's reaction.

"Do ya'll know this nigga left me in a ditch!" Mia yelled.

"Don't wake the baby up Mia." Cali said, holding a baby monitor.

"At Night!" Mia continued to yell, getting up from the couch.

"And he busted my eardrum!!" Mia yelled into her phone.

"Girl what!?"

"Hell naw!" Everyone started yelling.

"Yes! I'm done with hood niggas yo'! But no ya'll let me start from the beginning, when I was still in Georgia. Okay so I get a message from Egypt like Yo Dax is on the run for robbery. I'm like what!! Man fuck no!?"

Chapter 30

Mia

The next morning Mia woke up on Cali's couch and instantly smiled when she saw Egypt on the opposite end, knocked out.

She got up and went straight to the spare room where she found Malakai stretched out on the twin sized bed. Mia went over and placed the cover over him before grabbing her toothbrush out of her gym bag. She went into the bathroom and opened the linen closet and grabbed a rag to wash her face. She frowned as she tried to remember the ending of the previous night. All she could remember was Egypt popping up at the door an hour after hanging up the facetime call and them eating, drinking and catching up.

She brushed her teeth and headed down the hall to Zay and Cali's room. She tapped twice before peeking inside and to her surprise Teal and Cali were wide awake watching t.v.

"Sissss!" Mia whispered, as she looked at Zay who was still asleep with his back to them.

"Thanks for keeping Teal, because lastnight was to lit. Whew." Mia said, as she quietly danced in place.

"Hey mommy's baby." She said leaning down to

Teal.

"I need the practice anyway." Cali said, thinking of her own baby that would arrive next month.

"I had so much fun that I don't remember the ending." Mia said.

"Mmhm, ask Black when he comes." Cali said, giving me the side eye.

Mia bucked her eyes at Cali and smiled.

"Don't get me wrong Mia Black is cool as hell, but he has the female version of Dax for a baby mom. You don't need all that drama." Cali said.

Typical Cali, I can't date anybody. Mia thought.

"Girl I'm about to be a divorced lady, I'm trying to have fun." Mia admitted.

"Black is definitely fun but ol' girl is lifetime movie crazy." Cali said.

"I hear you sis." Mia said, before heading back downstairs.

"Wake up shorty." Mia said, slightly nudging Egypt. She was happy her best friend popped up the night before. They had a ball catching up. Mia already made up her mind she would start coming to Baltimore every other weekend so they could continue to have fun.

"What time is it?" Egypt said, stretching as she sat up and looked for her phone.

"It's almost 11:00." Mia said. "Girl lastnight was just what I needed." Mia said, once again dancing. "We need to go out."

“Shoot, you might as well move on this side of the bridge with me and Cali.” Egypt said, “but I have to go because I didn’t plan on staying, I didn’t bring clothes or anything.”

“I have something you can wear, don’t leave.” Mia said, putting her hand on her arm.

Tap, tap, tap

Mia and Egypt looked at each other before Mia shrugged and Egypt got up to answer.

“Who is it?” She asked.

“It’s Black.” They heard him say on the other side of the door.

“That's your man, he was cool lastnight and he seem like he don't play, so that's right up your alley.” Egypt whispered.

"What was he saying?" Mia whispered, before Egypt snatched the door open.

“What’s up Slim?” Black said to Egypt as he stepped in.

“Alright Mia I’m back, why aren’t you dressed?” Black asked Mia as soon as their eyes met.

“What are you talking about?” Mia asked him confused.

“You were talking cash shit about being a shooter lastnight, I told you we was gone see. You thought I was playing?” Black asked, holding his hands up.

Egypt died laughing as she gathered her belongings.

“We’re going to the gun range.” Black confirmed. “Cali already said she would watch the kids for us. You just need to get dressed.” Black said, sitting on the arm of the couch.

"Oh lord, you gone make my bestfriend worse." Egypt said, watching Mia as she did her little dance before all three of them started laughing.

Dax

A few days later, Dax was laying in the bed with Kizzy when his burner phone started ringing.

"Yooo." He said, after answering.

"Yoo, Mia filed them papers on you D and she used this address. Mercedes opened the packet, knowing damn well it wasn't her business." Spook said, looking at his girl.

"Anything that comes to my house is my business." She said, while rolling her neck.

"What papers?" Dax said, with the phone to his ear as he laid with one arm across his forehead.

"These are divorce papers bro." Spook said.

"Divorce!!?" Dax said, instantly sitting up.

"This bitch must be out her rabbit ass mind. Gone send me divorce papers." He said, as he stood up and started to get dressed.

"What time is it?" Dax said, looking over at the clock on the dresser.

"She's driving that funky ass cab too, oh yeah, i'm bout to catch her. I'm on her ass bro. I'll get up with you." Dax said.

"You knocked her brains loose bro, you had to know it was coming." Spook said, with a chuckle before Dax hung up on him.

"Yo let me use your car Kizzy." Dax said, looking at her.

"I can take you but I don't let nobody drive my car." Kizzy said, rolling her eyes.

"Why the fuck would I bring your stupid ass to find my wife?" Dax asked, snatching her coach bag off her nightstand and grabbing her keys.

"Nigga you're going the fuck to jail." Kizzy said, standing to her feet.

"Aha! You'll be a dead bitch." Dax said, pointing at her before he headed out the front door.

Dax hopped into Kizzy's black Altima, connected his phone to the bluetooth and turned on Kodak's "Killin the Rats," before pulling off.

After riding around aimlessly for a little while he decided to make it easier on himself.

"Ay let me get cab 6 to Thirsty's store." Dax said, into the phone before hanging up.

Less than 20 minutes later, Mia pulled up to the store and put the car in park.

Dax hopped out and headed towards her car. He knew it was fucked up to leave her in the ditch on top of hitting her as hard as he did but it was never as serious as a divorce in his eyes.

"You gone divorce me?" Dax said, as he approached her vehicle with his hands out.

He watched her as she rolled her window down with her top lip up in the air.

"What I disgust you now bitch!?" Dax yelled, standing a couple feet away from her as he scratched his stomach underneath his shirt.

"You chasing me down in a bitch's car?" Mia asked, nodding towards Kizzy's car. "And you wonder why we done?" Mia said, squinting her eyes as she looked up at him.

"We will never be done. We're married!" Dax said.

"Man what!!? You fucked my cousin! You won't leave the drugs alone and you have a hand problem! You better sign them papers." Mia snapped.

"You really got me fucked up but I'll see you in court! It's over. I done moved on." Mia said, rolling her window up before she began to put the car in reverse.

"You moved on? With who?? Niggas in this city know not to fuck with me!!" Dax said, before he spit at the car.

"Go get help! You're foaming at the mouth!!" Mia yelled before she skirted off down Church street.

Mia

The next morning, Mia sat across from the older lady that reminded her of Mrs. Pat from her old job.

"Here are your keys. These two are for the front door, this one is to the laundry room and this one is to the outside storage closet." She said as she handed her the four keys.

Mia had been smiling so much her cheeks hurt. Her, Malakai and Teal would finally have a place to call home. No more staying at the roach motel.

"Thank you so much!" Mia said.

"You're very welcome now let me know if you need anything." The lady said, as Mia stood to leave.

She was in a hurry to go inside the place. She had a lot to do to it before she went to pick up the kids.

She already had her facetime group chat ringing as she put the key in the door to get inside.

"Ayyyyeeee!!!!" Everybody yelled as Mia held the phone up so they all could see the apartment.

"3 bedrooms bookie!!" Mia said, before she bent down and started twerking.

"The housewarming finna be lit!!!!" She continued.

"We'll be over there." Lola said.

"Alright ya'll well, I have the whole truck full of stuff. Love ya'll! I'll call ya'll back!!" Mia said, before hanging up.

She felt butterflies as she stood in the empty apartment. She had to start completely over from scratch, no furniture, dishes, appliances or anything. But she was determined to get it all back, and then some. Never would she ever again let another man drag her down so far. She had received her tax refund just in time and knew exactly what couch and dining room table she wanted. She planned to do the living room in black and pink everything and she could not wait.

Mia gushed with excitement as she made the trips back and forth from the house to her truck. She felt her phone vibrate in her back pocket and saw that an unknown number had sent her a long paragraph. "Man what?" Mia said, out loud to herself as she read the text in her head.

This is Black's babymom and wife! I'm only going to give you one warning to leave my husband the fuck alone! He only wants to fuck you trust me, we've been together for seven years and I've been through this multiple times. Do you really want to be the home wrecker that destroys a happy home? Aren't you married yourself? Yeah, I thought so. I've done my research on you, so bitch don't play with me!!! I'm pregnant right now but that won't stop me from taking that ride to your little town if it really comes to that. Don't make me come put my foot in your country ass hoe!

Mia couldn't believe what she was reading. She was so glad she hadn't fucked his lying no good ass.

Man watch your mouth because your face ain't pregnant. You are welcome to pull up anytime!!!! You really got me fucked up, ask about me!!! But if you've done your research like you say, I'm sure you know what I look like right? So, you should be able to tell that I don't have to steal anybody's man dummy!! Wifeyyy shit only!!! What the fuck I look like being a niggas sidepiece? Thanks for telling me and by all means bitch keep him!!!!!!!!!

The message exchange had Mia seething. How dare this nigga try to play her by having a whole pregnant bitch at home!!!! She scrolled to Blacks name and sent him a message as well.

I just talked to your pregnant babymom/WIFE? Boy you really played! I'm glad she told me but yo' you might want to get her under control being that she's pregnant because if she pulls up in my city… I promise you, I ain't gone think about none of that!!! I won't hesitate to do whatever needs to be done. But other than that fuck you! And no need to text back, you're blocked!!!

Mia blocked him immediately after the message was delivered and slid the phone back into her back pocket. She couldn't believe he had lied, she was lowkey hurt. She was feeling him, he was the perfect gentlemen he hadn't even tried to come onto her after their date. He was funny, he was sexy as hell, he didn't have any social media accounts, she didn't have the guilty feeling she felt with Reese and she had quickly became accustomed to the idea of dating someone outside of her city. With all the drama Dax caused her in their own city, Black was the breath of fresh air Mia wanted and desired. She rolled her eyes, as she began to think back to their date.

Black stood behind Mia as she held onto the Glock aimed at the target 50 feet away.

"Alright so you're going to take your right hand and leave your finger off the trigger until your ready to shoot. But take your bottom three fingers and grip the base of the gun put your thumb right here." He said, guiding her hands with own. "Now take your left hand and put it right here. Alright now you want to find your dominant eye and use it aim. You close your left eye and look down the little notches on the gun. Hold it steady and try to get your target between the two notches before you fire."

"Alright I think I'm ready." Mia said, already having one eye closed as he was talking.

The gun range they went to already gave them a quick safety class so she felt like she had it.

"Alright let's see what you got Killa." Black said, laughing because she was so serious.

Pop, pop, pop, pop

Mia placed the gun down onto the shelf and shifted her weight to one side as she placed her hand on her hip watching Black press the button to reel in the target paper.

Mia's shots weren't in the bull's eye but they were still inside the circles.

"You're a natural." Black said.

Mia watched him as he ripped off Mia's the sheet and put a new sheet in its place, before reeling it back out. He picked up the gun removed the clip and replaced it before getting into the shooting stance.

Pop, pop, pop, pop

Mia could already see that all of his bullets hit right inside the red bull's eye.

"Mmm mmm mmm." Mia said, licking her lips. This nigga is too much, she thought.

Chapter 31

Dax

The next day, Dax paced Kizzy's living room in front of the window as he waited for Spook to pull up.

"This shit is crazy." He mumbled under his breath.

Kizzy sat on her couch watching him, as she had done for the past few hours.

"He's on the way." Dax said, still walking back and forth.

"I need some more molly."

"You've taken more than enough." Kizzy said, leaning on her hand as she shook her head at Dax's disheveled appearance. He had been murmuring to himself a lot while constantly swallowing molly and pain killers. He hadn't taken a shower or tried to touch her since he arrived at her house 2 days previously.

"There he goes." Dax said, before heading out of the front door.

"Damn bro, you alright? You need to just come to my crib and change." Spook said, looking over at Dax after he slid into the passenger seat.

"I'm straight bro." Dax said, "Let's go see Nearee."

Spook looked over at Dax and examined him before he pulled off. He had on the same nike tracksuit he had on when he left Mia in the ditch, he put it back on without it being washed or anything. He had his hands stuffed into his pockets, as his bloodshot eyes stared off towards the windshield.

"I think you really might need to check-in somewhere. You not even moving how you normally would." Spook hated to see Dax in the state he was in.

Dax closed his eyes fighting back tears. He couldn't remember the last time he cried. He clenched his teeth together as he removed his gun from his pocket. He kept the gun low to his lap as he pointed it at Spook.

"What the-"

Pop, pop, pop

Dax hopped out the car and jogged the few blocks back to the few Kizzy's house. Leaving Spook in the car as it slow rolled into the sidewalk and came to a holt by itself.

Mia was in the kitchen cooking, when she heard a knock at her door.

Tap, tap, tap, tap

She went to the door and looked through the peek hole and busted out laughing at Ransom standing on the other side of the door.

"How the hell did you know where I live? We just

got here yesterday." Mia said, after she opened the door.

"Don't much get pass me. It's smells good as shit though. What are you cooking?" Ransom said, inviting himself in, walking past Mia. She trusted him, so she didn't object but it was embarrassing that she didn't have any furniture.

Mia closed the door and locked the dead bolt. Following Ransom to the kitchen.

"Where you been at M-beezy?" Ransom asked Mia, as he lifted the lids to look inside the pots that were on the stove. Mia had never been around Ransom outside of the taxi so she never realized how tall he was. He had to be at least 6'3.

"Boy get out my pots! It's only been one day." She said, with a frown. "I just wanted to have one day to get settled. Which is normal Ransom, I work every day."

"Nah, I know you do." Ransom said, "you should've told me you were moving. You know I would've came and helped you. You good? You need something?" He asked, turning to face her.

Mia had on a white tank top and pink striped pajama shorts.

"I appreciate it, but actually you've done enough. You ain't even know it but I was staying in a fuckin motel this whole time. You over-paying every night, helped me get the spot." Mia admitted, looking around.

"I did know. Like I said, don't much get pass me. But yo' I wanted to ask you what's up with me and you M Beezy?" He asked, leaning on the kitchen counter and folding his arms.

"Ayo, I heard you was married." Mia said with her top lip raised. She was taken aback by the question. Most niggas that knew Dax wouldn't dare ask her out. She was attracted to his boldness but at the same time she knew she would never be able to trust a man like Ransom.

"And? You're married too but we aren't with them." He said, shrugging.

"I'm dating somebody and I filed for my divorce already." Mia said, folding her arms. She thought about the fact that Black played her but kept that part to herself.

"Whoever the nigga is, won't do you better than I will." Ransom said, standing up straight.

Bang, bang, Bang!

"Mia!!" They heard Dax's voice, from the other side of the door.

Bang!

Ransom headed towards the door.

Mia's eyes bucked, "What are you doing!? Don't open it." She whispered.

Random lifted his hoodie to show Mia the gun on his waist.

"No!!" Mia whispered, signaling with her hands. Divorced or not she would never want anything to happen to Dax on account of her.

Bang, bang!!

"I have to, so open the door." Dax mumbled to himself, as he paced in front of Mia's door holding his gun.

Malakai ran out into the living room, holding his PlayStation controller. "Mommy, Teal is moving now. She's waking up."

'Okay Kai Kai, shhhhh." Mia whispered, leaning down to him with her index finger over her lips.

Ransom watched Dax through the peephole.

Dax stopped pacing and tapped the gun on his forehead as he contemplated his options. He pulled the notepad out of his coat pocket and looked down at it. He had a long way to go on his list.

He began to pace again before walking off, throwing the notepad down on the sidewalk.

"Nigga buggin." Ransom said, shaking his head.

Mia peeped out the blinds after silence filled the other side of the door, "he's leaving." She said, breathing a sigh of relief.

"He dropped something out there." Ransom said as he opened the door, before walking out to the sidewalk and picking up the yellow pad Dax dropped.

Mia's phone rang in her back pocket before she answered it. She could smell her rice and cabbage starting to burn in the pot. She walked over to the stove and turned off all the burners, before moving the pan of rice and cabbage to the back burner.

"Hello." Mia said, as she headed to the back room to check on Teal.

"He did what!!?" She yelled, into the phone.

She gently scooped Teal into her arms before

walking to the door. She watched Ransom as he read whatever was in his hand.

Ransom couldn't believe what he was seeing inside the notepad. He recognized almost all the names on the list but only Spook's name was crossed off at the bottom.

Mia's name was the name on top of Spooks.

"This nigga must've gotten ahold of some bad percs." Ransom said, out loud to no one in particular.

Dax walked through the entrance of the emergency doors at the hospital and walked over to the window. He had thrown his gun down the storm drain outside of Mia's apartment.

"How may we help you today?" The lady asked.

"I'm a danger to myself and others." Dax told her.

About 3 hours later Dax woke up in a hospital bed but he didn't remember how he got there. He had one hand handcuffed to the bed and he knew he had to go before the cops showed up. He pulled on the handcuff as he tried to slip his hand out.

"It's okay Mr. Truitt, you were having a psychotic episode. We've given you some Seroquel to treat that as well as some Suboxone for your detox. We found a prescription bottle of Percocet with someone else's name on them. Have you been abusing opioids for while Mr. Truitt?" The Nurse said, leaning over Dax's bed.

"Bitch! Get the fuck out my face and get this handcuff off me." Dax said, before hauling off and punching the nurse as hard as he could in the face.

"That's enough Mr. Truitt. You're not going anywhere." Officer Davis, said stepping into the room as he smiled and chewed his gum.

"Are you alright Sarah?" Another nurse asked rushing in.

"All ya'll bitches gone die fucking with me!" Dax yelled to the top of his lungs.

Epilogue

Dax stood at his cell door, looking through the small window as he waited for commissary call. He had been back at the county jail for a couple months, awaiting his next court date. The Psych meds the jail had him on had finally corrected the chemical imbalance he had when he first arrived. He hated that the whole city was calling him crazy for shooting Spook. The fucked up part about it was that he didn't even remember doing it, but if what they were saying was true about him having half of the city's name on his hit list with Mia included then he couldn't blame them and he also couldn't blame Mia for not answering the phone. He just wanted to apologize to her before their scheduled day in court for their divorce. He still refused to sign the papers. In his mind even though it looked like he came to shoot her, he didn't believe he would of ever done it. To him, she must've been the reason he checked his self in to the hospital in the first place. He could admit that the drugs had him fucked up, trying to harm the ones he loved the most. He was happy when he found out Spook survived but he felt all the more guilty that he was the reason Spook was also booked in the county jail and stuck living with a colostomy bag for the rest of his life.

"Commissary!" The C.O. said as he passed Dax's door pushing the huge cart. Dax couldn't believe he was right back where he started. The State of Maryland had hit him with a slew of new charges including, 1st degree attempted murder for Spook, plus 1st degree robbery with a deadly weapon for Sosa, 1st and 2nd degree assault on the nurse and police officers. They had found the gun and matched the shell casings from the robbery at the hotel with Sosa and to the shell casings left in Spook's car. His public defender also told him that he had confessed to everything after the police had taken him out of the hospital while he was highly medicated. He didn't remember any of it but apparently, they had it all on video. So, he knew right then and there, that they would try to throw the book at him this go around. They had been wanting to bury him and probably would succeed, but on his meds, he was in his right mind and decided that he would still try to beat the case by pleading not guilty by reason of insanity which was actually a fact. Plus, what the officers did was illegal, getting him to confessed when he wasn't competent. If he had a good lawyer he knew they could get that part of the evidence thrown out but if not he already had it in his mind that if he lost at trial, he would just appeal. He doubted they'd give him life. So for the time being he would let Mia go but in his mind she belonged to him, always had and always would.

Mia

"Surprise!!!!" Everybody yelled as soon as Mia opened the front door to walk into Cali's house. It was her 21st birthday and they had the living room completely engulfed with balloons, garland, streamers, fringe curtains and confetti.

"Oh ya'll went crazy on shein huh?" Mia said, smiling.

"Chile please!" Egypt said, rolling her eyes to the ceiling.

"Girl." Cali said, sucking her teeth making everybody bust out laughing.

"I'm just playing ya'll!!!" Mia said, hugging everybody in attendance which of course included, Alyssa, Lola, Ballow and Chanel. She peeped the biggest bottle of fireball she had ever seen on the deserts table and knew she was about to have a fun night.

"We missed you little sis!" Alyssa said.

"I missed ya'll too! We're about to have so much fun! Ya'll ready to turn up? Where the food at?" Mia said, looking around the room.

"All the food is back there."Ballow said, pointing.

"Mom!!!" Mia screamed, when she got to Corrie hiding in the back along with Justin and Keegan.

"Keegan! Justin!! What the fuck!!? Ya'll came all the way from Georgia!?" Mia screamed.

"Hunny we packed up a u-haul last week and came back. We've been staying here with Cali while we wait for our place in Dundulk to be move in ready. We wanted to surprise you." Corri said, as Mia hugged her.

"We're all together again." Mia sang, as she danced.

"I came back for my grandbabies." Corrie said, taking Teal out of Keegan's hands.

"Happy Birthday Slim." Mia heard Black say from behind. She rolled her eyes before turning around. She snatched the number 21 balloons and pink roses he was holding.

"Gee thanks, balloons and cake from a lying piece of shit." Mia said, pointing to the strawberry crunch cake he was holding in his other hand.

"Oh shit." Corrie said, as everybody got quiet and looked at the pair.

"Come here." Black said, grabbing Mia's wrist. She followed him into the kitchen, folding her arms before he pulled out his phone.

"She was lying. She's my baby mother yes. We have two kids but she's not pregnant and we were never married. I moved out last summer and she just won't let it go." Black said, looking Mia in the eyes.

Mia still had her mouth twisted in disgust as she looked at him.

"Alright look at these messages. I asked her why she told you she was pregnant and that we were married, and she replied," Black said, showing Mia his message thread, "that she doesn't know what the fuck I'm talking about. It's right here, look."

Mia was relieved because she really liked him but she didn't show it.

"Now how would I know if Surita?" Mia said, reading the name from his phone, "is really your babymom?"

Black pressed the call button on his phone before placing the call on speaker.

"Alright just listen." He said, as the phone rung.

"Hello." A female answered with a heavy Baltimore accent. Black locked eyes with Mia.

"Okay, what are the kids doing?" Black asked, to prove his point.

"They playing the game, what's up with you?" Surita asked.

"Alright so look, tell the truth Surita. We've been broke up for over a year. Right or wrong, keep it a buck. Never married, none of that shit right?" Black said.

Damnnn, Mia thought as she listened while looking down at the floor.

The phone was silent for a few seconds before they both heard her speak up.

"Both of ya'll bitches gone regret this whole day. Just wait." Surita said calmly, before ending the call.

Black shrugged and pulled Mia into his arms. Even though Black didn't speak on her threat Mia made a mental note. She would stay on her P's and Q's. Anybody that even looked suspicious would instantly catch a left jab, right hook and a knee to the face if she could get that lucky. In her mind, the "B.M." had met her match.

Mia inhaled the scent of the same Jean Paul

Gaultier cologne he wore on their date. That shit made her panties wet. *Damn,* she thought. It was a smell she could definitely get used too.

"Man you had me mad as fuck, I thought you tried to play with me." Mia admitted, after letting him go.

"I knew you was." He said, still hugging her. "I got a surprise for you after the party. I have it all lined up."

Mia's stomach had butterflies of excitement.

After catching up and partying with her friends and family, Mia was past tipsy as she headed up the stairs to take a shower before her date. An hour later, she sat once again in the passenger seat of Black's car as he took the exit towards D.C.

"Where are we going?" Mia asked, with a grin.

"We can go wherever you want to go. It's your b-day." Black told her, as he glanced over at her.

They pulled up to the Hyatt on the D.C. harbor in no time and Mia was gushing with excitement.

"Let's go." Black said, hoping out of the car and going over to Mia's side to open her door.

"Let's check in and then we can go do whatever you want." He said, as he grabbed her hand. They walked inside the hotel lobby hand in hand. As she looked around she was glad she had decided to drop her usual tomboy appearance and opted for a black skin tight crocodile textured long sleeve leather dress with a pair of black thigh high boots. Otherwise, she would've felt out of place in such a lavish place. She felt like she was officially back, as she felt her natural hair flowing down her back blowing in the cool night air as she walked. It was her birthday, she smelled good, she looked exceptional, and she truly felt like she was that girl.

After checking in the pair headed to the elevators which showcased a view of the Potomac river on the national harbor. Mia had never seen anything more magnificent. Her city didn't have anything like it.

“It feels like we're at the ritz-carlton! This is too much.” Mia said, covering her face. She had never stayed in a hotel so nice.

"You sicin' it." Black said, removing Mia’s hands from her face.

“And you are always covering your face, you know that? Do you realize how beautiful you are?” He asked her.

"What does sicin' it mean?" Mia asked, hugging him before he kissed the top of her head. The elevator dinged when they reached the 9th floor.

"Sicin' it means you're ji like making it more than it is." He said laughing.

“Come on. Cover your eyes.” Black said, walking behind her with his hand over her eyes.

Mia laughed as she carefully stepped forward.

“Alright right here.” He said, before he opened the door.

Mia stepped inside as he guided her hand into the room. She opened her eyes to a trial of red rose petals going all the way up to the bed with two happy birthday balloons on each side of the bed. No one had ever went to this extend for her birthday before.

Mia covered her face again, this time hiding tears.

“They wouldn’t let me light any candles.” Black said, as he walked back over to Mia and wrapped his arms around her.

"Candles? I just told you I really haven't seen nothing like this before."

“We got to get your passport because this is ji like nothing but I wanted to do something."

"Well it's a big deal to me." Mia said, looking in him the eyes.

“I’ve never met a female like you. It’s like you have all the characteristics I admire, you’re sweet but tough. You swear you’re a gangster but you don’t act like a hood rat. You are smart, ambitious, loyal, you’re a good mom. And then to put the icing on the cake, look at you. You have the kind of body that all the females are getting surgery to get. You’re so beautiful.” He said, once again removing her hands from her face.

"Alright, now *you* sicin' it." Mia said, looking at him.

He laughed before wiping a tear away with his thumb before he continued.

“So where do you want me to take you? The mall is still open its right around the corner, the MGM casino is right here. There’s a lot of restaurants, bars I just didn’t know what you would want to do.”

Mia wiped her eyes and looked at the ceiling as

she paused to think.

"I'm trying to see Riverdale. Take me to your hood." She said, looking over at him.

Black fell out laughing.

The next afternoon Mia was floating on a cloud as she walked to her truck hand in hand with Black.

"I don't even want to leave." She said.

"I know, I don't want you to either but I'm coming to you next weekend. Now you gotta show me your hood." Black said, with a slight chuckle.

"Don't be trying to play my city." Mia said, as she watched Corrie head out with Malakai, Cali, and Keegan as she held Teal.

"I'm not, I'm excited to see where you grew up. I told you I used to ride through there all the time. The area I seen looked like where Boosie from. Some Baton Rouge, across the tracks type shit."

"Are you coming back next weekend Mia?" Corrie asked as she opened the backdoor and placed Teal in her car seat.

"Go head and get in Kai Kai." Mia said, looking at him.

"I'm coming back the weekend after next mom." Mia said.

"Alright sista girl, see ya'll." Keegan said, hugging Mia.

"Give me a hug too." Corrie said.

"Not you wanting a hug big Corr." Mia said, squeezing her mom.

"Love you sis, see you next time." Cali said, before they headed inside. Leaving Mia and Black standing face to face.

"I miss you already." Mia said, before she leaned into Black.

"I miss you more. Call me we can stay on the phone during your drive." He said, pulling Mia into his chest.

"Alright, Kai." He said, leaning down and waving at Malakai after he released Mia.

Mia smiled as she watched his walk towards his car. *Abasi,* she thought, she loved his government name. She felt butterflies after she climbed into the driver's seat of her truck. Everything was lining up perfectly. Her family was officially back in Maryland, she had her apartment for her and her babies which she already laid out, she had her job and she started school next week. She ignored the "unknown" caller as her phone rung already knowing it was Dax. She had blocked the jail but he had been having someone 3-way call her repeatedly since he had gotten arrested. She contemplated changing her phone number, because what he had done this time was unforgivable. Even if he wasn't in his right mind, he had shot his best friend multiple times and then came to shoot her immediately afterwards. She hated to think about what could have happened if Ransom hadn't been there. So in her eyes there would never be anything to talk about. She would never be able to trust him or feel safe around him again.

She was counting down the days to their court date for their divorce she couldn't wait to get it over with. Even though he refused to sign, she was fairly certain the judge would grant her the divorce. Her marriage had taught her a lot, never would she ever normalize a man disrespecting her verbally calling her out of her name, cheating and putting their hands on her. She would definitely have to work on keeping her hands to herself as well but they would only get one chance. She felt like she was turning the page into a new chapter.

She put on her black sunglasses before she adjusted her review mirror to see Malakai in the backseat and Teal sitting comfortably in her car seat. She was glad she wasn't asleep as she picked up her phone and pressed play on Pop Smoke's, *"Tunnel Vision."* She checked the driver's side mirror before she pulled out into traffic and headed home.

What Mia didn't know was that Surita and her 2 sisters had been staked outside of her apartment for the last hour waiting for her to return.

The End.

Next up.....

Nearee

An i'm from Da' Bury Novel

Prologue

present

June 2022

I wiped sweat from the bridge of my nose before I sat up, I leaned onto my elbows as I watched Rah head into the bathroom.

"Alright I have to go, Cash is blowing me up." I told her after laying there for a few moments. I stood up, quickly gathering all of my belongings to leave. Rah started out as just the homie, but a drunk night turned into a one-night stand and then the one-night stand turned into a every night thing while Cash was away. She quickly rushed out of the bathroom wearing a grey sports bra with a white beater and some black basketball shorts.

"Why you always leaving in a rush Nearee? Come here." She asked me, while blocking the door.

"Come on now Rah move, see this is why I should've never came back over here. We just have to dead all this and act like it never happened. Cash comes home in a couple weeks and his ass will kill both of us." I said looking into her eyes, so she'd know that I was dead ass.

"Kill who?" Rah said with her hand on her chest

as she laughed. "You better ask about me shorty. But any who, I'm trying to be with you on some Mimi and Ty shit. I got the bread. And I already know you work and the nigga Cash be getting money but I am too you feel me?" She told me pointing back to the bed we had just occupied.

"Yeah I feel you." I told her.

"For real though Nearee. So you gonna come back and fuck with me again tonight?" She asked while pulling me into her arms.

"Man I'll try to slide through." I said lying through my teeth, before leaning in to kiss her. I had to play along so I could get up out of there.

"Alright, just hit me when you're about to get dressed later, we can figure out what we tryna do." She said opening her bedroom door to let me out.

"Alright, Bet." I told her.

As soon as I pulled out of her driveway, I stopped at the stop sign on the corner and blocked her from my phone and all my social media accounts. I know what ya'll are probably thinking, "Oh this bitch is triflin for that," but nah. I'm simply just playing the hand I was dealt but let me formally introduce myself, I'm Nearee Lashay Jackson from the Bury, yeah that's right I'm from the Eastern shore in the DMV area. I'm twenty-nine with no kids, out 'chea single as a bitch just living but that's how I got my reputation. I'm known in my city for being heartless just like the Kayne song. I don't even be doing much. The real problem is that my city is so small you can't keep anything a secret and dating is just a huge revolving door full of drama, std's and humiliation. One thing ya'll are going to quickly learn about me is that my momma didn't raise no dummy, I'm single by choice, what did Toni Romiti say? "If he a dog imma dog too." That's honestly what I been on for the past five years because these niggas are grimy and imma be grimy right along with 'em. I refuse to ever go back to being one of those bitches crying in the car, over a nigga, like Yvette. Not to sound cocky but I'm real pretty, plus my body is stacked and no shade but I didn't need to go see Dr. Miami for a damn thing. I came out of my momma's cooter with these chinky eyes and chocolate skin. My mom said she knew from day one I would be a problem. Now I ain't gone hold ya'll, I have fucked a few niggas that I knew had girlfriends and even one that had a wife but see ya'll have got to understand, I wasn't always like this. I've simply fallen for to many of the wrong niggas over the years. Every single mothafucker I've ever loved played with me, with the exception of one. So let me tell ya'll my story in my own words, from the beginning.

Nearee

Chapter 1

Summer 2008

See the summer of 08' was where it all started for me. I was sixteen at the time and still naïve to all the tricks and games niggas played to get what they wanted. Up until this point, I had always lived isolated, in a house surrounded by fields and trees with little to no neighbors. My mom assumed that keeping me on the outskirts of the city would prevent me from running wild in the streets, fighting and having sex like most teens while she was gone and it worked for the most part. With nothing in walking distance, I stayed cooped up in the house. It wasn't necessarily a bad thing because we had the best of everything. The entire house was decked out, we had internet and cable, my mom kept the fridge full and the pantry stocked with snacks. My bedroom had everything I could ever want, I had picked all white furniture with black decor. I had over a dozen pink fuzzy throw pillows with the matching comforter set, I chose a pink area rug, pink curtains, a pink lamp, shit even my alarm clock was pink sitting on my nightstand. I was fully aware that I had a great life but the older I became the more I began to crave my independence and freedom. I'd get invited to kickbacks and house parties all the time at school, I had even snuck out to a couple of them. Shit, I looked up our cab companies in the phone book and called them from the house phone. After they'd pick me up, I got them to stop me at any random house a few streets over from where I was going, tell them I'd be right back out with the money and dip on they asses. They caught onto me quick though and threatened to call the cops if I kept calling without having the money I owed them. I knew my uncle would fuck me up if he found out, so I was forced to continue to miss out on everything. So when my mom suddenly revealed that we would be relocating from the cornfields into one of the most popular, predominantly-black neighborhoods in my city, it was like a dream come true for me. I didn't know what brought on Niecy's sudden change of heart but I was grateful and more than ready to jump out there!

"Welcome to Doverdale Nearee." My mom said with a smile.